HONESTLY ALWAYS YOU

A CODEX ORIGIN LOVE STORY

MELISSA FREY

INDEPENDENTLY PUBLISHED IN THE UNITED STATES OF AMERICA

www.melissafrey.com

Honestly Always You / by Melissa Frey. —1st ed.

Summary: When Mandy Carlson's life implodes on graduation weekend, fellow college student Justin Stanford—who's pined for her from afar—offers to be her fake boyfriend to give her time to pick up the pieces.

ebook ISBN: 978-1-7324335-7-1

Paperback ISBN: 978-1-7324335-6-4

Interior Formatting: Wicked Dreams Publishing

Book Cover Design: Taylor Danae Colbert

Author Photo: Two Kin Photography

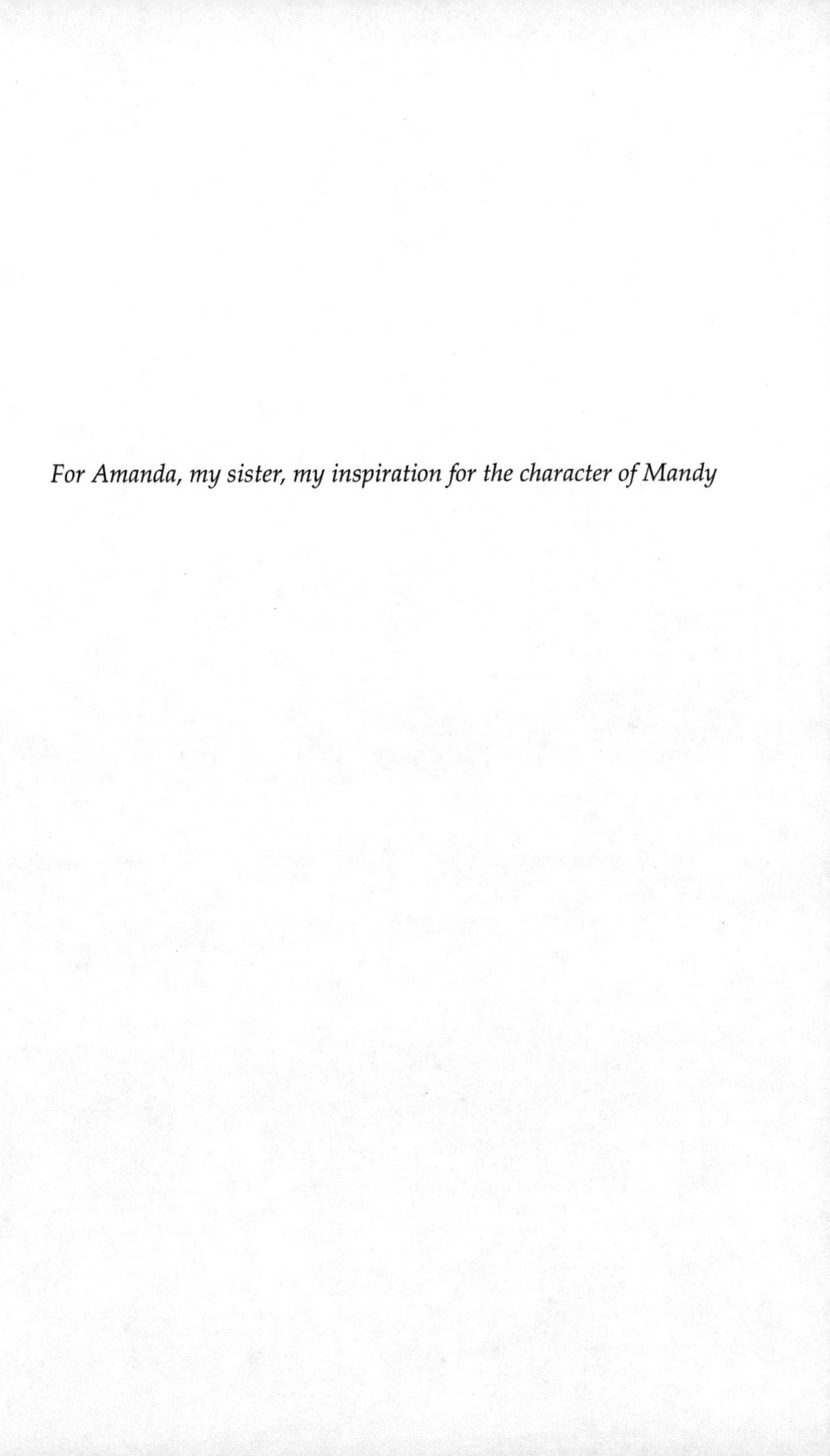

For Amanda, my sister, my inspiration for the character of Mandy

CONTENTS

AUTHOR'S NOTE

If you've read my other books, you'll quickly realize this book is quite different from my previous ones. The Codex Series does not include strong language or on-page sex; this book does. *Honestly Always You* is intended for mature audiences of 18 years of age and older.

I wrote *Honestly Always You* because I'd always wanted to know how Mandy and Justin (from The Codex Series) originally met and fell in love. The idea for it came in the midst of the global pandemic of 2020, and I wrote the first draft over 11 days in the summer of that year. It was a labor of love for me but also a way to escape the heaviness going on in the world at the time.

I hope this story gives you a happy escape as well.

HONESTLY ALWAYS YOU

CHAPTER ONE

MANDY CARLSON CHECKED HER SHOULDER-LENGTH, strawberry blonde hair in the tiny mirror over her apartment's bathroom sink and smiled. Despite the Florida May heat—sweltering even at eight PM—her curls were staying, at least for now. She knew it wouldn't last long, but she'd take what she could get.

She clicked the light off in the bathroom and stepped immediately into the living room. While most twenty-two-year-old almost-graduates were sharing apartments near UCF, she'd opted for her own place near the school. She'd sacrificed square footage to do it, but it was worth it. Her all-night study sessions didn't disturb anyone else—nor did her late-into-the-night sessions of another kind with her boyfriend, Dan.

And she probably wouldn't be here much longer anyway.

Her phone vibrated in the pocket of her skintight jeans, and her smile widened when she saw the text that'd come through.

I'm downstairs when you're ready. Dan had added a smiley face emoji.

Mandy had been dating Dan since sophomore year. She'd been failing English Lit miserably during the fall semester of her second year, and he'd stepped in like her knight in shining armor and tutored her until she passed.

Barely, but she did.

The guy had big plans after graduation, a cushy new job at one of the largest banks here in Orlando. Mandy had already been accepted into the graduate Anthropology program at the University of Central Florida, so she was staying local, too, at least for the foreseeable future. Beyond that, she wasn't sure what would come next.

She liked to know what came next. Ugh.

She quickly typed in her code to unlock her phone and shot a text back. **On my way.** She added a heart.

She repocketed her phone, shoved her ID, a couple of credit cards, and some cash in her tight back pocket, used her keys to lock up, then flew down three flights of stairs and into Dan's car.

"Hey." She leaned in for a quick kiss before buckling her seatbelt.

He smiled at her. "Hey. You look good."

Mandy glanced down at her silky, emerald-green tank top that she'd matched with her favorite jeans and uncharacteristic strappy gold heels and blushed. "Thanks."

Dan grinned from beside her, swiping his fingers across her warm cheek. "No need to be embarrassed, Mandy. Just wanted to compliment my girlfriend."

She offered a sheepish smile as he pulled out of the parking lot and onto the street lined with lights just blinking on.

They pulled up to Dan's elaborate fraternity house. Mandy hated to drive, even when she wouldn't be drinking, so he was always sweet enough to pick her up. She usually stayed the night after these things anyway—her walk-of-shame game had been perfected over the years.

Tomorrow was graduation, so tonight would be the biggest blowout of the year. Mandy was used to these frat parties—they were usually tolerable, sometimes even fun—but she was a little glad to be saying goodbye to this part of her life. She was ready to move on to bigger and better things—especially if Dan would be moving on with her.

He hadn't asked yet, but Mandy was hoping that he'd present a ring soon. She'd hinted at it, they'd skirted around the subject, but nothing had been decided. Mandy liked decided. She just wished he'd ask already.

Dan parked on the street and reached the passenger side just as Mandy was climbing out of the low-profile sports car, feeling like she was stepping out onto a red carpet.

No, literally—the guys had apparently set out a red carpet that extended all the way from the front door to the street. She knew they had a flair for the dramatic, but this was a little over the top, right?

Mandy eyed Dan as they walked to the door, his arm sliding around her thin waist.

"What?"

Mandy swiped her arm through the air to indicate the carpet beneath their feet. "What is this?"

Dan chuckled, pulling her closer and planting a kiss on her forehead. "For us, for all of the graduates. The guys thought it would be a good send-off."

Mandy grinned up at him. Even with her heels, he towered over her, but she didn't mind. She stretched up to plant a kiss on his lips as they reached the porch. "It was a good idea."

The door was already open, and sounds of loud music and a thousand conversations floated on the twilight air. Dan stepped through and immediately pulled the guy in front of him into one of those weird bro-hugs that start out as a handshake.

Dan clapped his friend on the back once then stepped away. "You can thank Justin here. This was his brainchild." His arm made a wide sweep of the room, and Mandy finally took in the space. And gasped.

The entire first floor of the frat house had been transformed. The red carpet theme continued in here, complete with golden stanchions, a large popcorn machine, and innumerable glittering stars hanging from the ceiling and on the walls.

Mandy blinked over at Justin as he swiped his blond hair out of his bright-blue eyes. The guy was a walking stereotype—she'd even heard he drove to the coast to go surfing on the weekends. "Wow, Justin—this is impressive." Mandy's brain searched a few of the interesting conversations the two of them had had over the years at parties just like this—notable for the simple fact that interesting conversations were few and far between at similar soirées—and wondered if he'd divulged his talent for party planning. She couldn't remember, but she suspected Justin's real talent was to keep everyone guessing.

He grinned widely, his perfectly white teeth on display. "Thanks, Mandy. Good to see you again. Enjoy the party." He took a swig of the beer in his hand then headed further inside after a single nod to the couple.

Mandy took a deep breath, wiping her suddenly sweaty palms on her jeans. She could party with the best of them, but tonight she just wanted to be alone. Tomorrow was a big day, one she was ready for, but she still got butterflies in her stomach when she thought about what would come next.

For the next few hours, she made her way around the party, greeting her friends, Dan's fraternity brothers, and her fellow classmates at UCF. She found Dan periodically, giving his hand a squeeze or sharing a silent kiss before getting lost in the revelry again. He smiled amiably every time, but his smile was increasingly off. And as the night progressed, Mandy felt a pit forming in her stomach.

JUSTIN STANFORD WAS ENJOYING the party, but he'd felt unsettled since it'd started. Since Dan had shown up with his girlfriend, the beautiful and untouchable Mandy Carlson.

His eyes drifted to her, finding her in the crowd as he had all night. She was talking to some sorority girls from the house next door but didn't seem to be enjoying the conversation. She was smarter than all of them put together—why did she bother?

After some small talk with one of his frat brothers, he found an empty seat and settled in with his beer. He'd been carrying around the same one all night—it was extremely warm and utterly undrinkable now, but holding it kept the guys off his back. He wasn't much of a drinker, but his brothers didn't know that. And he was happy to keep it that way.

Only a few more days, and he'd be out of here anyway.

His eyes followed Mandy as she crossed the room in strappy golden sandals that lifted her three inches off the ground. Justin thought they were sexy as hell, but they didn't seem like her. He liked a woman who knew who she was and wasn't afraid to say what she liked.

He was a big fan of hearing what they liked out loud, too. Especially in the bedroom.

Justin shifted in his seat, adjusting himself discreetly. He shouldn't be thinking these things about another guy's girlfriend. He wouldn't put himself—or her—in that situation, no matter what.

Which was why he'd been girlfriend-less for the past three

years. Three years was an infinitely long time to wait—not that he was exactly "waiting," but he certainly wasn't looking for any kind of commitment—yet he couldn't seem to get his mind off those gorgeous hazel eyes and light-brown hair a guy could tangle his fingers in and never let go.

He shook his head to clear it then stood up. Time for a distraction.

He headed to the kitchen in search of a new drink. All he could find was some whiskey, so he begrudgingly poured a little into a glass. At least the top-shelf liquor the guys kept in the house was decent, if a little strong.

Justin took the long way out of the kitchen, heading back to the party by way of the first-floor residence hallway, looking for a brief moment of peace. But the sounds coming from behind one of the closed doors were starting to get a little obscene, so he picked up the pace.

Sex and alcohol always seemed to mix in a group like this, and it was never a good idea.

When he finally made his way back to the living room, Justin spied Mandy sitting alone on a nearby velvet couch. He quickly surveyed the room, noting all the guys who were obviously drunk. Pretty much all of them.

Mandy shouldn't be by herself. Where the hell was Dan?

CHAPTER TWO

BY ELEVEN, Mandy was ready to go home. She'd stopped drinking over an hour ago out of boredom more than anything else, and she'd exhausted every topic of conversation she could think of with the girls that came from the sorority next door. They weren't exactly known for their scintillating conversational skills.

She'd never pledged, but being the girlfriend of a frat guy somehow made her part of the club.

Mandy glanced up from her sparkling water and surveyed the room. She didn't see Dan anywhere. She'd found this spot —on an on-brand velvet couch, no less; she had to admire Justin's commitment—and had claimed it as her own for nearly a half hour.

Just then, a buzzed Justin walked up and plopped down next to her without ceremony. *Speak of the devil,* she thought. But his drink didn't spill, so he couldn't be *that* drunk, right? "Hey, Mandy. Having fun?"

Mandy straightened, moving away from him slightly as she did. Seemed he was doing that sitting-too-close-because-he-was-drunk thing, and it was a little annoying. Or maybe she was imagining it because she was perturbed at Dan's sudden absence. Or maybe . . . who knew? The whole night felt off. "Yeah, tonight's been fun. You did a really good job."

"You think so?" He sat up a little, still leaning against the back of the couch, and took in the party, which was still going strong. "That's nice of you to say." He leaned in closer, and Mandy inched away again.

"You're drunk, Justin. Stay on your side of the couch." The guy was harmless, but still.

He backed away and raised a hand between them. "I'm not, actually, but no worries, Mandy. Sorry." He took a sip of his drink, a brown liquid that Mandy couldn't imagine was helping his situation, but then she saw him wince at the taste. Maybe he was sober after all. "Where's Dan?"

Mandy glanced around again. "Not sure."

At her words, Justin suddenly straightened, depositing his drink on the table beside him. Mandy's brow furrowed, and she stared at him, her eyes narrowing slightly. As he met her gaze, she could tell that he was absolutely *not* drunk—his eyes were the clearest blue she'd ever seen. Oceans.

"What is it, Justin?" Her eyes held his with the force of a thousand chains.

But he somehow managed to escape her glare and glanced away, toward the hallway. "I . . ."

"What, Justin? Out with it."

Then Justin's face fell. He shook his head. "Mandy, please don't . . ."

Mandy jumped to her feet. Which were killing her—stupid heels. "Justin, you know something." Her next words were ground out between gritted teeth. "Tell me what you know."

Loud music and colorful lights pulsed around them, and no

one seemed to notice their suddenly tense conversation. Mandy's world froze for an instant.

Then Justin stood up beside her, placing a gentle hand on her bare upper arm and catching her gaze again. Mandy's arm heated where he touched it, and soon the fire spread to her entire body.

She knew her face was getting red as she considered his non-response, so she broke their gaze and shoved past him, headed for the hallway. Whatever he was hiding, she needed to know. She didn't *want* to know—God, she really didn't want to —but she *needed* to.

The third door on the left was shut. She didn't know much about the house, though she'd spent a little time here, but she knew that room. That was Dan's room. And the noises coming from it could only mean one thing.

She staggered and fell back against the wall, and Justin was immediately at her side, grabbing her arm to hold her up. She thought she was going to be sick.

"Mandy—" Justin started.

"No. Don't you dare defend him, Justin." She straightened, finding her footing.

"I wasn't. I just . . ."

"You just what?" Mandy crossed her arms and turned her attention to the only man she could yell at in this moment. "You knew, and you didn't tell me? You were covering for him?"

"No, I—"

She waved a hand in front of his face, cutting him off. "Save it. You're just as bad as he is."

"Hey! I didn't do this!"

Mandy turned her back on him. She should apologize—he was right, after all—but she was just too angry.

At that moment, Dan's door opened. Out stumbled a leggy

blonde in a skintight, barely there hot-pink dress that hung haphazardly on her thin frame and Dan, his dark-brown hair and khaki pants rumpled and his polo shirt half-untucked.

Mandy's eyes shot wide. When the jerk finally glanced her way, his face fell. And Mandy realized abruptly that she couldn't stand here and listen to any excuses. She was done.

So she spun around to leave, smashing directly into Justin's chest. Which was harder than she expected it to be. "Let me go!"

Justin backed away, letting her pass. Mandy stumbled down the hall—she was cursing herself for wearing these damn shoes—then finally regained her footing as she headed for the front door.

She sprinted toward it, launching herself outside as if she couldn't breathe in that house.

Turned out, she couldn't.

JUSTIN WHIPPED back around toward Dan as the latter started toward Mandy. The tall blonde had scurried away before Mandy had even made it out of the hallway.

Justin stuck out his hand, pressing it against his frat brother's chest. "Don't."

"But she—"

"Do not go after her, Dan."

He shot his hand toward the entrance. "I have to explain . . ."

Justin moved to block his exit. "No. She doesn't want to talk to you."

Dan scowled at him for a moment, then a smirk spread

across his face. "This is perfect for you, isn't it? You've had a hard-on for her since we started dating."

Justin felt his cheeks heating. "I'm just trying to stop her from having to see your asshole face again."

Dan leaned in, his nose inches from Justin's though he was a few inches taller. Justin stood up straighter. "I'm just doing what any guy would do." He leaned in and stage-whispered his next words, his hand near his mouth. "She's a little boring in the sack."

Justin's chest heaved, and he had to clench both fists to keep from punching Dan in the jaw. Justin glared up at his former friend, his smug face still only inches away, and growled out his next words. "Watch your mouth, Dan."

The jerk backed away, shaking his head. Then he whistled through his teeth. "Fine. Good riddance. You can have her." He turned and sauntered down the hallway.

If only, Justin thought as he focused his breathing, tried to calm down. He knew Mandy was too good for Dan when they'd started dating, but he hadn't truly understood how far out of his league she really was until this moment.

She didn't deserve this. She was a girl to be loved, cherished, and worshipped, not used and discarded.

He turned back to the living room, scanning the room for her. He didn't see her anywhere. Where was she? He'd been watching her all night, and he hadn't noticed her being overly social with any women the whole time, at least not by choice.

Which meant she'd need a friend.

Justin stalked across the room and burst out the open front door.

Mandy circled the house, settling in the shadows on the side opposite the long driveway, and gasped for air through her tears. They just wouldn't stop.

Her thoughts were blank, as her breaking heart had taken over until her entire being was one aching ball of despair. She couldn't summon the energy to think her way out of this, so she instead let herself cry, the only sound in the darkness her quiet sobs.

She didn't know how long she'd been there, bawling, when she heard a twig snap only a few feet away. She jumped at the sound, her shriek piercing the night.

"Mandy!" a voice hissed in the darkness. "It's just me!"

The familiar sound brought some measure of comfort, but Mandy was still too angry to chat. "Go away, Justin."

But instead he stepped closer, into the light of the full moon shining overhead. "I'll leave if you want, but I wanted to apologize. Explain."

Mandy sniffed, unceremoniously wiping her nose with the back of her hand. "I don't want to talk." She did, but breaking down in front of Justin was just embarrassing. If her cheeks hadn't already been red from the crying, she knew they definitely would be now.

Justin nodded but didn't move, and Mandy felt his eyes on every inch of her exposed skin. The gesture could've been creepy—it probably should've felt that way—but she welcomed Justin's appraisal in that moment. What was happening?

She sighed, her shoulders relaxing. "But I guess you can." She flicked her hand in the space between them. "Talk."

Justin stepped closer still until he was less than a foot away, and his close proximity had every nerve ending buzzing. The guy seemed nice—and attractive, though she couldn't think about that now—but why did he care so much?

He stopped in front of her, brushing a stray hair off her forehead. Her heart warmed at the gesture coming from him, though she couldn't for the life of her figure out why. "I am so sorry, Mandy. Dan . . . you didn't deserve that. No one does. He's a jerk."

"No, he's an asshole."

A staccato laugh shot from Justin's throat. "I've never heard you swear before."

Mandy shrugged, starting to feel a little more like herself. "I usually don't."

Justin smiled at her. Though he was shorter than Dan, he was still a few inches taller than her. With her heels still on, though, high as they were, he had to look up slightly to catch her eye. In another life, that might have made a good kissing height . . .

Mandy blinked, pressing back against the house. Justin took the hint and stepped back.

"I just wanted to apologize for not telling you. I didn't know for sure," he quickly added, "but I heard something in the hallway. When you didn't know where Dan was, I put two and two together."

Mandy's heart broke again, and an unwelcome sob shook her shoulders. Justin reached for her, pulling her to his chest, and she leaned in to him as her tears broke loose again.

Justin just held her while she cried. She didn't know why. Despite the surprisingly enjoyable conversations they'd had over the years—about the weather, what professor was annoying them lately, or how their classes were going, generally—they'd never had an actual conversation about anything *real*.

But in this moment, she was thankful he was here. She'd been so wrapped up in her relationship with Dan and with finishing up her bachelor's degree that she didn't have anyone else.

Her tears subsided slowly, but eventually she pushed away from Justin. She winced at the mascara stains on his light-blue t-shirt. "I am so sorry, Justin. I'll pay for that to get cleaned."

Justin shook his head. "No worries, Mandy. It'll wash out."

She blinked at him through tear-filled eyes. "You sure?"

He shrugged like it didn't matter either way. Then he smiled at her, swiping a tear from her cheek. Her skin tingled long after he pulled his finger away.

Then he stepped back. "So how are you getting home?"

Mandy glanced around automatically, hoping the answer would be hidden in the shadows on the side of the massive house. Then she let her face fall. "Dan brought me."

Justin straightened. "Okay. I'll take you home."

Mandy shook her head, sniffing again. "No, that's okay. You've been really sweet, but I'm okay. I was planning on calling a car anyway."

Justin waved a hand in her face. "You're in no condition to get home on your own."

"Hey!" She smacked his arm.

He grinned. "I just meant it would be easier for you if you didn't have to explain the red eyes and tear-stained cheeks."

"Oh." Mandy swiped both hands across her cheeks, under her eyes. She had to have mascara *everywhere*. "Okay, then. I accept."

Justin offered her his hand. "Great." Mandy slid her hand into his, welcoming its warmth. "You know, that's the first time you've been easy all night."

Mandy's mouth fell open as they stepped out from the side of the house, still hand in hand. "I can't believe you just said that!" She smacked him again with her free hand.

Justin rolled his eyes as they approached the red carpet and crossed it. "You know what I meant. A girl like you is never easy."

Mandy hid her eyes as they approached the driveway. "I don't know whether that was a compliment or not."

Justin pulled a set of keys from his pocket and tapped the key fob. The lights on a tan Jeep flashed as he reached for the passenger door and held it open for her. "It was a compliment. I like a girl that makes you work for it."

Mandy's face turned beet red as she climbed up into the vehicle. An awkward silence settled between them as Justin jumped in and made his way to her apartment. He barely needed directions, which made her eyes narrow at him more than once, but she didn't ask. She was too busy trying to figure out what was with him tonight. Why was he being so nice to her?

And what was with that compliment thing? Was he saying she was high maintenance, but that he liked high maintenance women?

Was he saying that he liked *her*?

CHAPTER THREE

Justin pulled into a parking spot in front of Mandy's building—Dan had told him long ago where she lived "just in case," but in case of what, Justin didn't know—then glanced over at her. She was shaking her head, her pretty face drooping. He wished he could erase this entire night for her, spare her the pain.

Then she groaned.

"What?" Justin turned in his seat to face her.

Mandy covered her face with her hands, her response muffled. "I have to see my family tomorrow."

Justin chuckled quietly. "And that's a bad thing?"

Mandy shook her head, her hands still over her face. "No." She lifted her eyes and found his gaze. "But I tell my mom everything. If Dan's not with me tomorrow, she will bug me until I tell her what happened—and I just can't deal with that right now. It's just too raw, and she will have so many questions. They all will."

Justin nodded but kept his expression blank.

"What—no witty comeback?"

He just shrugged.

"Well, what do I do? You seem like a guy with all the answers."

Justin stared out the windshield for a moment. Then a thought popped into his head. *Justin, that's crazy,* he thought. *She'll never go for it. You need to keep it to yourse—* "I do have an idea."

Mandy's breath turned shallow, and Justin studied her carefully. Hyperventilation seemed a strong possibility at the moment. "Yes?"

He pushed one corner of his mouth up, and Mandy blushed. He'd been watching her for years, so he had a hunch what that meant. "You may not like it."

Mandy rolled her eyes and crossed her arms. "Just say it."

Justin took a deep breath and spoke before really thinking of the consequences. *Here goes nothing . . .* "What if—just for this weekend—we pretended to be together?"

"What?" she nearly shouted.

Justin smirked again then shrugged. "It would get your family off your back. You could tell them you and Dan broke up weeks ago, that we just started dating."

"My mom knows Dan and I are—were—dating! She knows I would've told her if we'd broken up."

Justin paused to consider her objection before answering. "So use part of the real story. Tell her what happened with him, but just act like it happened a few weeks ago and you were too embarrassed to tell her. Would that work?"

Mandy chewed on her bottom lip.

"Look, it's totally up to you. I'm just offering to help out."

Mandy eyed him. "And what do you get out of this?"

"A beautiful woman on my arm." Justin grinned, hiding the butterflies swarming in his stomach with humor, like he always did. He couldn't let Mandy know that an arrangement much like this one was what he'd been dreaming about for years.

Mandy chewed on her thumbnail and stared blankly at the dash. Justin felt his pulse start racing as he waited for her answer. What if she said no? He'd look like an idiot. But if she said yes, he might not be able to keep his true feelings hidden, and that wouldn't be fair to Mandy right now. Oh, shit—what if she said yes?

Then she took a breath. "Okay. Let's do it."

"Really?"

Mandy nodded exuberantly. "Yes. What's the worst that could happen?"

"Aw, Mandy. You just jinxed us!"

"I did not!"

Justin laughed. "Whatever you say."

Mandy smiled back, but then she frowned slightly. "So how do we do this?"

"Do what, exactly?" Justin pursed his lips.

"Pretend to be together. I think we need some ground rules." Mandy stared up at her apartment for a few moments. "Okay, you'll stay the night."

Justin jerked like something had been shot through his heart. "What?!" If Mandy was going to push the boundaries of this arrangement, he was screwed. He wasn't sure his heart could take it when they inevitably "broke up" if she was going to insist on getting so damn close.

Mandy shoved him. "Oh, don't be a prude. We need to get our stories straight, and I thought it'd be more comfortable to do in my apartment than sitting here in the car for hours."

"And why am I staying the night?"

"So we can pick up my parents at the airport first thing, silly. You don't think my amazing boyfriend wouldn't be practically living at my place anyway?" She didn't state the obvious: that Dan hadn't been.

And Justin wasn't about to mention it either. "Okay."

"Okay?"

Justin hesitated for just a moment then smiled despite the fact that this woman was going to be the death of him. He knew that with certainty. "Yeah. I can do one night with you, I *suppose*."

Mandy smacked his arm.

MANDY UNLOCKED THE DOOR, kicking off her heels as she entered her small one-bedroom apartment, and Justin followed her inside. She wasn't usually this spontaneous, but her asshole boyfriend of three years had just cheated on her the night before graduation. Though she wasn't ready to completely swear off men, the thought had occurred to her.

"Make yourself at home," she started, politeness taking over. "You want something to drink?"

Justin stood in the entryway/living room/hallway/office and surveyed the room. "Um, Mandy . . . where's the rest of it?"

"Oh, shush." But she couldn't hide her smile as she smacked her palm against his chest. How could she have forgotten how deliciously hard it was? "Drink or not?"

Justin took two steps and stood in front of the futon Mandy was using as a couch. "Just water, thank you." But just as he sat down, he yelped, popping back up. A lopsided throw pillow had fallen right beneath him.

Mandy laughed. "Here, come sit at the table." She set his glass on the tiny, round wooden table she'd gotten at a yard sale two summers ago. It fit perfectly in the apartment, which meant it was small. Or "cozy," as she preferred to call her space. Then she pulled open the junk drawer in her kitchen and pulled out a pad of paper and a pen. "We have a lot to work out anyway."

Justin sighed but crossed the room and sat on the hard wooden chair. "You're one of those planning types, aren't you?"

She grinned as she sat across the table from him. "How could you tell?"

He smiled back, but Mandy noticed for the first time his half-opened eyes.

"Look, Justin . . . if you're too tired, we could just go to bed."

He arched an eyebrow.

"Ugh! You know what I meant."

"Freudian slip, I'd say."

She glared at him.

He laughed. "I'm okay, I'm awake. I don't know for how long, though. I graduate tomorrow, too, you know."

"You do?"

Justin nodded, taking a big gulp of his water. Mandy watched his Adam's apple bob up and down as he swallowed. "Yep. B.S. in Statistics."

Mandy's jaw actually dropped. "Wow—seriously? So you're, like, smart."

Justin laughed again. "I suppose."

"And your plans after graduation?"

Justin shrugged. "Graduate school."

Mandy leaned back in her chair, crossing her arms while looking him over. She'd never seen his serious—or intelligent—side, just the carefree one that was always the life of every party. This man was chock-full of surprises. "At UCF?"

Justin nodded. "Yeah. I'm actually switching departments. I was accepted into the Anthropology graduate program."

"Really? Me, too."

"Seriously?"

Mandy smiled. "So I guess we'll be seeing a lot more of each other. There aren't a lot of us in the program, I've heard."

That crooked smile showed up again, and Mandy felt it below her waist. What was this guy doing to her? She'd been single for what—like an hour?

She shook her head to clear it then glanced down at the pad of paper. "Okay, let's get this all sorted out."

Justin took another drink. "What do we need to get sorted out?"

Mandy tapped the pencil against her chin. "Hmm . . . where did we meet?"

"Through Dan, of course."

Mandy nodded slowly, drawing in a slow inhale before writing it down.

"Hey—if you don't want to do this . . ."

She waved him off. "No, it's fine. That makes sense." She nodded again, more deliberately this time. "Next—when did we start dating?"

Justin pursed his lips, leaning back as he crossed his arms. "Like I mentioned in the car, why not use part of the truth?"

Mandy's eyes narrowed at him. "What do you mean?"

Justin leaned forward, the overhead light illuminating the back of his head as though he were in a dark interrogation room. "Just that you and Dan broke up because he was cheating on you, but I comforted you. A few days later, we realized what we both were feeling, and I asked you to dinner."

"Dinner? That's boring."

Justin chuckled, leaning back again and reaching for his water. "You have a better idea?"

Mandy scrunched her eyebrows together. "Skydiving?"

Justin nearly spit his water across the room, and he had to recover from a coughing fit before answering. "I don't think skydiving's very believable, Mandy."

Mandy frowned. "No, you're right."

THEY FELL silent as Justin looked her over. This woman was hilarious without even meaning to be. A girl as beautiful as her with a sense of humor, too? She was one in a billion, and it killed him that he couldn't make her his right now, right in this apartment. Three years was a long goddamn time.

He groaned internally. She was right across the table from him, but he couldn't do a damn thing about it. Fucking Dan.

"Oh! What if you asked me to dinner, but I said no because it was too boring? So you talked me into going with you to the beach the next day."

Justin's eyebrow shot up as her voice whipped him back to the present. "How do you know I go to the beach?"

Mandy shrugged. "You surf, right?"

"You remembered that?"

Mandy shrugged again, a sexy pout on her lips.

Justin eyed her for a moment before answering. "Okay, I like that. A picnic on the beach, hot sex on the sand—"

"Wait—what?!" she yelled.

"Too much?" He widened his eyes, pretended he didn't know he'd just deliberately pushed her buttons. He couldn't say he hated it, either.

Mandy crossed her arms. "You were the one who said I wasn't easy."

One corner of his mouth turned up. "Touché." *Damn, this woman keeps getting sexier.*

Her chest heaved as she drew in a breath. "But you do bring up an excellent point."

He blinked, and his heart started racing. He sensed something was coming. "What's that?"

When Mandy caught his gaze, Justin thought his heart might actually have stopped. "Sex."

Justin blanched for a split second, but then he shook himself out of it with a satisfying smirk. He knew just how to respond. "Pro."

Mandy laughed aloud, her face turning adorably red yet again. "You're so ridiculous!" She couldn't stop laughing and was soon gasping for air. Justin just watched her, his smile widening as he thoroughly enjoyed the sight of her happy.

When she'd composed herself, she reached for his water and took a drink. Then she gasped. "Oh! Sorry. I can get you another one."

"No, this is fine." He picked up the glass and tossed it back, and he could've sworn he tasted her on the glass.

Mandy scrutinized him as he did. Then: "For the record, I'm pro, too. But that's not what I was asking."

Really good to know. Justin gulped down the last of his water, staring at her as he set the glass back on the table. "You're wanting us to figure out how close we've been."

"Yes." Mandy's eyes were wide.

"Hmm . . ." Justin paused. "Kissing, for sure."

Mandy nodded. "Definitely."

Justin raised his eyebrow again, and his heart thumped loudly in his chest. He took a deep breath and continued.

"Well . . . we're a few weeks into our fantasy relationship—would you sleep with me that soon?"

Mandy blushed again, and Justin was fighting a grin. "That depends."

"On what?"

She straightened and looked him right in the eye. His heart leapt into his throat. "If I find you attractive enough."

Justin swallowed hard. "And?"

"And what?"

His eyes narrowed at her. "You know what. Do you find me attractive?"

CHAPTER FOUR

MANDY DIDN'T MISS that what Justin asked wasn't exactly the question she'd posed. But she had a feeling this guy would get really cocky if she admitted any attraction so soon, so . . . "You're alright."

Justin laughed in a short burst. "Just alright? Come on!"

Mandy shrugged, eyeing him up and down in a way he couldn't miss. He fidgeted in his seat, and she fought a grin. "You're attractive enough. So sex, yes." She picked up her pencil and started scribbling on the pad.

"You're writing that down?"

"What?" Mandy scrunched her nose at him. "It's the best part."

Justin's eyes widened, and Mandy laughed.

"Am I wrong?"

Justin just shook his head slowly, letting out a slow stream of air through his pursed lips as he did.

"Okay," Mandy scanned her minuscule list. "Family. Yours?"

Justin visibly relaxed in his chair, leaning back. "Dad: Roger. Mom: Jan. They live in Montana."

Mandy nodded, writing it down.

"Yours?"

She took a breath. "Glad you're sitting down."

Justin chuckled.

"Mom: Amy. She and my dad got divorced when I was really young, and she remarried later on. His name is Bill Thatcher, and he's an investment banker. They live in what's pretty much a mansion in Philadelphia. How I can afford to live in the lap of luxury here." She grinned.

"Where were you from originally?"

"I grew up in Atlanta."

Justin nodded. "It's pretty there. But busy."

Mandy nodded back. "Yep."

"And your dad?"

"I haven't seen him since he left."

"How old were you?"

Mandy exhaled. "Three."

Justin sucked in a breath through his teeth. "I'm sorry."

"It's okay."

"It's not."

Mandy just shrugged, frowning.

"Siblings?" Justin asked.

Mandy nodded, thankful for the change of subject. "One sister, Lucy—well, she's my stepsister. She's a few years younger than me and snarky, but she's pretty cool. You?"

Justin shook his head. "Just me."

"Explains why you're so cocky."

A laugh shot out of Justin. "Do you always say what you're thinking?"

Mandy shrugged, but a half smirk that she couldn't help broke through. "Usually. Does that scare you off?"

"Not at all."

Mandy chuckled then looked over her list. "Favorite foods?"

"Pizza."

"Figures."

Justin grinned. "You?"

Mandy stared off into space. "Barbecue ribs, cheesy potatoes, and corn on the cob."

"You're showing your Southern roots, girl."

Mandy caught his gaze. "Always, y'all," she drawled, raising her hand to her forehead to tip an imaginary hat to him.

"What foods don't you like?"

Mandy made a face. "Spinach. Anchovies. Lemon-flavored anything. Chicken. Almond milk—"

"Should I be writing this down?"

Mandy grinned. "You'll learn."

JUSTIN'S BROWS FURROWED, just a little, as he considered her response. If this was just for the weekend, how would he "learn" what she liked or didn't like? If this was just a temporary arrangement, Justin wouldn't have time to learn much of anything. Unless Mandy was considering making it more permanent . . . *Stop it, Justin. She* just *broke up with Dan. Like an hour ago. Don't be a bastard.*

Mandy continued her interrogation. "You?"

"Mostly just celery. Oh, and anchovies is a good one."

Mandy threw her head back and laughed.

Justin smiled back. Smiles came easy with her around.

"What else should we know?" Mandy asked, glancing at her phone.

Justin pulled his own phone out of his pocket and set it on the table. It was almost one. He yawned as a question popped into his head. "How often do I sleep over?"

Mandy blushed again. "I'd say you have a drawer."

"So often, then."

Mandy pursed her lips then nodded. "Yeah, that feels right."

"How often do you sleep over at my place?"

"Well, we'd probably reciprocate. Although . . . I wouldn't want to stay in the same house as Dan, right?"

Justin pointed at her. "Right."

JUSTIN FELL SILENT, but Mandy could tell the wheels in his brain were spinning. "What?"

His cheeks actually got a little red. "Nothing."

"Oh, come on! It's *something,*" Mandy goaded.

Justin shook his head.

"Okay, new rule."

"We have rules?"

She ignored him. "We have to be honest."

He looked her right in the eye. "That's a dangerous game, Mandy."

Mandy shrugged, but her words came out softly, fervent. "If people were honest with me, we wouldn't be in this situation."

Justin was quiet for a moment. Then: "Okay."

"Good. So what were you thinking about?"

He took a breath. She had somehow managed to embarrass the unembarrassable twice in the same night. "Just guy stuff."

"Guy stuff?"

"Yeah." Justin swallowed. "Can I get a refill?"

Mandy grabbed his glass and pushed off the table. "Sure. But you still have to answer my question."

Justin nodded, but the way he fidgeted in his seat told her he really didn't want to.

Mandy came back with a full glass, setting it on the table in front of him, and Justin took a long swig.

"Out with it, Justin."

He swallowed again. "I was just wondering . . . what we'd be like in the bedroom."

Mandy blinked, her eyes wide. "Oh . . ."

"Yeah."

Now Mandy swallowed then took a sip of Justin's water. She could've gotten her own, but she hadn't considered it. Plus, she kind of liked sharing with him. Not that she'd admit that to anyone. "But you brought up another good point."

"I did?"

Mandy nodded, setting the glass back down. "A couple knows each other completely. Both outside the bedroom"—she waved her hand around the room—"and inside it." Her face was heated, but she was committed now—no going back.

Justin hesitated. "What do you propose? I am not having sex with you the night you broke up with your boyfriend."

Mandy waved him off. "I wasn't proposing that, goofball. But . . ."

"But what?" His eyes were wide as he studied her.

"Just that . . . if we're gonna do this, we need to . . . um . . . practice."

Justin's mouth fell open. "I won't 'practice' having sex with you either, Mandy."

"No! That's not what I meant. I just meant . . . if we're not comfortable around each other, how will people buy us as a couple?"

Justin's shoulders relaxed. What—did he *not* want to have sex with her? Was she reading all his signals wrong?

She scrutinized him again. No, she wasn't reading him incorrectly, she was certain of that. But he was right—sex had to be off the table for the time being. She shook her head at herself. She *just* broke up with Dan, for heaven's sake.

"Okay," he answered. "So we need to get . . . close."

Mandy nodded slowly, her eyes wide. She couldn't believe she'd actually suggested this. She had no clue what it even meant, but to her middle-of-the-night, sleep-deprived brain, the logic was solid.

Justin put his hand on the table, tentatively reaching for hers. She extended her hand to his and felt his fingers close around hers.

"This is weird."

Justin chuckled but left his hand on hers. "Yes, it is."

Mandy pulled her hand away. "This needs to be more spontaneous."

Justin leaned back in his chair. "You can't plan spontaneity, Mandy."

"Before that . . . we need nicknames for each other. Like 'baby' or 'babe'—that's simple enough, right?"

Justin pursed his lips then nodded. "I like it, baby."

Mandy scrunched her face for a split second. "We'll work on it."

"Okay, *babe*." Then his eyes shot wide. "I know how to make this work."

"Make what work?"

"The spontaneity."

Mandy blushed, and Justin grinned at her.

"Do you trust me?"

"Trust you with what?"

Justin stood, shaking his head. "Trust isn't trust if it's qualified." He stuck out his hand.

Mandy took it, letting him pull her to her feet. She was thankful she'd dropped her heels at the front door.

"Come with me." He led her the few steps it took to get out into the living room, into the only space big enough for two people to stand comfortably. He wrapped his arm around her waist, pulling her closer to his chest, and guided her arms up to his neck. "Dance with me."

"We're dancing?" Mandy asked as they started swaying in the silent, dark apartment. "But there's no music."

"We're not here to actually dance, babe." Justin smiled down at her. "We're getting comfortable being close."

"Oh . . ." Mandy stretched the word out as she finally got it.

Justin chuckled, and Mandy felt it reverberate through her. And instantly, she thought of Dan. He'd been sweet, kind, and gentle with her. They'd danced like this more than a few times. What had gone wrong? Why hadn't she been enough?

One by one, tears started to fall down her cheeks. She was about to cry on Justin's shirt yet again, but she couldn't stop herself. The tears kept falling, and soon she was shaking enough that Justin noticed.

He pulled her away slightly so he could see her face. "Mandy, are you okay?"

She lifted her tear-stained cheeks and brought her wet eyes to his. "I was just thinking about what happened, about Dan."

Justin nodded then pulled her head to his chest. She softly cried into his shirt. Again.

After a few moments, she sniffed and pulled back. "I'm sorry. This isn't fair to you."

Justin took a step back and led her to the couch. Once they'd both sat down, he turned to face her, holding her hands in his lap. He waited to speak until Mandy looked at him again. "Listen, Mandy. You have nothing to apologize for. You've been through a lot tonight."

"But I—"

"No." Justin cut her off. "Stop apologizing. It's okay to feel what you feel. And stop worrying about what's fair to me. I chose to be here with you. I'm okay with letting you cry."

"Why?" Mandy sniffled, reaching for a tissue on the coffee table.

Justin took a breath. "I haven't known you that long, Mandy, at least not well, but what Dan did to you was unacceptable. I thought you could use a friend."

"But why would you care?"

Justin shrugged. "I just do."

Mandy wiped her nose with the tissue then made a face at it. "Let me go clean up."

Justin nodded. "Of course."

JUSTIN WATCHED MANDY WALK AWAY, luxuriating in the way her perfectly round ass filled out her jeans. This woman was going to kill him before all this was over.

He slouched down on the couch, resting his head against the back of the futon. It had been a long night. He thought back to just this afternoon, back to when things had been barely tolerable but infinitely simpler.

This afternoon, he'd been pining after a woman who was utterly unavailable. Then, in the most horrific yet serendipitous of moments, the Universe had presented him everything he'd ever wanted on a silver platter. He just had to play this right.

Despite how Mandy was carrying on about their "rules," he would have to set a few of his own if he was going to come out of this unscathed. He would have to put a wall up around his heart if he was going to have to walk away from her, away from everything he'd been hoping for since he spotted her in that classroom freshman year.

She'd barely even known he existed then, and since, she'd only had eyes for Dan. Justin had seen it every time she looked at him. She'd been enamored with the guy—perhaps even in love—and the asshole had torn the kind, generous heart she'd graciously offered him to shreds.

And Justin had been there to pick up the pieces. Fortuitous timing in some ways, terrible in others. For as much as he wanted her, he would have to force himself to keep his distance.

He'd dug his own grave by volunteering to be her boyfriend for the weekend. If he wasn't careful, he would fall in love with her before she even had a chance to get over Dan.

And yet, despite everything, he wouldn't trade where they'd ended up for the world.

Though if he could've saved Mandy the heartache, he would've done it in an instant.

MANDY STARED at herself in her bathroom mirror, wondering how the evening had gotten so off course. After she'd removed the rest of her mascara—which was mostly under her eyes anyway—she surveyed her bare face in the mirror, still red from wiping it with a towel. And an overwhelming gratitude flowed through her. Gratitude for Justin, specifically—that he'd noticed she needed help tonight and offered it without hesitation.

She took a deep breath, steeling herself, then headed back out to the living room.

Justin was already asleep on the couch.

Mandy smiled, pulling the throw blanket off the back of the futon and laying it over him. Then she turned the lights out in the kitchen and headed to bed.

They could finish the list in the morning.

CHAPTER FIVE

MORNING CAME WAY TOO SOON, and the sunlight streaming through Mandy's lone bedroom window was blinding. She stretched in the bed, smiling to herself before the memories came rushing back.

Dan . . . cheating . . . crying . . . graduation . . . Justin.

Mandy jumped out of bed, throwing off the blankets as she did, then flew to the door.

Justin was still asleep on the sofa and looked like he hadn't moved since she'd covered him up last night.

But apparently her crazed sprint to her door had woken him up. He stirred on the couch, blinking slowly at first then pulling himself up to a seated position. "Where . . . oh, hi." He shot Mandy a sleepy grin that went all the way down to her toes. And other places. Damn. She'd thought that was just a last-night thing.

"Sleep okay?"

Justin nodded. "Yes. Your futon is surprisingly comfortable."

Mandy grinned, still leaning against her doorframe with her

arms folded across her chest. As Justin's eyes scanned her from head to toe—a seemingly subconscious action—her thin black racerback tank top and super-short silk shorts suddenly didn't cover enough skin. She shifted her weight, pulling her arms tighter around her.

"Are you hungry?"

Justin nodded. "Yeah, but mostly thirsty. And I kinda need to use the bathroom."

Mandy stepped back and motioned at the doorway next to her. "Be my guest."

But he didn't get up right away.

"Something wrong?"

"Uh . . . well, give me a minute."

Mandy blinked, then the realization hit. And her face turned beet red. "Oh! Sorry." She turned away. "Take all the time you need." She stepped into the bathroom, quickly grabbed a clean hand towel from the small rack mounted over the toilet, a new toothbrush she had stashed in the medicine cabinet, and her tube of toothpaste and laid them all out on the counter for him. Then she retreated to her bedroom, shutting the door to give him some privacy.

It had been a while since a guy had actually stayed over at her apartment, come to think of it. Actually, it had never happened. Dan had always had an excuse. That's probably why they never moved in together, either.

At the thought of Dan, she felt a stabbing in her chest. She was furious with him—most definitely—but her heart still sensed the loss sharply.

She let a few tears fall, but she quickly wiped them away as she headed to the closet to don her clothes and grab her graduation gown and cap. Today was a day for happy endings and new beginnings.

Even if one beginning was fake.

JUSTIN SPLASHED water on his face over Mandy's bathroom sink then stared at himself in the mirror. He couldn't believe he'd spent the night with this woman just hours after she'd broken up with her boyfriend. In separate rooms, but still. What the hell was he doing?

"Justin! You want breakfast before we head out?" Mandy called through the closed door, though this place was so small she could've been in the kitchen and he still would've heard her.

He reached for the towel Mandy had laid out for him and dried his face. "Sure!" he called. "Be out in a minute!"

He pulled the bathroom door open thirty seconds later, and immediately the smell of something burning hit his nose. He rushed to the kitchen—which took about a second because it was only five steps away.

"Mandy! You okay?"

Mandy was whipping a kitchen towel at a toaster on the small sliver of countertop that sat between her fridge and sink. She tossed the towel in the stainless steel sink, flipping on the water to douse it. Because it was on fire.

Justin covered his mouth to hide a smile. Cooking: 1, Mandy: 0.

Mandy sighed, her shoulders falling. Her hair was an adorable mess. The toaster smoldered on the counter as Mandy flipped the water off, but when she looked up at Justin, who was fighting his laughter and losing, a grin spread across her face. Then she started laughing.

Soon they were both in tears, and Mandy was bent in two,

trying to catch her breath. Justin was struggling to breathe himself.

"I . . . am . . . so . . . sorry . . ." Mandy gasped between breaths. Then she straightened, composing herself at least enough to talk. "Cereal it is. That okay?" She chuckled again, shaking her head at the mess in her tiny kitchen.

Justin nodded, still laughing. "Now I know why you didn't go to culinary school."

"Shut up!" She smacked his arm. "This was a one-time . . . okay, like four-time thing."

Justin laughed again. "Noted." His face settled into a smile. "Cereal would actually be great. It's my favorite food."

"I thought it was pizza?" Mandy cocked her head then moved to grab a few boxes from the top of the fridge.

"Second-favorite, then," Justin conceded, grinning as he stepped next to her. "Bowls? Silverware?"

Mandy nodded to the single cabinet on the other side of the sink as she pulled open the drawer next to the fridge and grabbed two mismatched spoons. Justin selected a couple of well-worn bowls—mismatched as well—and set them on the table. He sunk into his chair from last night as Mandy grabbed the milk from the fridge.

"Okay, I have frosted shredded wheat or a sugary one with marshmallows."

"Marshmallows, please."

Mandy rolled her eyes as she set the box in front of him. "I should've guessed."

Justin just grinned, his teeth on full display as he opened the box and poured himself a bowl.

Mandy dropped to the chair opposite him and smiled, grabbing the box of frosted wheat. He could feel her eyes on him as he poured milk over his cereal and shoved the first spoonful in his mouth.

"What?"

Mandy just smiled, shaking her head as she poured her own milk. "Nothing."

"Honesty, remember?"

Her smile widened. "I was just thinking that this is nice."

Justin smiled back, his face softening. "It is. Is this a normal breakfast for you?"

Mandy shrugged. "If I have time. Or an energy bar if I'm rushing out the door." She shoved a bite into her mouth then chewed and swallowed before continuing. "I'm really glad to be done with school, at least for the summer. Though I have a work study, it'll be nice to have a break from classes."

Justin nodded, chewing his own bite.

"You have any summer plans?"

Justin swallowed. "Yeah, I'm going to see my parents in Montana, spend most of the summer there."

"Oh, that'll be fun!" Mandy paused, cocking her head. "That'll be fun, right?"

Justin smiled. "Yeah. My parents are really cool."

"What do they do?"

Justin stood, pulled a glass from her only other upper cabinet, and poured himself some water from the faucet. "They're kinda 'independently wealthy,' so to speak. They made some really good investments several years ago that paid off. They're living off the proceeds."

"That's pretty cool." Mandy smiled at him, and he didn't quite understand the look on her face. So since they were doing this honesty thing, he thought he'd ask.

"What are you thinking?"

Mandy leaned back in her chair, pursing her lips and

crossing her arms beneath her ample chest. "Whew, this honesty thing is gonna bite me in the ass."

Justin just grinned as he finished off the last of his cereal.

"I just like this."

"What?"

"Us, like this. That you knew where to go to get yourself some water. That you felt comfortable enough here to do it." Mandy shrugged, and Justin thought he saw a tear forming in the corner of her eye.

"Aw, Mandy, I'm sorry. I didn't mean to bring up something painful."

Mandy nodded, sniffling. Then she wiped her nose and blinked hard a few times. "No, it's fine. I was just remembering how Dan never wanted to spend any time here."

Justin nodded. He'd figured that's where her thoughts had gone. "I'm sorry. He was an asshole."

Mandy offered a watery chuckle. "Yeah." She wiped her eyes with a napkin. "It's like I'm now looking at the relationship through a whole different filter. I'm questioning everything he said and did. It's emotionally exhausting."

Justin just nodded again, unsure of what to say.

Mandy sniffed once. "But I'm okay. This is a day for celebration." She smiled, standing and reaching for their bowls.

But Justin snatched them first, carrying them to the sink.

"What are you doing?"

Justin just grinned over his shoulder as he pulled the soaked towel from the sink, wringing it out before setting it on the counter. "You made breakfast, so I do the dishes."

Mandy laughed, leaning back against the table. The sight of her happiness warmed Justin's insides as he turned back to the sink and flipped on the water. "I would hardly call what I did 'making breakfast,' but I'm not complaining that you've taken over dish duty."

Justin soaped up a sponge and started on the first bowl. "When I make you dinner, you can do dishes."

Mandy pulled a clean towel from a drawer nearby, brushing Justin's arm as she did, and sparks spread from his arm throughout his whole body as he handed her the first bowl. She grinned over at him as she dried it. "Deal."

CHAPTER SIX

THEY DECIDED that Justin would drive to the airport—it would fit with Mandy's aversion to driving anyway, and he had the bigger vehicle. Plus, what a perfect opportunity to introduce the family to her new boyfriend, right? No time like the present . . .

Justin stopped off at his house to change and get a quick shower. Mandy thought his blond hair was cute all messed up from sleeping on her couch—which she still couldn't believe had happened—but he literally took her breath away when he exited the frat house thirty minutes later with his hair gelled and perfectly in place. He wore a fitted gray suit with an open dark-brown dress shirt stretched across his clearly muscled chest, a brown belt, and brown dress shoes that somehow all worked together.

Mandy reached over and turned up the AC. The guy could rock a suit.

Soon they were headed into early Saturday morning traffic —which, in Orlando, was considerable. As they sat on the interstate, waiting for the truck in front of them to move, Mandy pulled her notebook and pencil from her large faux-leather purse.

Justin laughed when he noticed. "We're still doing this?"

Mandy nodded several times. "Yes, Justin. We need to be prepared."

"Babe."

"Babe," Mandy conceded.

"Okay." Justin nodded, pulling forward a few feet before stopping again. "So far, I know you like barbecue ribs and hate lemon anything and chicken. Who hates chicken, by the way?"

Mandy ignored him. "And you like pizza and sugary cereal that rots your teeth but hate celery, was that it?"

Justin nodded again and chuckled, his eyes out the windshield. "And we're picking up your mom, Amy, and her husband, Bill. Plus, your sister, Lucy."

"Right." The car inched forward again as Mandy eyed him. "Are your parents coming to graduation?"

Justin kept his eyes on the road, but Mandy saw his jaw clench. "They can't make it."

"Sorry."

"For what?"

Mandy looked out the windshield as well. "For whatever's keeping them away. Seems like a sore subject."

Justin sighed then glanced over at her, his eyes tired. "My mom's in the hospital."

Mandy gasped. "Justin! I'm so sorry!"

"It's okay. She had to have emergency surgery, but she's recovering well. She can't travel, though, and my dad didn't want to leave her."

Mandy nodded. "I understand that. Have you seen her yet?"

Justin shook his head and pulled forward. "We had a video

call yesterday. She's sad she'll miss it. She knows how hard I've worked." His voice broke at the end.

Mandy leaned over and squeezed his leg. "I'm sorry they can't be here."

Justin's jaw was still tight, but he released it after a moment and exhaled. "It's okay." He reached down and covered Mandy's hand with his. "It made me available to help you." He smiled her way.

Mandy grinned back. "I really appreciate this, you know. You didn't have to do this."

"I know, but I wanted to. This is kinda fun, actually."

Mandy gasped again. "This is my life!"

Justin's smile widened. "Temporarily."

"True." Mandy took a deep breath then released it. "Let's just take this one day at a time. We'll worry about what happens next when this weekend is over."

Justin nodded then pressed on the gas. Traffic was moving again, which was good. The flight was landing in thirty minutes, and they were still twenty minutes away.

MANDY'S FAMILY had been ecstatic to meet Justin—a little confused at first but then ecstatic. He even saw Mandy's sister give her an elbow to the ribs and mouth "hot" when he was trapped in a hug from her mom.

They were back on the interstate in no time at all.

"Thank you so much for picking us up—Justin, was it? I'm sorry; Mandy just never told us about you."

Mandy rolled her eyes from the passenger seat, and Justin hid a grin. "It's new, Mom."

"You said that already, sweetheart."

Justin reached over and grabbed Mandy's hand, squeezing it. But he didn't let go. Mandy needed the support today, and he was more than happy to give it. Truth be told, he probably needed it, too. Plus, now their hands were front and center, on full display for her entire family.

"So what happened to Dan?" Lucy asked from behind Justin's seat.

Mandy turned toward her sister but kept Justin's hand in hers. "Dan cheated on me."

Amy Thatcher gasped. "That jerk . . ."

Justin smiled over at Mandy. "That's what I said."

"So what . . . you guys just hooked up right after Dan cheated on you?" Lucy was pressing for all the gory details, and Justin cringed internally, eyeing Mandy. He'd watch her closely so he would know when she needed him to run interference.

She wasn't kidding about the questions.

Mandy shifted in her seat. "Pretty much, yeah. A few days later."

"Aw, that's sweet. Isn't that sweet, honey?" Amy turned to her husband, who was focused on his phone.

"Uh, hmm? Oh, yes, sweet," Bill muttered, only taking his eyes off his phone's screen for a second.

Amy dismissed him with a wave of her hand. "Don't mind him. He works twenty-four-seven."

Justin saw Lucy in the rearview mirror nodding vigorously at Mandy, leaning back so she was out of their mother's eyeline. He saw Mandy put her free hand to her mouth, her eyes smiling.

Justin changed the subject. "So how old are you, Lucy?"

She straightened in her seat. "Seventeen, almost eighteen."

"Then you must be graduating . . . this year, right?"

Lucy smiled. "Yes."

"Any college plans?"

Lucy started rattling off all the places she'd applied to, some of which she heard back from long ago for early acceptance, then launched into why she picked the one she did and how excited she was to move out of the house in the fall. Justin just smiled and asked appropriate questions along the way, squeezing Mandy's hand at periodic intervals without even thinking about it.

Though he barely knew this family, he discovered he liked getting to know them. Mandy had suddenly become extremely important to him—or not so suddenly—and his new mission in life was to make her happy. He could tell her family was important to her, which made them important to him.

So inane conversations or not, he was eager to find out all he could about them, connect with her family—for their sake and for hers. And as the conversation turned toward Amy's hobbies and the things that kept her busy, he felt a smile spread slowly across his face. He could get used to this.

MANDY'D HEARD all of Lucy's college plans before and knew she was headed to Georgetown University in D.C., so she tuned her sister out and stared out the windshield. She started thinking about her future, what would happen after today.

And as she'd come to expect over the last twelve hours, thoughts of Dan and what she'd lost resurfaced. As she felt tears spring to her eyes, she felt Justin squeeze her hand again. She glanced over at him, giving him a teary smile. And her heart filled with gratitude for him once again. She'd have to figure out how to thank him properly when this was all over.

They pulled into the parking lot at UCF with time to spare. With the way traffic was today, they'd opted to store her family's luggage in the back of Justin's Jeep and head directly to the school.

Mandy's mom was snapping pictures the whole way, even getting shots of the palm trees along the interstate.

"Mandy, let's get a picture of you and Justin before you put your gowns on!" Amy shouted, motioning vehemently for them to get together under a nearby tree.

"Mom! We're still in the parking lot." Mandy pointed toward a nearby grove of trees. "Let's go over there."

Amy squinted across the cement lot then nodded her approval. Mandy glanced over at Justin and mouthed a "sorry." He just grinned and waved her off.

After beating the world record for most graduation pictures taken in one sitting, Lucy announced she needed to find a restroom. Mandy pointed her sister—and consequently her mother and stepfather, too—in the direction of the closest building she knew would be open. They sauntered off as a group, Bill a few paces behind the women, still enthralled with his phone.

Mandy sat down on the edge of the large cement planter box that marked the center of one of many campus quads. Justin dropped down beside her.

"I am so sorry for my family."

Justin waved his hand in the air between them. "Don't worry about it. It's kinda nice. I wasn't exactly looking forward to having to spend this day alone."

Mandy nodded solemnly as silence fell between them. After several minutes, Mandy glanced in the direction her family had gone. What was taking them so long?

"Mandy, can I ask you a question?"

She nodded.

"It's personal."

She sucked in a breath. "Okay. Honesty was my rule anyway—seems only fair."

Justin leaned forward, his elbows on his knees, and gazed out over the parking lot. "Did you love Dan?"

Mandy's breath caught at the question, and she thought a minute before answering. "I don't know."

"You don't know?" He turned to her.

Mandy paused for a moment then shook her head. "No. I thought maybe I did, but now . . ."

". . . you don't know."

"Right."

"Then why were you with him for so long?"

"How do you know how long we were together?"

Justin raised an eyebrow. "I was there when you two met and started dating. Before, actually."

Mandy chuckled nervously. "Oh. Yeah."

"So why?"

Mandy took another deep breath. The air was already thick with humidity, and she was glad she wore a lightweight, white sundress covered in a large floral print with strappy heels. Justin must be dying in that admittedly sexy suit. "I'm not sure—he felt comfortable. I thought he loved me. I thought I saw a future together."

Justin straightened and looked over at her. "I'm sorry for what happened to you. I'm sorry you didn't get your happy ending."

Now Mandy stared out at the parking lot. Her next words were a whisper. "I thought he was going to ask me to marry him."

"Really?"

Mandy nodded, a single tear escaping down her cheek. She wiped it away quickly. She would not ruin her mascara two days in a row. "I thought because of graduation, the new chapter in our lives, he would be ready to take that next step. I guess I know now why he didn't."

Justin reached for her hand. "I really am so sorry."

Mandy squeezed it back. "Thank you for doing this. Turns out I really needed the support today."

Justin grinned, and Mandy could feel everything inside her clench. How had she never noticed him before? "No problem. Like I said, happy to be here. With you."

Just then, her family came into view past a collection of bushes not too far away. Amy held up her phone. "It's time for you two to get in line."

Mandy whipped out her own phone to check the time then leapt to her feet. "Thanks, Mom!" She ran over to give her a kiss on the cheek then held out her hand for Justin, who pushed to his feet. "Ready to go, babe?"

Justin grinned again, and Mandy didn't know how she'd get through this day without kissing that grin off his lips. "Ready, babe."

Mandy grinned back.

JUSTIN LEFT Mandy with the Cs and made his way to the Ss.

"Oh, look who it is."

Justin cringed before he turned toward the voice. "Dan." He should've known Dan would be right here. His last name was Stanley.

"Guess we're graduating together, *buddy*."

Justin could hear the sarcasm dripping off that last word.

"Guess we are." He took a breath and decided to take the high road. "Congratulations."

Dan raised an eyebrow. "Congratulations? That's all you're gonna say?"

Justin shrugged as he checked in with the attendant then found his place in line. Dan stood right behind him, so Justin turned to respond. "What else should I say?"

Dan's eyes suddenly widened, and Justin's stomach dipped. *Uh-oh.* "Did you *sleep* with her last night, man?"

Justin's mouth fell open as he stared his former friend down. "What?! No way—absolutely not!"

Dan's smirk was wicked. "You're not fooling anyone. No one acts like that without screwing a guy's girlfriend behind his back."

Justin snorted. "After last night, she is definitely *not* your girlfriend."

Dan just shrugged, his face relaxing into a passive frown.

"And that's *your* MO, not mine." Justin sighed. "She's just trying to move on, Dan. You should, too." Justin turned around, facing the front of the line. Wasn't it time yet?

"To you?" Dan goaded from over his shoulder.

Justin sighed and slowly turned back around. "Mandy makes her own choices. She's free to date anyone she'd like."

"Well, not anyone."

Justin's eyes narrowed. "What does that mean?"

Dan shrugged, turning his attention to the front of the line just as the attendant motioned for the line to start. Justin didn't move.

"What. Did. You. Do." He growled out the words through gritted teeth.

Dan blew out a gust of air. "She's a whore. The guys needed to know it."

Justin squeezed his hands into fists at his sides. He'd never considered hitting anyone, but this guy was making a good case for it. He certainly deserved it. "Do not *ever* call her that again." Justin glared up at him. He didn't care that Dan was taller—he wasn't backing down.

"What are you gonna do about it, huh? The brothers are on my side now. If you want her, you can have her. She's not my problem anymore."

Justin whipped around to face the front of the line, his heart rate finally slowing. Dan was still an asshole, but his last words had calmed him. Dan wasn't *her* problem anymore. And that thought alone made Justin's chest loosen, just a little.

He followed the instructions of the assistant as the line started moving, and Dan didn't say another word during the entire ceremony.

Though what Dan had said still didn't sit right with him. An entire fraternity thought Mandy was cheap and slept around. He knew better—she'd never do that to anyone, say nothing of the guy she'd thought she was going to marry—but the thought was still unsettling. He hated that Dan had ruined her reputation like that, even if she never saw any of those guys again.

But at least Dan was done with her. Mandy deserved to move on without his interference.

Justin just hoped that when she was ready, she'd want to move on to him. And he'd wait for her, however long it took.

He didn't have any other choice.

THE CEREMONY TOOK FOREVER, but it was also over before Mandy knew it. She knew she'd barely remember it—that was what happened with important occasions, right?—but it didn't matter. She'd remember the most important thing: that Justin was willing to pretend to be her boyfriend just to keep her family off her back. Oh—and that she graduated, of course. Minor detail.

They already had reservations at a local restaurant, and Mandy had booked it for five, so switching out Dan for Justin was easy. But she felt a pang in her chest at the thought that her scumbag of an ex-boyfriend was no longer in the picture and wanted to scream. The dichotomy of missing him while hating him was grating on her nerves.

"So where are your parents, Justin?" Bill asked, his phone set aside for the moment.

Justin looked over at Mandy and grabbed her hand under the table. Mandy was surprised by how much they were touching without anyone looking, but she welcomed the feeling of his hand in hers. "My mother just had her appendix out. She's doing fine but couldn't travel."

Amy reached out and patted Justin's hand, the one that was still on top of the table. "I'm so sorry to hear that, honey. I'm sure she is very proud."

"Yes, ma'am, she is." Justin smiled.

"Oh, no need to call me 'ma'am.' Amy is just fine, sweetie."

"Amy, thank you."

Justin held Mandy's hand until their dinner came, then he found it again repeatedly as they ate. Was it possible he needed her company as much today as she needed his?

When dinner was finished, Mandy's family wanted to check in to their hotel. And Justin, being characteristically charming, offered to drive Mandy around this weekend so they could borrow Mandy's car.

"Are you sure?" she asked Justin out of earshot of her family before they hopped in the car after them.

"Of course! Anything for my baby." Justin winked at her as they split to opposite sides of the Jeep, and Mandy shivered despite the heat.

She straightened her spine to shake off her reaction to a simple wink then rolled her eyes as she yanked open the passenger side door and climbed into his Jeep.

CHAPTER SEVEN

"So where to now?" Justin asked as they sat in his SUV in the parking lot of her apartment. Her family had just pulled out in her car, headed to their hotel.

Mandy glanced down at her phone. "It's only three now, so I'm sure they'll want to meet up for dinner around seven or close to it. So we have four hours to kill."

Justin just nodded, ideas of how they could spend the next four hours bombarding his mind without his permission.

"I'm really sorry about this—you didn't have to offer to drive me around all weekend."

"Nonsense, it's fine. Really. What else was I going to do today?"

"Really?"

"Yes, of course. Stop worrying about it, babe."

Mandy grinned. "Okay, babe."

Justin grinned right back. "I think we're getting the hang of that."

"I think so, too." Mandy leaned back in her seat, a smile lighting up her already beautiful face.

"You wanna watch a movie or something?"

Mandy sat up. "Ooo—that's a great idea! Theater or my house?"

"Would you rather watch a movie inside?" He nodded up at her apartment.

Mandy nodded. "Yes. That way I can get out of this dress." She glanced down at the large pink and blue flowers before her eyes shot wide and her cheeks turned an adorable shade of red.

Justin chuckled then leaned forward and turned off the vehicle. "Your house it is. Clothing optional."

Mandy smacked his arm.

AFTER MANDY HAD CHANGED and way too much discussion, they settled on an action movie. Justin draped his suit coat over one of the chairs in her kitchen and rolled up his sleeves, and the thin fabric stretched tight over his pecs gave Mandy a perfect view of his chest. In fact, she couldn't stop herself from staring at him every chance she got.

"See something you like?" Justin asked without taking his eyes off the screen. Mandy jerked her gaze away, her cheeks heating yet again—a common occurrence in this man's presence. When she didn't answer, Justin turned to her with a grin.

"Sorry." Mandy covered her eyes with both hands.

Justin paused the movie with the remote then reached for Mandy's hands, pulling them gently off her face. "Don't be. I actually like when you look at me."

"You do?" Mandy barely squeaked out.

Justin nodded, leaning back on the couch, his arms stretched out on the back of the futon.

"Why?"

Justin glanced over at her. "It's not important."

"Honesty, remember?"

Justin sat up and turned to face her. "I will always be honest with you, Mandy, but this isn't something I should share right now."

"Why not?"

Justin sighed, but he shifted even more in his seat to face her head on. "Because, babe, I'm trying to be a gentleman here."

"What does that mean?"

"Do you always ask this many questions?"

Mandy nodded, biting her lip. She saw Justin's eyes flash down to her mouth then back up to hers, a fire now burning in his eyes that hadn't been there before.

Justin's chest heaved and suddenly the air felt heavy around them. Mandy held her breath. "You just broke up with Dan, Mandy."

"I know that, Justin."

"So . . ."

"So . . . ?" She didn't get it.

"So I will not take advantage of you right now."

Mandy blinked. "What does that mean?"

Justin exhaled again. Mandy could see she was testing his patience, but she really had no clue what he was talking about. "Look, Mandy. This has been fun, it really has. And I'm happy to continue. But maybe we need more rules."

"Um, okay?"

"Rules like how far this thing should go."

"What thing?"

Justin's eyes flashed. "Do you really not know what I'm talking about?"

Mandy shook her head, her eyes apologetic.

Justin's whole body deflated. "I'm sorry, Mandy, really. I

just, I find you . . . attractive . . . but I refuse to take advantage of that, of you, when you *just* broke up with Dan last night. You deserve a friend right now, not someone who wants to . . . be with you."

Mandy blinked, blood rushing to her cheeks yet again. Seemed to be happening often in Justin's presence. "You want to be with me?" she whispered.

Justin squeezed his eyes shut and laid his head on the back of the couch. Seconds ticked by as Mandy's heart raced faster with every beat.

Then Justin spoke. "Honestly? Yes." He opened his eyes and found hers. "But you need to know I would never ask that of you, not now."

"And later?" Mandy wasn't about to stop now. This honesty thing was working out pretty well for her so far.

Justin's eyes softened as he inched closer. "Definitely."

Mandy's entire body heated up in an instant, and she was sure she would combust. How could she feel so close to this man in just what, like fifteen hours?

She stared him down, her eyes boring holes into his. His heated gaze lit her on fire. And Mandy was convinced that being with Justin would consume her whole—mind, body, and spirit.

But he was right, as always. She closed her eyes and pulled away, tucking her hair behind her ears.

"Well?"

Mandy eyed him. "Well, what?"

"You're just not going to say anything?"

Mandy glanced over at the frozen TV to avoid Justin's piercing gaze. "I don't know what to say."

"You don't have any thoughts about it at all?"

Mandy didn't respond.

"Honesty works both ways, Mandy."

"Fine—yes! If you asked, I would probably say yes."

"Probably?"

This honesty thing just got real. Mandy swallowed hard. "Definitely." She caught his gaze and held it. "I don't know what is even happening between us, Justin, or what it could be, but if you asked—later—I wouldn't say no."

Justin smiled that crooked smile she loved, and he leaned back. "Good to know."

"Gah!" Mandy smacked his arm. "See—cocky!"

Justin grinned and actually wiggled his eyebrows at her.

Mandy gasped when she caught his meaning. "You have a dirty mind!"

Justin just settled back into the couch. "Always, babe. Now let's finish the movie."

MANDY'S FAMILY chose a Mexican restaurant for dinner. Though not his favorite, Justin didn't mind. Anything to make Mandy happy. Besides—who didn't like tacos?

"So, Justin, a B.S. in Statistics, huh?" Bill asked, tucking his phone in the pocket of his jeans.

Justin nodded, answering before tilting his head to take a bite of his hard-shelled taco. "Yes."

Bill just nodded. "What do you want to do with that?"

Justin swallowed then took a sip of his water. "I'm actually headed to graduate school in the fall."

"Oh, that's interesting! What in?"

Justin looked over at Mandy, grabbing her hand under the table. "Anthropology, actually, same as Mandy." He smiled at her. She grinned back, squeezing his hand.

Bill nodded his approval. "Excellent. I've found my MBA to be extremely helpful in my work. Do you have a career track yet?"

Justin blinked, but then he realized that getting an interrogation from Mandy's stepfather meant that her family was taking them seriously as a couple. And Justin liked that more than he should.

"No, sir, not yet."

"Please, call me Bill. None of this 'sir' and 'ma'am' stuff. You're practically family."

"Bill!" Mandy gasped. "We've only been dating a few weeks!"

He grinned at her as Amy spoke up. "We're just happy for you both, dear. We can tell you have something special."

Mandy's eyes widened, so Justin squeezed her hand, though he wasn't quite sure why. Probably to ground her and help her focus.

She blinked, and Justin watched her come back to herself. "We do?"

Amy smiled, nodding. Lucy had been on her phone for the past ten minutes, so she wasn't even paying attention. "Yes, sweetie. I like Justin for you, so much better than that jerk, Dan. I can tell you really love each other."

Justin froze, his eyes shooting to Mandy. Her face was beet red as she hissed at her mother. "Mom . . ." she gritted out through her teeth. "Like I said, it has only been a few weeks."

Amy just smiled, scooping up a forkful of Mexican rice as she shrugged. "When you know, you just know."

Justin couldn't agree more.

CHAPTER EIGHT

AFTER DINNER, Mandy's mother insisted on seeing her place. She had already warned her family about how tiny it was, but Amy said she didn't care—even in the thunderstorm that was currently pelting the area with torrential rain, she still wanted to see inside her daughter's home. So, of course, Mandy obliged.

But only ten minutes into the visit, the power blinked out. The sun hadn't officially set yet, but with the sky so dark with clouds, Mandy could barely see. She stumbled into the kitchen to find a flashlight then used it to locate her candle stash.

Thankfully, her love of candles was a little close to obsession, so she had a ton. She also found a lighter, and soon she and Justin were placing candles all over her small apartment and lighting them up. Mandy felt a thrill trickle through her at the sight—it was actually kind of romantic.

Bill held up his phone. "Um, bad news, everyone. Looks like the streets by the hotel are flooded. We're not getting there tonight unless this rain lets up. But it doesn't look like it will until morning."

Mandy groaned to herself, but Amy perked up from the couch. "No matter—we'll just stay here."

Mandy balked. "Um, what?"

"Sure, honey, you don't mind, right? I doubt Justin will be able to make it back to his house, so we should all stay here together."

"But, Mom, this place is *tiny*. We would never all fit!"

"Look around, sweetie, we are already! If you have a few extra blankets and pillows, your dad and I can unfold the futon, and Lucy can sleep on the floor here."

"And Justin?"

Amy flipped her hand in the air. "He'll sleep with you, silly. I swear—sometimes I think you've lost your mind."

Mandy shot a pointed glance Justin's way as her mother set to collecting blankets and pillows. She mouthed a "sorry" his direction, but he just smiled back, shaking his head slightly.

Just as Amy reached her nearby closet, Mandy jumped up. She didn't need her mother to know all her secrets. Mandy quickly pulled her only extra blankets and pillows from the closet and handed them to her mother, who smiled her thanks and walked them back to the futon.

"It's kinda early for bed, isn't it?" Lucy asked from the living room floor. "What did you people do before cell phones? Mine's almost dead."

Mandy snickered as she turned around. "We could play a game if you'd like, but all I have is a deck of cards."

"Perfect." Lucy jumped in without hesitation. "I'll teach you all a game I saw online. It's supposed to be really easy."

Mandy nodded, grabbing the deck from the hall/coat closet before she shut the door. A lot of places served double duty in this apartment.

She set the unopened deck on the coffee table, careful to

avoid the five candles they had burning there. "You guys get it set up. I'm gonna talk to Justin."

Lucy nodded and tore into the plastic-wrapped deck as Mandy pulled Justin into her room then pushed the door shut.

"Wow. One night and I already get to see the bedroom. And behind closed doors, no less." Justin was surveying her candlelit room, his eyes reflecting the flames.

"Justin, quit it!" She tapped his chest to get his attention. "Be serious for a minute."

He squinted his eyes at her, pursing his lips dramatically. "Okay, I'm serious."

"Quit!" But Mandy giggled at his expression—she couldn't help it. "I want to know if you're okay with this."

"Okay with what?" Justin crossed his arms, accentuating his chest.

Focus, Mandy. And not on his chest. "Staying over. With . . . me."

Justin reached up and tucked her hair behind her ear, his face softening. His fingertips lingered, trailing along her jawline and down to her chin. "Do you want me to stay with you?"

Mandy's heart was racing as she gazed up at him. His hand was still on her chin, but now his thumb reached up and tentatively brushed her bottom lip. Mandy shuddered, her eyes falling closed.

"Mandy . . ." Justin whispered, and her eyes fluttered open. "I told you I wouldn't ask to be with you until later, but I'd really like to kiss you right now."

Mandy blinked up at him. She wanted that, too, more than anything. "Then kiss me."

Justin's thumb rubbed her lip again, rougher this time, as though he wanted to leave his mark there before claiming her mouth with his own.

Then he leaned in, both hands moving to cup her face, and closed the distance between them. Mandy didn't have to stretch at all for him to reach her lips, and she decided he was definitely the perfect height for this just as he pressed his mouth to hers.

His kiss was soft and gentle at first, and Mandy sighed. His lips on hers felt right, perfect. Like home.

Then his hands grasped her cheeks a little harder, his body inched a little closer, and Mandy felt her hormones shift into overdrive. Her heart hammered in her chest as her entire being responded to him, and she ached for more.

Her mouth opened slightly, and Justin let out a low moan as his lips parted to match hers. She gently traced her tongue along his lips, exploring, and he immediately slipped inside her mouth.

Mandy's body heated up exponentially.

Justin plunged his tongue into her mouth, his motions desperate and frantic. One hand moved to cup the back of her neck and the other landed just below it as he pulled her closer to him, as he explored her mouth with his own. Mandy moaned slightly, quietly, but she could tell he heard it. He groaned and pressed even closer, until the distance between them nearly disappeared.

Mandy didn't want this to end—ever—so she reached to pull him closer, too. First, she found the planes of his chest and shuddered as she explored him then clutched his shirt in her hands. Then she moved to the back of his neck and raked her hands through his hair, grabbing fistfuls. Justin moaned again, further deepening the kiss until Mandy felt their souls had melded together as one.

But then, like the snap of a rubber band, Mandy came back to herself. This was crazy. She was with someone else not even twenty-four hours ago. This was definitely fun—and her body craved it—but Justin deserved better than the rebound she could give him. So she pulled away.

They stood, foreheads touching, as their chests heaved in unison and their breathing slowed. Once she could breathe normally again, Mandy broke the silence.

"In case that didn't answer your question, yes. I want you to stay with me."

Justin searched her eyes, and Mandy could tell when he found the answer he was looking for there. "Okay. You want me to take the floor?"

Mandy bit her lip, considering her options. "No." Questions flashed in Justin's eyes. "The bed."

"Mandy—"

She waved him off. "If my parents or sister walk in here in the middle of the night and see you on the floor, they'll have questions that will lead to the truth. So . . ." She took a breath. "We share the bed."

"Are you sure?"

Mandy nodded. "Absolutely. It's not like we're gonna try anything with my mom, stepdad, and sister out in the living room. These walls aren't exactly thick."

Justin trailed his fingers across her cheek with the lightest of touches. "Are you worried we'd want to try something?"

Too late to skip the honesty now. "Yes. I know I do."

Justin swallowed hard, leaning down to press a soft, unbelievably sweet kiss to her lips. "For the record, I do, too. But I'll be good, I promise."

"Mandy! You guys coming?" her mom shouted from the living room.

"Coming, Mom!" she shouted back.

"Well, technically not . . ." A devilish grin flashed across Justin's face.

Mandy gasped and smacked his arm yet again. She had a feeling this would be a regular occurrence with him.

AFTER SEVERAL ROUNDS of a game Justin was positive Lucy made up, the family headed to bed a little early. Mandy made sure everyone had what they needed before Justin followed her into her room, and she shut the door.

"You mind if I sleep without a shirt?" he asked. He knew Mandy wouldn't care, but he wanted to see how she'd react to the question.

And he wasn't disappointed. Mandy's cheeks heated, but she unsuccessfully tried to hide them as she grabbed her night-clothes out of her dresser. "No, go ahead."

Justin was pulling his white undershirt off over his head as Mandy spun around. And suddenly looked a little unsteady on her feet.

"Hey, Mandy—are you okay?" Justin asked, circling the bed and stepping to her side. He touched his hand to her elbow and furrowed his eyebrows. Was this normal? Did he need to call a doctor or something?

She took a deep breath, her chest heaving. "I'm okay, Justin. Really." She swallowed hard as her eyes fell to his chest.

Justin chuckled when he caught her staring, and her eyes flicked up to his. "Ogle much?"

"Oh, stop." Mandy smacked his chest, her touch light enough that Justin barely felt it.

But he felt it enough. His eyes fell shut at the feel of her warm hand on his bare skin.

"Screw it," she announced, pulling her other hand to his chest and dropping her nightclothes on the ground with a dull thud. She explored his skin with both her eyes and her hands, and by the looks of the barely there smile gracing her pretty face, she was thoroughly enjoying herself. "You have a really nice chest."

Justin's chuckle was low and guttural. Her touch was doing things to him below the waist, and soon he wouldn't be able to hide it from her. "Thank you."

Then she pulled her hands away. "Sorry. I said I wouldn't try anything."

"Actually, I think *I'm* the one who promised to be good. You didn't agree to be, if I'm remembering correctly." Justin flashed the wicked grin he sensed got Mandy hot. He wasn't *actually* going to be good.

Mandy's eyes fell shut. "You are too damn tempting." Then her eyes blinked open, and Justin caught her gaze. He swore he was staring straight into her soul.

He reached up, smoothing his hand over her hair. "No, baby, you are." He followed the silky strands to her shoulders then traced his fingertips down her arm. She shivered at his touch, and he smiled. "As much as I'd like this to continue, I made a promise. So let's just get some sleep."

MANDY SWALLOWED HARD THEN BACKED up a step, leaning down to grab her clothes off the floor. "I'll just go change. I'll be back."

"Hurry, baby. I'll miss you."

She rolled her eyes at him. "You really are ridiculous."

"And also dead serious."

Mandy blinked at him, but his eyes held no hint of teasing. Damn, he really *was* serious. "I'll be back in just a few minutes. You can last that long without me."

Justin stalked around the bed to his designated side. "I doubt it."

Mandy just rolled her eyes again and slowly opened the door to her bedroom, slinking to the bathroom.

She was back only a few minutes later as promised, but Justin appeared to be resting so comfortably in the bed that she wondered if he was already asleep. She tiptoed quietly to the bed so she didn't wake him, setting her clothes in the hamper on the way.

"Mandy?" Justin stirred as she climbed under the covers.

"Shh—go back to sleep." She laid back, her head hitting her pillow. Her bed definitely felt a lot different with someone else in it.

Come to think of it, she'd never had someone actually sleep in this bed with her all night. Dan had always wanted sex then to go back to his own bed. They'd never taken more than a nap here. Selfish bastard.

"I don't want to sleep," Justin mumbled, his voice groggy, belying his words. "I want to cuddle with you."

"What?" Mandy craned her neck to look at him, but she couldn't see his face in the near blackness.

In response, he reached for her. She scooted closer to him until their bodies were touching, unable to deny this man the touch he seemed to crave, unable to ignore the longing she felt for it herself. As his hand brushed her bare stomach, the fire she always felt at Justin's touch scorched her skin.

His arm tightened around her waist. He was lying halfway on his side, halfway on his back, and his chest pressed against her back as he pulled her even closer. And though his chest was one of the hardest she'd ever felt, it felt immeasurably soft against her back.

It had been a long night followed by a long day followed by another long night, and though she'd made her plans, the future was changing. But tonight, in Justin's arms, she felt safe. Comforted. Like everything was going to be okay.

She fell asleep listening to him breathe.

CHAPTER NINE

Mandy woke to the sunrise. She had a tendency to wake up early and loved how quiet the world was before everyone else woke up.

She started to stretch but stopped herself when she felt an arm splayed across her waist. Somehow her shirt had risen in the night, and Justin's arm now covered her bare torso.

And once she saw it, she felt his skin scorching hers. Would this man always set her on fire?

She turned her head to glance over at him. He was lying on his stomach, his head facing her, his eyes closed and breathing slow and even. Mandy took the opportunity to stare at him.

His eyebrows were the same sandy blond as his hair, which he kept mostly short and slicked back, but sometimes fell into his eyes, like now. His face was angled in all the right ways—a strong jaw and dimpled chin were accented by a perfect nose and a mouth that she only now noticed was just a little lopsided. She found it adorable and relentlessly kissable.

Dammit, she *did* want to try something now.

Instead of jumping his bones, she turned her whole body

toward him, tucking her hands under her head to continue her staring. She'd be content basking in the quiet for a few moments longer, especially with this view.

"Take a pic, babe, it'll last longer," Justin mumbled, his eyes still closed.

Mandy giggled softly. "Oh, I'm sorry—did I wake you?"

Justin grunted, and one eye popped open. "Mm-hmm."

Mandy grinned at him. "Well, good morning, babe."

Justin squeezed his eyes shut. "Are you always this chipper in the morning?"

"Yup." Mandy's nod shook the entire bed.

Justin groaned, then he tightened his arm around Mandy's waist and pulled her to him.

"Hey!" she whisper-yelled. She definitely did not want to ruin this moment by waking her family.

Justin buried his face in her hair, her head lying on top of his. "Mmm . . . you smell nice."

Mandy froze for a moment. This felt completely foreign to her—she'd never once been with a guy who wanted to cuddle with her.

"Relax, baby." She heard Justin take a deep breath in, inhaling the scent of her hair. "You smell like . . . vanilla and coconut."

Mandy smiled, her shoulders relaxing—but only slightly. "My shampoo."

Justin nodded beneath her, his arm still holding her tightly against his chest.

"This can't be comfortable for you."

Justin loosened his vice grip, but only a little. Mandy pushed back until she could see his face, which was inches away. His bright-blue eyes sparkled. "That better?"

Mandy lay her head on his pillow, their noses nearly touching, then nodded. "I like this better."

"Why?"

Mandy smiled, eyes searching his. "I like looking at you."

Justin smirked back, that crooked smile that got Mandy all hot and bothered. "Good to know."

Mandy rolled her eyes, but the smile stayed on her lips.

Justin reached up and brushed a stray hair from her face, his smile softening. "I like waking up to you."

Mandy blushed, but she was so close to him that she didn't have the option of looking away. So she just kept staring. Then she whispered a confession. "I do, too. Probably more than I should."

Justin's brow furrowed, and Mandy's heart squeezed.

"Justin, I didn't mean—"

"It's okay, Mandy."

"No." She held his gaze. "I want to explain."

Justin's forehead smoothed. "Okay."

Mandy bit her lip. "I've never . . . *felt* anything like this. I've never known anyone like you. But with everything with Dan being so new and everything . . ."

Justin placed his hand on her shoulder, heating her skin yet again. "Mandy, I know. I get it."

She took a deep breath. "Honesty?"

His breath caught for only an instant, but Mandy saw it. "Sure."

"If things were different, if the timing was different, I would definitely be trying something right now."

Justin grinned widely, his white teeth glinting in the sunlight streaming through her window. "Yeah?"

Mandy swallowed hard, nodding. "Yeah." Mandy grinned back. "But we . . . you deserve better than a rebound."

Justin ran his hand along the side of her head, gliding his fingers through her silky hair. "It would be one hell of a rebound, though."

Mandy blushed again but nodded. "Damn right."

JUSTIN SMILED at her for a moment before he moved to sit up against the headboard. The thin white sheet fell off his chest at the same time Mandy's mouth fell open. He didn't hate that.

He studied her pretty face as she stared at his bare chest in the sunlight then chuckled. "You're always going to undress me with your eyes now, aren't you?"

Mandy's eyes shot to his as she pushed herself to a seated position facing him then nodded. "Absolutely. Your fault."

Justin's mouth fell open. "How is this *my* fault?"

Mandy waved the back of her hand in his direction. "You can't tell me you only do this for yourself."

Justin's mouth snapped shut. Couldn't argue with her logic. Dammit.

When he didn't answer, Mandy pressed him. "You must get any woman you want."

"Not any woman."

Mandy blinked. "Do you mean me?"

Justin's eyes just held hers.

Mandy froze, and Justin noticed she was barely breathing. But then she drew in a slow breath and broke their gaze with another wave of her hand. "Well, you've probably had your pick of women over the years. What about the sorority next door to your house?"

Justin bit his lip and shrugged. He wasn't exactly eager to

share the details. But yes, he did have his pick of women. Turned out, he'd been holding out for one in particular.

Mandy gasped. "How many?"

Justin's mouth fell open. "Are we seriously having the 'past sexual partners' talk right now?"

Mandy glanced over at the clock beside her bed. "It's early, and my family probably won't be up for a while. I'm game if you are."

Justin straightened, sitting up taller against the headboard. He swallowed once before answering. "Okay. Honesty time."

Mandy nodded.

Then he smirked. "Ladies first."

"What? No way! I asked you."

"You're the morning person."

Mandy chuckled. "Are you one of those must-have-coffee-to-function people?"

Justin shrugged, a smirk on his lips. "Just caffeine. Usually some form of energy drink or soda."

"Your dentist must love you."

Justin chuckled.

Mandy shifted in her seat. "Okay, if you *insist* . . . I'll go first." She took a breath then started ticking each relationship off on her fingers. "Well, there was Dan."

Justin nodded. "I figured. The walls aren't exactly thick at the house, either."

Mandy gasped and smacked Justin's chest then immediately threw her hand over her mouth.

"You're going to wake your parents if you keep spanking me, babe."

Mandy's mouth fell open. "I was not!"

Justin just grinned. He absolutely loved teasing her—her reactions were adorable. "Fine. Continue."

Mandy bit her lip, hesitating. "Um, well . . ."

Now Justin gasped. "Don't tell me Dan was your first!"

"Not easy, remember?" Mandy smiled as she pointed at herself. "But no, *technically* he wasn't my first."

Justin raised an eyebrow. "Okay, I need this story."

Mandy twisted the sheet with her left hand, fiddling with it. "His name was Tom."

"Tom?"

Mandy chuckled. "Yeah, *Tom*."

"Well, he sounds lovely."

Mandy snorted then clamped her hand over her mouth again. Justin's shoulders shook as he tried to hold in his laughter.

"Hey! He was pretty cute. He followed me around all freshman year, back when he was one of those annoying math geeks."

"And then?"

Mandy shrugged, her mouth twisting. "Sophomore year he bulked up. Gave up math club for soccer."

"I knew you went for jocks."

Mandy rolled her eyes, but he knew he wasn't wrong—Dan had been on a baseball scholarship. "So he asked me out after one of our games."

"Wait." Justin threw up a hand. "Were you . . . a *cheerleader*?"

Mandy blushed, nodding.

Justin whistled but kept his voice low. "Damn, babe, that's pretty hot."

Mandy smacked his arm—quietly this time. "So you were the jock that went after cheerleaders."

"We'll get to me next. Continue."

MANDY FELT butterflies rush through her as she braced herself for the next part. "I said yes, of course, since dating him would no longer have been social suicide."

"How honorable of you."

"Shush." Mandy waved him off. "We dated for a little over a year."

Justin rolled his hand, urging her to continue.

Mandy just shrugged.

"And? You're gonna leave me hanging before the good stuff?"

Mandy huffed. "Fine." She took a breath. "There was this old treehouse in our neighborhood. We had it to ourselves one night, junior year."

Justin gasped dramatically. "How romantic."

"You are so ridiculous."

"Keep going. This is getting good."

"You're disgusting."

"We've already established that, babe."

"Well . . ." Mandy hesitated, biting her lip. She didn't miss the quick flick of Justin's eyes to her mouth. "Neither of us had done much of anything before. So it was awkward and confusing and not that pleasurable at all."

Justin frowned. "That sucks. Sorry."

"What—your first time was so much better?"

He grinned, clearly remembering. "Her name was Joslyn. Seventh grade."

Mandy gasped quietly. "You were young!"

Justin shrugged, smirking. "I was a jock."

Mandy shook her head, a humorless chuckle escaping her. "So how about you?"

"Were you done?"

Mandy blushed at the memories that flooded her mind.

"Well, Tom and I tried again a few times, got better at it, but we broke up not too long after that. Then there was Chase."

Justin blinked at her. "Um, Chase?"

Mandy grinned. She'd deliberately held this back—served him right for being so cocky all the time. "Yup."

"Who was Chase?"

"A one-night stand when I got to UCF. Actually, turned out to be several nights, but it was over quickly."

Justin snorted. "What—like two, three minutes?"

Mandy smacked his arm again. "Ugh! That's not what I meant!"

Justin grinned widely, his teeth showing. "Are there any other guys I should know about? Trying to size up the competition here."

"Competition?"

Justin shook his head at her. "Mandy, you can be so clueless sometimes. *Later*, remember?"

Mandy's mouth fell open for a second, then she snapped it shut as the realization settled in her gut. "Oh."

"Yeah."

"No, no other guys. Unless you count Rick and Corey."

Justin's eyes and mouth shot wide.

Mandy giggled, clamping her hand over her mouth to keep quiet. "You should see your face."

Justin's mouth was still wide open. "You mean there wasn't a Rick or Corey?"

Mandy could feel her cheeks burning as she shook her head, her giggles turning into a full-blown laughing fit.

"You are an evil creature."

Mandy guffawed silently, if such a thing was possible, and fell sideways onto the bed, her body shaking as she tried to keep quiet.

"Shh!" Justin hissed at her. "You'll wake your family."

Mandy nodded, the effort of holding in her laughter making her eyes tear up. But she'd finally calmed down enough to talk. "Okay, sorry. That was just hilarious. Your face . . ."

Justin scowled at her, but she could see a smile fighting to break through.

"I said sorry!" Mandy took a breath. "Your turn."

It was Justin's turn to inhale. "Well, Joslyn. One-time thing. Then Candi with an 'i'—"

"You can't be serious. That was her real name?"

Justin nodded, a smile turning up the corner of his mouth. "We dated for a while freshman year, as much as it could be called 'dating' at fifteen."

Mandy nodded back.

"Then Ashley, the cheerleader, was junior and senior year."

"Wow—an actual girlfriend?"

Justin raised his hand. "Scout's honor."

"That's the wrong hand."

Justin glanced at his hand then waved the motion away. "Yeah, we were fairly serious. We broke up at our senior prom, actually."

Mandy gasped. "Wow, that sucks. I'm so sorry."

Justin shrugged. "Feels like forever ago. And we weren't meant to be anyway."

"But still . . ."

Justin offered a sweet smile. "Thanks."

Mandy cocked her head. "So that's high school. What about college?"

He drew in a deep breath, and Mandy thought he might be hesitating, maybe gathering the courage to share the truth, which didn't bode well. Mandy braced herself for his answer as his clear voice broke the silence. "Allison, Courtney, Dana, Courtney again, Dana again, Jessica, and Mallory."

Mandy's mouth fell open. "Are you kidding me?"

Justin threw his hands in the air. "What?"

"You're not serious. *All* of them? That's like"—she paused to do the math in her head—"eight women!"

Justin's cheeks turned pink, just a little. "Yeah."

She eyed him, the question she just had to ask burning her tongue before it tumbled out. "Are you clean?"

Justin's mouth fell open again. "What kind of question is that?"

"I just thought since we're being honest . . . plus, you know, if *later* ever happens." Mandy shrugged.

Justin's gaze got heated for a split second, and Mandy shivered involuntarily. "Yes, I always use protection. I'm clean."

Mandy nodded. "So am I." She bit her lip. "Uh, Justin?"

"Hmm?"

"Can I ask you a question?"

"More invasive than that one?"

Mandy smiled, but it faded quickly. "Those women . . ." She paused, willing Justin to pick up on the meaning behind what she was going to say. "None of them were at the same time, right?" She was staring intently at a random piece of decor on her wall by the time she was done.

Justin leaned forward, capturing her chin and pulling her gaze back to his. He seemed to *always* pick up on what she was trying to say. "Never. Mandy, listen to me. I would never do that. No one deserves that."

Mandy nodded, her eyes starting to tear up. Despite whatever this was between her and Justin, it didn't change the fact that she had been with Dan only thirty-six hours ago.

"Hey, it's okay, baby," Justin cooed, scooting closer and wrapping his arms around her.

Mandy let him hold her as she cried. It was becoming a regular occurrence with them, and she couldn't for the life of her figure out why Justin was even sticking around for it.

But there weren't as many tears this time, and they didn't last as long, either.

Justin pulled back when she was done, grabbing a tissue from the nightstand and wiping her eyes with it. Mandy chuckled through her drying tears. "Thanks."

Justin smiled kindly. "Anytime."

"Why are you so sweet to me?"

Justin blinked for an instant before his face softened. "I told you—I like you. And you didn't deserve all this—the least I could do was give you a shoulder to cry on." He shrugged.

Mandy blinked at him but decided to let it go for now.

"Uh, Mandy?"

"Yeah?"

"I just wanted you to know . . ." Justin's voice trailed off before he cleared his throat. "I was searching for something in my life when I was with all those women. Something real. I didn't find it with them, obviously, but I didn't stop trying for a while."

"What *did* make you stop?"

He paused, staring at the far wall for a few moments. Then he found her gaze. "I figured out that what I was looking for wasn't with them."

Cryptic. "Did you figure out what you *were* looking for?"

Justin nodded slowly, his eyes locked on hers, but didn't say a word.

And suddenly Mandy realized she wasn't ready to know. "So," she started, "what's the plan for today?"

"That's it?"

Mandy climbed out of bed, reaching for the hair tie resting on her nightstand and throwing her hair into a messy bun on the top of her head. "Yeah, that's it. We've covered a lot of ground this morning already. Figured we could use a break."

"But why'd you get out of bed?" Justin patted the mattress next to him. "I was hoping we'd stay in bed a bit longer."

Mandy glanced at the clock: seven fifteen. It was one of those atomic clocks that didn't need setting—but the fact that she could see the display meant the power was back on.

Seven fifteen was too early to wake her family up on a Sunday. "Okay." Mandy hopped back in the bed, pulling the covers over her. Justin quickly slid until he was lying down again then reached out his arm for her. She snuggled deeper into the bed then turned to lean against Justin's hard body, laying her head on his chest. His arm wrapped around her, and she finally felt safe once again. Like all her problems had vanished at his touch.

How did he do that?

CHAPTER TEN

JUSTIN WOKE AGAIN an hour and a half later—according to the time glowing on Mandy's nightstand clock—to the sound of someone banging pots and pans. Mandy was still on top of him, so he figured her family was up and attempting to make breakfast in the world's smallest kitchen.

Mandy stirred, lifting up to catch his gaze. "Looks like we fell back to sleep."

Justin smiled at her, his head still a little foggy. "Looks like it. Haven't slept that good in weeks."

Mandy returned his smile. "Neither have I."

He chuckled, his chest shaking. "Maybe we should make this a regular occurrence."

Mandy lifted up higher, her hands finding their way to his chest as if they were magnets. "I wouldn't be opposed to that. You know, later."

Justin groaned at the feeling, and he felt himself hardening in his boxer briefs. "You're making it very hard to wait until later, babe."

"What?" Mandy asked, her lashes fluttering comically. She

shot her eyes wide as she stroked his bare chest, tracing circles on it with her index finger.

Justin growled—she knew exactly what she was doing to him. "You know what." Without warning, Justin grabbed Mandy's upper arms and pulled her to him, planting a hard kiss on her lips. He pulled away just as abruptly, eyeing Mandy as her chest heaved. "There."

"There, what?" She was still staring at him, eyes wide.

"Had to be done."

Mandy smirked from only inches away, her upper body lying on his chest. "Agree." At that, she leaned in closer and kissed him back, but she took her time. She pressed her lips to his, massaging them gently with her own, and Justin realized Dan had been right—he definitely had a hard-on for her.

But then she maneuvered her body so she was even more on top of him, moving closer to his mouth so she didn't have to stretch, and Justin had to physically restrain himself from tearing off her incredibly alluring thin black tank top—that clearly had no bra beneath it; oh yeah, she *definitely* knew what she was doing—and silky shorts that had the most adorable heart pattern on them and were so short they nearly showed her ass. Instead, he leaned in closer, deepening the kiss, his hands slipping to the back of her neck as he tried to be good. He just didn't want to, dammit.

Mandy pulled away after a few moments, her chest heaving. Their chests rose and fell in unison as each tried to catch their breath.

"Definitely don't mind waking up this way," Justin whispered, his hand on her face again, caressing it as if it were the most valuable of treasures. Because to him, the woman on top of him was priceless.

Mandy smiled sweetly. "Me neither."

Then, in one swift motion, she lifted the sheets and slid her leg over Justin's torso, straddling him. Justin's eyes grew wide as she gazed down at him, her hands still splayed on his chest. He dropped his hands to the bed, his fingertips inches away from her soft, bare legs, and stifled a moan. She was definitely feeling him beneath her—he couldn't hide it now.

"Wanna try something?"

"Mandy!" Justin hissed, so worried about starting something he wouldn't be able to stop that he glued his hands to the bed at his sides. "Your parents and sister are right in the other room—and they're awake!"

Mandy raised one eyebrow, a devilish smirk stretching across her face. "Then we'll have to be quiet."

Justin could feel fire suddenly flaring in his eyes as he took her in. He warred with himself as she stared right back—he wanted her right now, not later, but he was too much of a gentleman to impose that on her. He couldn't be her rebound, not when he hoped there could be real feelings between them. But did that mean they couldn't fool around a little?

Mandy had apparently had the same thought because she leaned down, and their lips met again. Justin groaned quietly as they did, which only seemed to spur her on, and he gave in, placing his hands on her hourglass hips and squeezing.

She squirmed on top of him, her most sensitive part settling below his waist as her hands grazed his chest. She rocked on him a few times, the glorious friction sparking something in him that he'd never felt so strongly before, and he wanted to claim her right now, this very moment. He didn't want to be the nice guy, the sensible one, the friend. He wanted to consume her entire being, burn her from the inside out.

She pulled away, breathing hard, and climbed off of him. The sheets gathered around her waist when she crossed her legs, then she caught his gaze. He was overwhelmingly conflicted but also exceedingly grateful. If they'd kept going even seconds longer, he wouldn't have been able to stop.

Justin scrubbed a hand across his face. "Damn, Mandy. That was . . ."

". . . hot."

Justin just looked up at her from where he still lay, nodding slowly.

Mandy gulped. "Sorry."

"For what?" His eyebrows furrowed.

"I probably shouldn't have done that. Not now." Mandy frowned, then she bit her lip. "I just couldn't seem to help myself."

Justin sat up against the headboard then cupped his hands around her cheeks, forcing her gaze to his. "Don't apologize, Mandy. That little act will headline in my fantasies for a long time."

Mandy blushed, and he grinned at the sight.

"Mandy, Justin! Breakfast is ready!" her mother called from the kitchen.

Mandy stretched her foot out of the covers and onto the floor, moaning. "I was hoping I'd never have to leave this room."

Justin climbed over and got out of bed on her side, standing up beside her, invading her space. He brushed a stray hair from her cheek, an excuse to touch her and see her reaction to him. "Oh, and why is that?"

Mandy blushed, just as he knew she would, and he got even harder at the sight. "You know what I meant."

He leaned in quickly, placing a chaste kiss on her lips. Her touch heated him up anyway, but she already knew what she did to him, so he didn't try to hide it. Honesty wasn't always a bad thing. "I do, actually. And I'd be on board with that." He smiled his famous crooked smile, and Mandy shifted her weight, clenching her legs together so subtly he almost missed it—but he definitely didn't. She really did like that smile. Noted.

"We need to get out there. They'll think something's going on in here if we don't."

Justin tucked her hair behind her ear. "Isn't it?"

Mandy blushed again, sighing. "It just might be."

CHAPTER ELEVEN

After a leisurely pancakes-and-eggs breakfast—Mandy still couldn't believe her mom had found and cooked up a pancake mix in her mess of a kitchen—the group set to making the plan for the day. And her mom sprung an idea on her from the tiny table she and her husband shared: They wanted her to go to all the amusement parks in town with them this week.

Mandy involuntarily glanced over at Justin at her mom's request. She hadn't even thought about their plans past today—her work study didn't start for another week and a half. "I'm not sure, Mom . . ."

"Come on, Mandy! It'll be fun!" Lucy's uncharacteristic enthusiasm brought a genuine smile to Mandy's face. Her sister had found a spot on the floor near the coffee table while they ate, basically at Justin's feet.

"Okay, then. That sounds fun. As long as Justin won't miss me too badly."

"He could come, too! Or meet us for dinner or something afterward," Lucy said, smiling up at Mandy. Seemed like her little sister had a crush.

Justin smirked from where he sat next to Mandy on her now-righted futon. Knowing him, he could probably tell, too. "Dinner would be nice." He turned to Mandy. "I think I'll bow out of the parks, though. I've gotta pack."

Mandy nodded for her family's sake. She assumed he was talking about moving or going to Montana, but she wasn't entirely sure.

Her mother asked for her. "Where are you going?"

Justin glanced her way. "I'm headed out to Montana to spend some time with my mom as she recovers. My flight leaves Thursday, so I have time to pack up my room."

"Where are you moving, Justin?" Bill asked.

Justin shrugged. "The plan was to stay on a friend's couch until I left, then I'd find an apartment sometime when I got back." He reached for his orange juice, gulping down the last of it.

"Why don't you just stay here with Mandy?" Lucy asked.

Mandy choked on her water.

"You okay, baby?" Justin asked, reaching out to rub her back.

Mandy coughed several times before she nodded. "Just went down the wrong tube."

Justin's hand kept circling her back as he answered her sister's question. "This apartment's pretty tiny for the two of us. I have more stuff than I should at twenty-two."

Mandy, recovered from her coughing fit, jumped in. "Yeah, we talked about it. Unless Justin's willing to part with his designer shoe collection, the answer's no." She glanced over at Justin, her eyes playful. She hid her smile behind a final cough.

Justin's eyes sparkled in response. "And since that's completely unreasonable, I said no."

Mandy laughed, and soon they all joined in.

"So what should we do today?" Mandy asked the group when they'd all quieted down.

"I was thinking we could—"

Justin's phone rang just then, cutting Amy off mid-sentence. Mandy eyed him, her forehead creased. If he was anything like her, a phone call was never good news.

His forehead creased, too, as his eyes flicked down to read the number. Justin immediately pushed to his feet and glanced toward the bedroom before seeking out Mandy with his inquiring gaze. "I need to take this."

She nodded once, and Justin took the three steps necessary to cross the room then shut the bedroom door behind him.

Mandy couldn't make out what he was saying even through the thin walls, but she could feel her heart beating wildly in her chest. Something was wrong—she could feel it.

Justin exited the room less than a minute later, his face white. Mandy's stomach dropped as all eyes shifted to him.

"Everything okay, baby?" Mandy asked.

Justin barely shook his head. "No. My mom—she's taken a turn for the worse, apparently. That was my dad. He wants me to come right away."

Mandy gasped, flying to her feet and crossing the room to his side. "Oh no! I'm so sorry, Justin. What can I do?"

Justin pulled her into a one-armed hug and planted a kiss on the side of her head. "I'll be okay. I need to go pack and get my stuff out and call the airline and . . ." His voice trailed off, but Mandy could see the wheels still turning.

She shifted into caregiver mode. Happened every time someone needed help. "Okay, let's do this," Mandy declared.

"What?" Justin blinked over at her. Mandy could see in his eyes that he wasn't getting it.

"I'll help you with everything. Packing for Montana,

moving your stuff—you can certainly keep your stuff here if you need to."

Amy stood. "We'll all help. We didn't have any plans today anyway."

Justin's eyes scanned the room, lighting on each member of Mandy's family individually before turning back to Mandy. "Are you all sure? That's too much to ask."

"That's why we're offering instead, sweetie. Just tell us what we need to do." Amy was already gathering what few things they'd had with them before the storm stranded them.

Justin swallowed. "Um . . . okay. My room is mostly packed, and what isn't packed will probably go home with me."

Mandy nodded. "Okay, family, head to the hotel and get cleaned up. We'll meet you at Justin's place when you're done —I'll text Mom the address."

Amy, Bill, and Lucy nodded in unison on their way toward the front door.

"Great. Justin"—she turned to him—"we'll get you packed in no time. And if it's okay with you, I can drive you to your house so you can call the airline and get an earlier flight."

Justin just stared, a blank expression on his face as she said her temporary goodbyes to her family.

Once the door shut behind them, Mandy realized she was finally alone with Justin in her apartment. But all she could think of was Jan, Justin's mother. She hoped she was okay.

"Justin, how serious is it?" She hadn't wanted to ask in front of her family.

He ran his fingers through his hair, a move Mandy now recognized as a response to stress. "I don't know. Didn't sound like my dad knew much. I'm sure I'll get a more detailed story later on, but it didn't sound good."

Mandy slid her arms around Justin's waist and pulled him close. "I am so sorry, Justin. Really."

Justin kissed her forehead then pulled away. "I know. I'll get this all sorted out. And Mandy?"

"Yes?"

"Thank you for helping, for offering to help. It means more than you know."

"Of course! What kind of girlfriend would I be if I didn't help the man I love get home?"

Justin grinned. "A bad one, I suppose."

"Exactly." Mandy was enjoying herself so much that she barely noticed she'd dropped the l-word. "Come on. Let's get you home."

SIX HOURS LATER, Justin was fully moved into his friend David's house and on his way to Montana. Mandy felt a pang of longing shoot through her chest at the thought of him leaving—indefinitely, if his mother's condition deteriorated any more—and wondered how she could miss someone who was barely on her radar two days ago.

With her family back at the hotel for the night, Mandy slumped down to her old futon with a glass of wine and stared at the wall for who knew how long. She just kept staring, the sudden silence unsettling and unrelenting. How could this apartment, so full of life this morning, be filled with such despair tonight?

She'd hoped Justin would've been able to stick around for a few more days, to play nice with the parents, but his own parents needed him. She couldn't fault that.

But she missed him, more than she should. And, as much as

she hated it, she missed Dan, too. She thought back to all the times in her relationship where she'd thought he loved her. Come to think of it, they were few and far between. Had she really been wearing rose-colored glasses this whole time?

She spent the rest of the night with a full bottle of red wine, a heavy heart, a couple of sobbing sessions, and an all-pervading loneliness that threatened to consume her in all the worst ways.

But at least she had the wine.

CHAPTER TWELVE

JUSTIN RAN his hands through his unwashed hair. Weeks of countless tests and results that told them nothing had worn him down. His mom wasn't getting better, and the doctors didn't know why. He honestly didn't know how he was handling it. Considering he was wearing the clothes he'd had on three days ago, he would say not well.

His bloodshot eyes stung as he glanced up when he heard a stirring at the door. His dad walked in with a paper coffee cup in hand, eyes drooping and sad. Justin's heart broke yet again as he followed his dad's gaze, which always turned to his wife every time he entered the room.

He'd never seen his dad like this. The past six weeks had proven that he loved her completely, overwhelmingly—that much was certain. He'd barely left this room since Jan'd been here, say nothing of the hospital. Justin had had to make the trips home to get a change of clothes, do laundry, bring them food.

It was exhausting for both of them.

"Any change?" Roger asked, staring at his wife lying

unmoving on the bed, the heart monitor beeping steadily in the background.

Justin shook his head, tears threatening yet again, but never releasing. "No. The nurse was in just a second ago—they still don't know what to think."

"Dammit," he cursed under his breath.

Justin just nodded slowly, staring off into space.

Roger visibly sighed, his chest rising and falling before he turned toward Justin and shuffled over. He sat next to him on the plastic bench seat under the window and put a hand on his son's knee, repeating the mantra he'd said every day since Justin had arrived. "She's gonna be okay. She's gonna pull out of this."

Justin nodded as he always did, but he wasn't as certain. He wished he could be. His mom was one of the most important people in his life, and he couldn't lose her. It would kill both him and his father.

Then he heard a small, raspy voice. "Roger? Justin?"

Their eyes shot wide in unison, and they jumped up, simultaneously flying to the bed. "Jan, honey?" his dad asked. "Baby?" Roger reached for her hand and squeezed it gently. Justin saw his mom just barely squeeze it back.

His entire being relaxed as he caught his father's gaze then flew out into the hallway in search of a nurse.

When he got back to the room, his mom was actually propped up on a few pillows, her chin-length, nearly white blonde hair splayed out over them. Roger was still at her side, still holding her hand. Justin's heart warmed as he stood by the door, giving the nurse some room to work.

Her doctor, Dr. Coolidge, came in a minute later to check everything, and Justin slowly made his way back toward the window.

"Everything okay, Doctor? Do you know what happened?" Justin asked.

At his words, Roger seemed to register that his son was back in the room. He turned and extended his free hand toward him. Justin took it, letting him pull him back to the bedside.

The doctor consulted his chart. "We're not sure, and it might be too early to say, but I might consider using the words 'miraculous recovery.'"

Justin looked at his parents, grinning as they both grinned back. Aside from her pale complexion and cracked lips, Jan seemed almost normal. How could that happen so quickly?

Roger caught the man's gaze. "Thank you, Doctor, thank you."

Dr. Coolidge smiled, turning to his patient. "We'll definitely want to keep you here for a while, run some tests. We want to make sure everything is good before we send you home."

Justin just nodded, though he knew no one was looking at him. He felt like a tremendous weight had been lifted off his shoulders as he slunk back to the uncomfortable bench.

And, as it had been prone to do over the last six weeks, his mind drifted to Mandy. In all the chaos, he hadn't remembered to ask for her phone number, so they'd had no contact in all this time. He idly wondered what she was doing, how she was spending her summer. They'd only spent the one weekend together, but he missed her. Badly.

He pulled out his phone and tapped on his favorite social media app. He opened the search and typed in her name. Several Mandy Carlsons came up, but none were her, of that he was certain. Most had selfies for profile pics, and the ones that didn't only took a little more digging to realize that "momming hard in Tulsa" and "just a profile for me and my cat" weren't her, either.

Justin checked another app, but all he found was a profile that hadn't been updated in years that may or may not have been her. He sighed, locking his phone and setting it on the bench next to him. He should've known that nothing would've changed since he checked yesterday.

The next morning, after he'd talked his dad into going home to sleep in an actual bed and get a shower, Justin awoke from his uncomfortable position—sprawled out on the too-short plastic bench—to his mother stirring. The sun was just peeking above the horizon, and early-morning shadows danced on the linoleum floor through the gently moving blinds. Mid-summer in Montana meant AC, and Justin was grateful. They were in the middle of a heat wave.

He quickly sat up, tossing off the throw blanket he'd brought from the house and bolting to her side.

She smiled weakly at him, raising her hand slightly. "Sweetie, it's okay. No need to kill yourself getting to me." Her voice was quiet, but Justin could tell she sounded stronger than yesterday.

He sat beside her, reaching for her hand and stroking the back of it with his thumb. "Are you doing okay? How are you feeling? Can I get you something?"

Jan chuckled, her matted hair swishing around her face. She coughed quietly. "It's okay, baby." She patted his hand. "I'm okay."

Justin grabbed her water anyway, guiding the straw to her lips. She needed to hydrate. She obliged as he yawned, the adrenaline surge finally wearing off.

Jan laughed again. "You're still tired. Go back to sleep, baby. I'm sure someone will be in soon to check on me and wake you up again."

Justin smiled, blinking to help his vision clear. "I'm fine,

Mom. You've been asleep for six weeks—I can stay awake to keep you company."

She smiled back at her son, and Justin's heart warmed at the sight. He'd almost lost her.

Jan smoothed the blankets around her legs. "So shall we talk about your girl?"

Justin's mouth fell open. "What? Who are you talking about?"

Jan just shook her head at him, a knowing smile spreading across her face. "You know who I mean, Justin. How's Mandy?"

Justin blinked. "What are you talking about?"

Jan's hand fluttered in the air between them, her tongue clicking. "Your dad told me what happened during graduation weekend. I'm sorry I missed it, but I'm glad you were able to connect with her." She smiled.

Justin smiled back, the memories of Mandy on top of him coming back in a rush. He shifted in his seat, swallowing hard. This was not the time or place.

Jan eyed him, her smile widening. He'd inherited her intuition, which, at the moment, was a little uncomfortable. Didn't exactly make for an easy childhood when your mom could read you like a book, either—especially since he was always getting into trouble. "Tell me what happened."

Justin settled back in his seat. "What did Dad tell you?"

"Just that something happened with her boyfriend, and you were there to pick up the pieces."

Justin snorted. "That's not exactly the whole story."

"Then tell me." Her bright-blue eyes, same as Justin's, were alert as she caught his gaze.

Justin sighed. "Dan cheated on her."

Jan gasped. They talked often, so she not only knew about

Dan and Mandy but also Justin's three-and-a-half-year unrequited crush on her. "That's horrible! That poor girl."

Justin nodded. "It was at a party at our house, the night before graduation." Jan gasped again, but Justin continued. "She was a mess, so I took her home."

She stared him down. "I hope you were a gentleman, Justin."

Justin's gaze didn't waver. "You know you raised me to be. Of course, I was."

Jan nodded as if to approve. "Continue."

"But . . ." He cringed as he spoke his next words. "I sort of offered to be her fake boyfriend for the weekend."

"Justin Andrew!"

"What?" He grinned—he couldn't help it. "Her family was coming into town for graduation, and she couldn't handle the questions."

Jan nodded slowly. "I suppose that *was* the gentlemanly thing to do."

"Always, Mom." His grin grew wider.

His mom eyed him again and didn't say anything for a moment. Justin shifted under her scrutinizing gaze. "Okay, out with it, Justin."

He smiled at the memory of Mandy saying that same thing to him. They were a lot alike. Then he took a breath, his smile fading. "She's . . . I . . ."

Jan smiled over at him. "I know, sweetie. You've been hung up on her for years."

Justin nodded slowly. "Yes, and I waited all those years for her to finally see me."

Jan cocked her head. "And you think she finally has?"

"I don't know." Justin pursed his lips. "Maybe."

Jan stared at him a moment then smiled. "Justin, baby, any

woman would be lucky to have you. Of course, I'm your mother, so I have to say that." Her grin widened.

Justin smiled back, but he could tell it didn't fill his face. "Thanks, Mom. I just need her to see that."

Jan nodded.

"And after that weekend . . ." His voice trailed off as his mind flew back there. "There's something special between us, Mom. Something big. I've felt it before, but with her so close, it was so strong."

"Justin Andrew, please tell me you did not sleep with her the same night she broke up with her boyfriend."

"Mom!" Justin's cheeks heated. "I would never do that!" Then his mouth snapped shut, and his voice got quiet. "Not with her," he whispered. "Like I said, we have something special. Maybe not yet, but we will. I can *sense* it, Mom. I can't explain it, but I know we're meant to be together."

Jan just nodded, adjusting the thin white knitted hospital blanket over her legs. "I can see that, Justin." She paused to look at him. "Do you love her?"

Justin's mouth opened slightly. How did his mom know he'd been mulling over the same question? "It's way too early for that, Mom."

"Is it?"

Justin blinked at her response and didn't answer right away. Then he took a breath. "I think I could fall in love with her very easily." He bit his lip then nodded. "That's the best I can do for now. I haven't even spoken to her since I got here."

Jan gasped. "Why not?"

Justin shrugged, scrunching his face as he did. "I kinda forgot to get her number."

"Justin Andrew Stanford!"

"Stop using my full name like I'm four, Mom."

"I will use the full name I gave you whenever I'd like, young man."

Justin smiled at her contrived sternness.

She smiled back. "Then message her on social media."

He frowned. "Can't. She doesn't have any."

"Really?" His mom paused, and Justin could see the wheels spinning in her head. His mother had never met a social media platform she liked and had consequently recused herself from the entire construct. "I like her even better."

Justin grinned.

"Tell me about her. Do you have a picture?"

Justin shook his head, then he froze. "Wait—they put pictures of all the graduates in the ceremony program. I brought one for you and dad to keep." He stood and went to his book bag, which was lying up against his army-green duffel bag. He hadn't bothered to unpack anything at the house, thinking it was best to keep his things with him. He slept here half the time anyway.

Jan clapped her hands once, but Justin could tell her body was still a little weak. Her mind, however, seemed sharp as ever.

He pulled out the thick, letter-sized pamphlet with the UCF logo engraved in a deep black on the front cover. He set it on her lap with a smile. "Under the College of Anthropology."

Jan raised an eyebrow as she cracked the cover. "So you'll be in the same program this fall."

Justin crossed his arms, still standing, and shook his head at her. "How do you always know everything?"

Jan shrugged, turning back to the pamphlet and flipping through it. Then she gasped. "Oh, Justin," she breathed, "she's absolutely beautiful."

Justin leaned over her shoulder to gaze at the picture.

Mandy was in the middle of a green field with trees and large bushes forming a perfect background. Her body was facing away from the camera, but she'd turned her head over her shoulder and flashed a wide grin just as they'd snapped the picture. Justin's heart—and other things—warmed at the sight. "Yes, she is."

Jan set the open pamphlet down in her lap and gazed off into the distance. "You will make beautiful babies."

"Mom!"

Jan chuckled. "A mother can't hope for grandchildren?"

Justin's face turned red, and he turned away. "Let's just wait and see if she even remembers me when I get back."

Jan grinned widely. "Oh, she will."

Justin rolled his eyes. "Is that a 'mom' thing? Are you predicting that because you think I'm irresistible?"

"No, actually, though I do believe that. Nope, I just have a feeling about you two. Call it mother's intuition."

Justin sunk back down to the chair by her bed as he heard someone at the door. As the nurse came in to check on his mother, he whispered, "Let's hope you're right."

CHAPTER THIRTEEN

A LOT COULD HAPPEN in four months.

The plan all along was for Mandy to tell her family—namely her mother, which meant the whole family would know shortly after—that she had broken up with Justin right after they'd gone back to Philly. It'd seemed believable enough—starting a relationship right after a breakup, especially after dating someone for three years, was never a good idea.

But she just couldn't bring herself to do it.

She hated lying to her mom. Communication in the past four months had become increasingly difficult, and Mandy found herself missing phone calls or failing to return texts when her mother checked in. She felt horrible, but she wasn't sure what to do. "I broke up with Justin" just seemed wrong on her lips, and she didn't know why. They hadn't been together in the first place.

Justin was another issue. In their rush to get him to Montana, Mandy had neglected to ask for his phone number. And it wasn't like she was going to ask Dan for it, so she spent the whole summer wondering if his mom was okay.

But why didn't *he* ask Dan for her number? She knew Justin hated the guy after what he'd done to her, but she also knew they'd been friends a long time. Wasn't there some sort of "blood brothers" pact after being in a fraternity together?

For the first few weeks, the notion had haunted her. As she worked through her summer work study program, she wondered endlessly what he was doing, if he was thinking about her at all. Had she read him all wrong? Did their weekend together not mean anything to him? Maybe he was just busy with his mom?

She eventually decided that if he *had* been thinking about her, he'd have found her phone number and reached out.

So in month two, she decided she was officially swearing off men.

Until Logan, who whisked into her life a couple of weeks later at a bar she never went to, all muscles, tattoos, and brawn, and made her forget about both of the men from her graduation weekend. For about a minute and a few decent lays. Then she stopped answering his texts.

Rebound, check.

Her only satisfaction anymore was that school had started last week, and one of her professors was so easy on the eyes she found herself staring at him during each class, for the entire class. As luck would have it—well, honestly, luck wasn't really involved; there weren't a ton of professors in this department—she had the devastatingly handsome Dr. Grady McGready for Quantitative Research in Archaeology on Monday, Wednesday, and Friday afternoons for the fall semester. Ogling her brown-haired, blue-eyed professor for the rest of the year would certainly help her forget Justin.

Which worked until Justin showed up Monday for that

same class. Ugh. How was she supposed to drool at Professor McDreamy with Justin only a few feet away?

"Hey, Mandy," he said as he walked up to the table where her laptop was already open and ready to go, ten minutes before class was set to start.

Mandy just reached for her iced coffee, taking a sip while staring at her screensaver.

Out of the corner of her eye, she saw him sit down beside her at the long table, setting his backpack on the table in front of him. He waved his hand in front of her eyes. "You okay?"

She glared at him. "Peachy. Why?"

Justin's eyebrows furrowed. "You're mad."

Mandy huffed, crossing her arms. "Now why do you think that would be?"

Justin sighed. "I honestly don't know."

Mandy just turned and stared at the wall.

"Mandy, talk to me! What happened? Why are you so upset?"

Mandy growled, thankful the room was still empty as she turned back to him. "You can be a little dense sometimes, Justin."

Justin's forehead creased further.

"Fine, I'll spell it out for you." She took a breath. "You just left and didn't reach out at all! I was worried sick all summer about your mom."

"You were?"

His whispered response nearly stopped her heart. "Of course, I was! Is she okay?"

Justin nodded, his forehead smoothing. "Yes. It was scary, but she pulled through."

Mandy's chest released, just a little, but she still felt like punching someone. "Good. But you still should have told me."

"How?" Justin leaned toward her. "I didn't have your number."

"You couldn't have asked one of your frat brothers? You couldn't have asked Dan?" Three months ago, uttering Dan's name would've sent shockwaves through her system. Now, not so much. That bastard could rot in hell for all she cared—she hadn't given him a second thought in over a month.

Justin sighed again, crossing his arms and leaning back in his chair. "No, I couldn't. Mandy, Dan lied to the brothers about what happened, so all of them supported Dan and his warped side of the story. I stopped talking to all of them."

"Oh."

"Yeah. And I couldn't find you on social media, so . . ."

"You looked me up?"

"I tried."

"Oh," Mandy said again. She'd never been one to put her life on display on the internet. The last time she'd posted to any of her accounts was years ago. "Sorry."

Justin huffed, looking away. "You should've given me the benefit of the doubt, Mandy."

Mandy's heart sunk. She should've. "I know. I'm sorry."

"It's fine. If that's how you feel, fine. We don't have to be friends or anything."

Mandy shook her head slowly. "I don't want that," she whispered.

Justin's fiery gaze caught hers then. "Are you sure? Because you sounded pretty damn certain I was the worst human being on the face of the planet like ten seconds ago."

"I said I was sorry!" she shot back.

"I know, Mandy. So you did."

Tears were fighting to the surface, and she didn't know why. "Justin, I—"

Justin threw his hand in the air. "Save it, Mandy." He took a breath. "You know, I was actually looking forward to seeing you."

"You were?"

He nodded. "Honesty, remember? I haven't forgotten the rules."

Instantly, Mandy was transported back to her graduation weekend. How did four months feel like a lifetime ago?

"But now . . . Mandy, I don't like games. If you want to be friends, we'll be friends. If you don't want me to ever speak to you again, I can deal with that, too. But don't jerk me around. Don't get mad at some imaginary scenario you've conjured up in your head so you don't have to actually deal with your feelings."

Mandy gasped. "Are you kidding me? What are you even talking about?"

Justin shook his head. "Never mind, Mandy."

"No!" she nearly shouted. "Tell me what you meant."

"Mandy, I—"

Just then, the door opened at the front of the tiered classroom and none other than the well-built, sexy professor strolled in. Mandy just stared.

And Justin, embarrassingly, noticed. "Ogle much?"

She pulled her eyes away from the professor with a little effort, her cheeks heating as she tried to ignore his comment. "Justin, I'm . . . I'm sorry. I don't want to fight with you. I'd like to be friends, really."

He raised an eyebrow. "Really? Are you sure you wouldn't rather be friends with"—he checked the syllabus he'd brought with him—"Dr. McGready there?"

Mandy's face turned beet red. Damn hormones giving her away.

A small grin finally broke on Justin's face, and Mandy's shoulders instantly relaxed. "I guess he is kinda sexy."

Mandy gasped and punched him lightly in the shoulder. "You are ridiculous."

Justin's grin widened, and Mandy couldn't help but smile back. "Already established." Then his smile fell. "And I'm sorry, too, Mandy. It's been a rough summer."

Mandy simply nodded in response. His mother had nearly died—she could give him a break.

As a comfortable silence settled between them and their fellow students started trickling in, Mandy glanced at the clock on her computer screen. They had about five minutes before class started.

"Hey." Justin leaned toward her as the seats around them filled. "Wanna get coffee after this? Catch up?"

"Coffee? Isn't that a little . . . boring?"

Justin's eyes flashed to hers, and she smirked. He leaned back in his chair, tapping his pen on the table and staring toward the front of the room. "Fine. Hot sex on the beach it is."

Mandy gasped, smacking him again. "Shh! Someone's going to hear you! And I can't believe you remembered that."

Justin grinned at her. "Hot sex where you're concerned? Of course, I did, babe."

He winked at her, and she swore her panties flew right off. She crossed her jean-clad legs to ease the ache she suddenly felt between them.

Justin's eyes roved over her as she did, and his grin just got wider. Did the guy miss anything? She was certain her face was so red it matched her flowy fire-engine-red tank top.

She swallowed hard, turning to face the front of the classroom as the squeak of a dry-erase marker being uncapped sounded and Professor McDreamy started writing on the whiteboard.

Justin leaned over again. “Let’s just start with coffee, babe.”

Mandy nodded, her eyes still trained ahead.

She heard Justin snicker beside her, and she wished she could just disappear into the carpet.

CHAPTER FOURTEEN

JUSTIN FOLLOWED her to her favorite coffeehouse, which was located just off campus on a well-shaded, tree-lined street flanked by brick two-story buildings. She'd become addicted to their iced mochas over the past four years, and she swore she kept them in business.

Justin parked on the street a few cars down from her and climbed out of his Jeep to feed the meter. As he pulled up the app on his phone—Mandy was here so much she paid for an annual parking pass—she took the opportunity to look him over.

He'd changed a little over the summer. His skin was darker, sun-kissed, as though he'd spent his summer outside. His thin, light-blue polo—she decided she loved that color on him—stretched across his chest, a chest that could possibly be even more ripped than it was a few months ago. As he turned away from her, Mandy noticed how well his khakis stretched across his backside.

It was already sweltering out here, but if Mandy didn't get in air conditioning soon, she'd probably burst into flames.

"Ready?"

Mandy jumped, Justin's voice startling her out of her perusal. She blushed as she turned toward the coffee shop.

Justin leaned down to her ear. "Were you just checking me out?"

Mandy's face got redder as they reached the door.

Justin chuckled, that low, sexy laugh she felt between her legs. Dammit, this guy was going to kill her.

She yanked the door open, and the bell over the door jingled as it swung wide. Justin followed her to the back counter.

"Mandy—hi!" Vikki, the girl who'd worked here since last summer, greeted her as she approached.

Justin raised an eyebrow. "Come here often?"

Mandy rolled her eyes. "Hey, Vikki. The usual for me."

She nodded, tapping away on the touchscreen in front of her.

Justin scanned the menu then turned to Mandy. "What's good here?"

"It's a coffee shop. It's all good."

Justin shrugged. "I just don't drink much coffee."

Mandy sighed. "I can't take you anywhere." She turned to him, mouthing a "sorry" to Vikki on the way. "You like it sweet or black?"

Justin grinned over at her. "Sweet."

Mandy rolled her eyes. "Why does that not surprise me?" She grinned back. "Then try the mocha I get. You'll love it."

Justin cocked his head to one side. "Okay. But I like it hot."

"I bet you do," Mandy murmured under her breath.

Justin nudged her with his elbow as Vikki punched in his order and gave them the total. Like the complete gentleman he was, Justin produced his credit card to cover the mochas, then they headed to the other end of the counter to wait for their drinks.

Justin leaned against the counter and crossed his arms, his eyes sizing her up. She folded her arms over her tank top as she crossed her legs to match. Justin's eyes shot south for a brief second, then he raised an eyebrow at her.

"What?"

He smirked. "You know what."

Mandy shook her head. "I really don't."

Justin's crooked smile widened. "Your body gives you away, babe."

Mandy glanced down at the counter as her face turned pink. "You don't know what you're talking about, *babe*."

Justin chuckled. "Whatever you say, *Mandy*."

The barista handed their drinks over the counter. Mandy grabbed a straw, opening the paper and punching the plastic through the lid of her drink, then headed to the sleek, minimalist couch near the front window. Justin followed close behind.

"This okay?"

Justin motioned to the couch with a dramatic flair. "After you, my dear."

Mandy smiled. She really had missed him over the past few months. "So . . ." she started as they sat down, keenly aware of how little space was between them.

"So . . ." he repeated.

Mandy sipped her drink and turned her body toward him. "How was your summer?"

Justin pursed his lips. "Well, my mom was in the hospital for most of it, so I was as well."

"Really? You look so tan."

One corner of his mouth turned up. "I went surfing yesterday."

"Ah." Mandy took another sip, closing her eyes as she enjoyed the feel of the cold beverage on her throat and the vision of a shirtless Justin in board shorts. "What happened to your mom, if you don't mind me asking?"

Justin sipped his hot coffee carefully. "She got an infection in the hospital, and she was in a coma for like six weeks. It got pretty serious, but she's a fighter. My dad was a wreck, though—they really love each other. She's his whole world."

Mandy smiled wistfully. "That's sweet."

Justin nodded as he took another sip. "It's why I'm a romantic at heart."

Mandy raised an eyebrow. "Really? I never would've guessed." She smirked, belying her words.

Justin snorted. "You know I am, babe."

Her smile widened. "Anything else of note happen this summer?"

He frowned.

"What?"

Justin stared down at the lid of his coffee cup. "Um, well . . . I saw Ashley."

Mandy's heart stopped for an instant as Justin caught her gaze, holding it. She swallowed past the sudden lump in her throat—she remembered exactly who that was, but she wasn't sure how to respond. So she settled for: "How was she?"

Justin swallowed hard then slowly took another sip of coffee. Why was he being evasive? He took a breath. "Are we still doing the honesty thing?"

Mandy pulled in a sharp breath. "I'd appreciate it."

Justin's shoulders lifted and fell before he responded, and

his hand went to the back of his neck. "We, uh, kinda hooked up while I was home."

Mandy's mouth fell open, but she quickly snapped it shut before Justin could see. "Oh." She glanced around at the other patrons clicking away on their laptops, couples having quiet conversations. "And how was that?"

Justin's eyes widened, and he stared at her as his hand dropped into his lap. "Still saying whatever pops into your head, I see."

Mandy smiled at him, shrugging. "Life's too short."

Justin blew air out of his mouth, leaning back against the couch. "I did say I liked when you made me work for it."

Mandy grinned.

"To answer your question, it was . . . weird. She'd just broken up with her boyfriend and had moved back home after college, and I was messed up over my mom. It just sort of happened."

"What—she tripped and fell into your bed?"

Justin jerked, almost spitting out his coffee. "Something like that, I suppose. You can't tell me you spent an entire summer here alone."

Mandy blushed.

He gasped. "You didn't, did you? I knew it!"

Mandy sipped her mocha.

"Come on, I told you mine. Honesty, remember?"

Mandy stared at the brick wall beside them, pulling in another long drink through her straw.

"Mandy."

She dragged her gaze to his. "Ugh, okay, fine! Yes, there was a Logan."

Justin's jaw dropped. "*Another* guy?"

Mandy smacked his arm. "You say that like I'm easy!"

He grinned at her. "We both know you aren't easy."

She rolled her eyes. "I needed a rebound."

Justin shrugged, tipping his disposable cup to his lips. "I get that." He grinned. "So did you get it out of your system?"

"What—sex?"

Justin choked on his coffee and started coughing.

She reached over and patted him on the back. "You okay?"

Justin nodded, his eyes tearing up. She watched his Adam's apple bob up and down as he swallowed to clear his throat. "Yes. But no, not sex. The rebound part."

"Oh." Mandy smiled. "Yeah."

Silence fell between them as Mandy enjoyed the sweet liquid on her tongue, and soon her drink was gone. She wished again they offered free refills—one iced mocha was never enough.

MANDY TOOK her last sip and set her cup on the floor by the leg of the couch before asking another question. "So when did you get back in town?"

Justin tipped his coffee back, finishing it off. He had to admit—this place made a pretty decent mocha. "Saturday. I thought about getting an earlier flight so I'd be back when classes started, but Mom was just released from rehab on Thursday, and I didn't want to miss that."

Mandy gasped. "Rehab?"

Justin nodded, his eyes sad. "Yeah. Because she was in a coma for so long, she needed weeks of rehab to get her functioning normally again."

"Justin . . . I'm so sorry." She reached out and rubbed his bicep.

He put his hand over hers, holding it in place. "Thanks. She almost died." He thought back to the worst six weeks of his life and frowned.

Mandy nodded, her eyes wide. "But she's okay now?"

Justin nodded back. "Yeah. A little weak, but a lot better. My dad's a good caregiver, so I'm sure she'll be back to one-hundred-percent really soon."

Mandy just nodded again.

"What about your family? How are they? And how was your week of amusement parks?" He smirked.

Mandy smiled back. "They're good, and it was fine. Fun. I got really tanned, but as you can see, it's pretty much gone."

Her skin was perfect from where he was sitting. "So what else did you do this summer besides Logan?"

Mandy snickered, and Justin couldn't help but smile in response despite how much he wished it'd been him instead. "Just my work study. I'm applying for a fellowship this semester, and a summer work study looks good on my transcript."

Justin nodded. "I'm sure you'll finish before me. They let me get my prereqs in online this summer, but I still feel behind considering I don't have an anthropology degree."

Mandy leaned against the back of the couch and crossed her arms, her eyes scanning him. "But your advisor wouldn't have recommended you if they didn't think you could do it."

"I suppose that's true." Justin smiled lightly, simply enjoying being in her presence, seeing her face-to-face. She was so much better in person than she was in his fantasies.

Though those were pretty fucking hot, too.

Mandy took a breath. "So how does a guy who loves surfing but grows up in Montana make his way to Florida and end up studying archaeology?"

Justin smiled. "I didn't say I grew up in Montana."

"Oh? Where did you grow up?"

"SoCal, baby."

"Ah." Mandy nodded. "That explains literally everything."

"Hey! I'm not easy, either."

"Oh, I didn't say that."

Justin grinned at her.

Mandy grinned back. "When did you move from California?"

Justin stared off into space, trying to remember. "Um, it was eighth grade, I think."

"So Joslyn was there?"

A jolt of something that felt a lot like love shot through Justin. *Stop, it's too soon.* "You remembered."

Mandy tapped her temple. "Memory like an elephant."

Justin's eyebrows raised. "I'll have to remember that."

"So you moved to Montana for eighth grade?"

Justin shook his head. "No. We moved to Hawaii."

"Oooooh-kay," Mandy drawled, stretching out the first syllable. "The man that is Justin Stanford"—she swiped her hand in the air between them—"makes so much more sense to me now."

"Happy to solve the mystery for ya." He grinned, setting his empty cup on the floor. "From Hawaii, we moved to Montana. After my freshman year."

"Explains the lack of a girlfriend that year."

"Yep." He inhaled slowly. "How about you?"

"I didn't have a girlfriend sophomore year either."

Justin laughed out loud, and a couple of the other patrons glanced over.

Mandy hid her eyes. "Shh!"

"Oh, I'm not hurting anyone. You're just hilarious." He grinned wider. "No, I meant what's your story?"

Mandy took a breath and leaned back, settling in. "I lived just outside Atlanta my whole life—in the same neighborhood, even after my dad left. When I was seventeen, my mom met Bill. He came into Atlanta for a business trip—my mom met him at the law firm where she worked."

Justin nodded, his eyes focused on hers.

"My mom waited to move to Philly until I graduated so I could finish up school in the same place."

"That was nice of her." Justin leaned his arm across the back of the couch, his arm up against the brick wall behind them, his fingers grazing her hair. It was more silky than he'd remembered. Damn. "So you've never lived in Philadelphia?"

"Nope." Mandy shivered. Justin wondered if she was cold, but the sun beating down on them through the wide glass front windows was so intense he was starting to sweat a little. She continued before he could ask. "Lucy had been living with her dad all that time. Her mom passed away several years before he met my mom."

"Oh, that's terrible."

"Yeah, really sad. My mom said he was really devastated for a lot of years, but that his heart came alive again when he met her."

"Aw, you come from a family of romantics, too."

Mandy smiled sweetly. "I guess you could say that."

SILENCE FELL BETWEEN THEM, and Mandy searched for another topic of conversation. As much as she loved chatting with Justin, getting to know him, she couldn't help but wonder where this was headed. She'd already tasted him, and she was eager for another sample.

She chastised herself. She always did this. *This doesn't have to go anywhere, Mandy,* she told herself. *Just enjoy the journey, girl.*

"What's going through that beautiful head of yours?"

Mandy blushed. "You don't want to know."

Justin pursed his lips, his eyes squinting. "Honesty, remember?"

She sighed. "I was telling myself to enjoy the journey." Well, it was partially the truth.

But Justin wouldn't let it go. "Why would you have to tell yourself that?"

Another shiver skated across her skin as Justin twirled her hair around his fingers. "Because of that."

Justin's brow furrowed. "Because of what?"

"That." Mandy nodded toward his hand.

"Oh." Justin's fingers froze, then he chuckled. "I didn't even realize I was doing that."

Mandy's cheeks heated slightly. "I didn't ask you to stop."

Justin smiled as his fingers resumed their exploration of her soft, strawberry blonde hair. "I'm glad. I kinda like it."

"Me, too."

"You know, Mandy . . ."

"Hmm?"

"I think we should continue this."

"What specifically?"

"Us."

"Oh." Mandy's mouth formed around the O. "Is there an 'us'?"

Justin twirled another lock of hair around his finger. "I'd like there to be, if you're up for it." When she didn't answer right away, he quickly added, "We can keep it as casual as you'd like."

Mandy bit her bottom lip, fighting the smile threatening to spread across her lips, and cocked her head at him. She couldn't stop herself from toying with him.

"You have to think about it?"

Mandy let a smile break through. "Just trying to figure out if it's 'later' yet."

One corner of Justin's mouth turned up. "And?"

Her grin widened. "Verdict's still out."

At her words, Justin pursed his lips. Then he grinned. "Okay."

Mandy stared over at him. "Okay, what?"

He shrugged, an adorable frown stretching across his lips as his brow furrowed. "Okay, now I know what my job is."

Mandy tilted her head to the side. "And what is that?"

Justin's gaze caught hers, and Mandy saw a new fire flash to life in them. "To convince you."

Mandy flushed, but it had nothing to do with the sweltering heat coming in through the front windows. "Oh, really? Are you really so *cocky*"—she emphasized the word on purpose—"that you think you can?"

Justin just flashed her a characteristically "Justin" grin. "Oh, absolutely, babe. Be prepared to be wowed."

Mandy rolled her eyes. But she wasn't about to complain.

CHAPTER FIFTEEN

As they left the coffee shop and went their separate ways—with a hug that kept Justin warm long after Mandy'd stepped away from him and climbed back in her car—Justin's brain started spinning. He needed a plan.

A coffee get-together to gauge Mandy's interest, check.

Oh, she definitely was interested.

Next step, wooing her.

Mandy was special; Justin had known that forever. But since that conversation with his mom this summer—the one where he'd confessed he'd felt an almost supernatural connection to Mandy—the stakes were now infinitely higher.

He couldn't screw this up. He would treat her like the goddess she was, worship her as a person before worshipping her body.

Which he hoped he'd get to do very soon.

He pulled into the driveway of David's house, slowly piecing together a plan. First up, flowers.

Wooing a woman always started with flowers. His mom had taught him that.

Mandy was sprawled out on the couch with a piece of pizza and her favorite show later that night when her mom called. She sighed, setting down the slice and pausing the show she was bingeing.

"Hey, Mom."

"Mandy, sweetie, hi! How are you? Are you okay?"

Mandy frowned to the empty room. "Why would you say that?"

Amy cleared her throat. "I just haven't heard from you in a while. How are classes going? They started last week, right?"

Mandy cringed. If this was like last semester, she would've already talked to her mom about classes at least five times by now. But this year . . . a pang of guilt shot through her chest. "I'm really sorry, Mom—I've just been busy." Another lie to add to the pile. "But yeah, classes started last week. It will be a hectic semester, but I'm excited about it. I have some good professors." Not to mention, some good-*looking* ones . . .

"That's wonderful, dear. You've always been so good at school; I know you'll do great."

"Thanks, Mom." Mandy smiled.

"And how's Justin?"

The smile died on her lips. This was exactly why she hadn't been answering her mother's calls. "He's . . ." Then she had a stroke of genius. "We have a class together, so that's nice." There. Wasn't even a lie at all.

"Oh, that *is* nice!" her mom exclaimed on a dramatic exhale.

Maybe this would all work out fine. Maybe this thing with Justin would actually turn into something and she wouldn't have to lie to her mom anymore.

She shook her head. Who was she kidding? A lie was a lie, and she knew she'd have to come clean eventually.

Just not right now.

"How's Bill?"

Her mother paused, and Mandy's heart lurched, just a little. Was Bill okay? "He's doing fine, sweetheart. But Lucy's struggling a little at school. I think she misses being home."

"Oh no! I remember it was like that for me, too, though. She'll adjust quickly. What classes is she taking?"

As the conversation shifted to her sister, her mother's book club, and just about every other thing under the sun, Mandy noticed Amy didn't bring up her husband again.

Then she heard the doorbell. *Who the hell was here at*—she glanced at her phone—*nine PM*? Wasn't it too late for the post office to be delivering a package?

"Mom, I gotta go. Someone's at the door."

"Okay, dear. Have a great night. Love you."

"Love you, too." Mandy hung up the phone and pushed off the couch, stretching as she padded to the front door and opened it.

"Delivery for a Mandy Carlson."

She yawned, covering her mouth with her fingers. "That's me."

The delivery man smiled at her and handed her a white package the width of a shoebox but much longer. "Have a nice night."

She took the offered box with a smile and a nod, and he hurried back down the stairs.

Mandy closed the door behind her, staring at the large box the whole time. She walked it over to her kitchen and set it down, staring at the box that dwarfed her tiny table as if she could intuit what was inside. She'd never gotten a delivery like this before.

Then it started ringing.

Mandy jumped at the sound, glaring at the box like a snake would jump out of it and bite her, before she reached to pull it open.

Inside was at least two dozen flowers in a variety of colors and types. She gasped, then the phone rang again, louder this time. She dug through the greenery and found the culprit, an old-style flip phone. She smiled as she picked it up, flipping it open.

"Hi."

Mandy grinned. "Hey, yourself."

Justin chuckled over the line. "Since I never got your number, I figured this was the best way to call you."

"Elaborate plan."

"You like the flowers?"

Mandy nodded to the empty apartment. "Very much. Carnations are my favorite."

"Noted." She heard the smile in his voice. "Convinced yet?"

She hesitated for a second to keep him in suspense. "I'd say it earns you my phone number, at least."

"What—you don't like chatting on this flip phone? It's vintage."

Mandy laughed. "Um, no, thank you. I'm good with my smartphone."

Justin laughed back. "So does it earn me a date?"

She pursed her lips. "What was the coffee shop today?"

"A pre-date."

"Those exist?"

Justin sighed dramatically. "Oh, yes. That was the warm up to the main event."

Mandy shivered at the thought of Justin warming her up. As if he didn't already. "Hmm . . ." She stretched out the word. "Okay. I'd say it earns you a date. *If* it's not boring."

Justin chuckled again. "Challenge accepted."

Suddenly, Mandy's heart was in her throat. "What does that mean? Justin—I was kidding about the skydiving thing."

He gasped. "I think I know you better than that."

"Do you?"

Justin snorted. "Yes, babe. Calm down. I've got you."

Mandy blushed. She liked that thought.

"Okay. Text me your number, and I'll get it set up. And like I said, prepare to be wowed."

"I can't wait." She said it a little sarcastically, but she didn't mean it sarcastically in the slightest.

She actually couldn't wait.

CHAPTER SIXTEEN

Mandy waited until morning to text Justin her number. She wasn't going to let him live down that he'd called her easy.

Besides, it was fun to make him sweat a little.

Hi :)

Justin responded back in less than a minute. **Who is this?**

Mandy quickly fluffed her newly done hair as she tapped open the camera app on her phone and switched it to selfie mode. She flashed her sexiest pout and sent it on without retaking it.

Damn.

Mandy just sent a winky face.

So are you ready for our date?

What—it's tonight? A girl could dream.

Someone excited?

Mandy bit her lip, considering her response. She sent a snarky face emoji.

Justin's response took a second. Then he sent a flame.

How could a single emoji turn her on? There must be something wrong with her brain.

Mandy clenched her thighs together as she shot a text back. **Just tell me what we're doing and when, babe.** She couldn't believe she'd just put that in print, without him saying it first, but she was past caring with him at this point. Besides, she was rather enjoying this banter between them. She hoped it wouldn't stay all talk, though—that man was . . .

His next text came through. **Are you free Thursday?**

Mandy hesitated a bit to make it seem like she was checking her calendar. Since it was too early in the semester to have a ton of homework yet—and she'd started working ahead already anyway—of course, she was free. Especially for him, but he didn't need to know that. **I think I could do that.**

You think??

Mandy grinned as she typed her response, starting with another winking emoji. **Looking forward to it. What are we doing?**

She stared at the three dots as they danced across the screen. **Not telling.**

She frowned. **Then how do I know what to wear?**

Clothing optional.

Mandy gasped to the empty apartment. **Justin!** She included the surprised emoji.

Justin sent the snarky emoji back then added, **Just kidding, babe. Nothing too casual but comfortable.**

Mandy carried her phone through her tiny apartment to her closet and frowned again. She'd need to go shopping.

Another text came through. **And come hungry, of course.**

So you're going with the boring option?

Justin's response put a smile on her face. **Baby, being with me will *never* be boring.**

Her stomach flipped, butterflies swarming. She had no doubt he was right.

Mandy was out the door ten minutes later. She had Concepts in K'iche and Mayan Hieroglyphics with another professor in the Anthropology department, a Dr. Kayla Harrington, on Tuesday and Thursday mornings. Mandy had heard she was the leading expert in the world on the Mayan language, so she was excited to learn everything she could from her. She'd been planning to specialize in Maya studies since she knew the university offered the program.

After class let out, Mandy headed to her favorite consignment clothing shop, located on the same street as the coffee shop she'd gone to yesterday with Justin. Someday she'd be happy living nearby, but for now, she settled for spending most of her time here.

She found the perfect outfit: a navy cap-sleeved wrap dress with tiny emerald-green-and-white flowers and a matching belt. She'd pair it with her favorite dark-tan flats, so the entire ensemble would only cost her fifteen dollars and forty-five cents. Dressy but comfortable, and graduate-student affordable.

She loved consignment shopping. And bonus: Justin would be drooling. It hugged her curves and breasts in all the right places.

As she paid for the dress and carried the cute, hand-stamped brown bag out to her car, she felt the butterflies again. She didn't know what Justin had planned, but she was certain it wouldn't be boring.

But what on earth would they be doing at seven thirty on a Thursday night? It's not like he could actually drive them to the ocean and be back in time for their classes the next afternoon like their imaginary first date.

After a leisurely stop for groceries and yet another mocha—she was definitely addicted—Mandy headed home. Once she'd wrestled all her packages inside, she hand-washed her dress, hanging it up to dry in the bathroom, then put the groceries away. She changed into something to lounge around the house in then ventured back into the living room, idly wondering how she was going to spend the rest of the evening.

Mandy trailed her fingers over the flowers Justin had given her that she'd set in water in the only glass pitcher she had. She probably should've bought a vase, but the pitcher gave it a classy but eclectic vibe she loved.

She sighed, sinking into one of the two chairs at the table. What would she do for the two days before their date? She didn't have any pressing homework, and she missed Justin. She'd missed him this summer, but after four months, the ache had lessened, just a little.

But then he'd crashed back into her life, and the feelings she'd been trying to tell herself all summer had just been in her head came rushing back. She almost felt an otherworldly connection to him, one that told her he was important to her, that they were meant to be together.

It was crazy—she knew that. And it was damn scary. But she just couldn't shake the feeling.

A knock sounded at her door, and she jumped up to get it.

Another delivery man with a now-familiar box of flowers. She signed for them, thanked him, then locked her door and set the flowers on the table, which was already crowded with the first bouquet.

Mandy opened the box and gasped. Two dozen white carnations filled the box.

She grinned.

David was nice enough, but his house was getting a little crowded with his new girlfriend always spending the night. Justin hadn't really felt welcome in the common areas even before they'd hooked up—which they now did on nearly every available surface; he'd seen way more skin from both of them than he ever cared to when he left for the library just this morning—so now Justin mostly just hid in his room, and tonight was no different.

He'd tried to read his textbooks, get ahead, but he was already bored. He had other things on his mind. Another person in particular.

His phone went off, and he snatched it up. **Thanks for the carnations.** Mandy'd followed her text with a smiley face emoji.

Justin smiled. **Anytime, babe. You deserve flowers every day of your life.**

The three dots popped up. Then: **I don't think I have enough vases for that.**

Justin laughed out loud. **Wanna hang out?**

Mandy didn't respond right away, and Justin's stomach dropped. Too soon?

But then her text came through. **That would be nice. I'm bored.**

Same. Lady's choice.

It took a few seconds for her to answer. **Keep it chill? Movie marathon at my house?**

Justin grinned to the empty room. That sounded perfect. **I'm in. Want me to bring pizza?**

Yes, please. She added another smiley face, and Justin thought it was adorable.

Just to clarify, this is still part of the pre-date.

Oh?

Justin typed out his message quickly. **Yes. I will not have our first date start with a "wanna hang out?" text.**

Mandy sent the laughing emoji. Then: **Okay, deal. Of course, that means sex is off the table.**

Justin's mouth fell open at that, but then he started chuckling to himself and shook his head as he thought of the perfect response. **I'm good with sex off the table. But I wouldn't mind it on the table, either.**

Justin! She sent the see-no-evil monkey emoji. **No sex on the table, either. Dirty mind.**

Justin just sent the snarky emoji as he reached for his keys, then he remembered something and pulled his phone back out, swiping it open. **What do you like on your pizza?**

Her response was nearly immediate. A pineapple emoji.

Justin blinked. **Like, just pineapple? No ham or anything?**

Nope.

Justin chuckled again. **Your wish is my command, babe.**

She just sent the sparkly emoji.

He was in real danger of falling in love with her tonight.

He arrived at her apartment twenty minutes later, pineapple-only pizza in hand. And a supreme for him, though he'd eat pretty much any pizza—except one with anchovies, of course. He'd also grabbed a salad, just in case either of them felt the need to offset the junk food. Unlikely, but he wanted to be prepared. And given Mandy's lack of cooking skills, the salad could keep her fed for an extra meal or two as well.

Mandy threw open the door with a smile. "Hi."

Justin grinned at her. She was barefoot and had on a pair of light-gray fitted sweats and a royal-blue racerback tank top. Justin almost had to physically stop himself from pulling her to him, planting a kiss on those gorgeous, full lips, running his hands underneath her flowy shirt, discovering if she was wearing a bra—

"Hey, babe," he managed, forcing the thoughts away, and stepped through the threshold.

Mandy closed the door behind him then motioned to her outfit. "Since this isn't a date, I figured casual was okay."

Justin set the pizza down on her kitchen counter. "Oh, absolutely. I think you look amazing." Understatement of the century.

Mandy blushed and stepped around him into the kitchen. She pulled a couple of plates from her upper cabinet, setting them on the countertop.

Then she moved to the fridge and opened it. "I got you something." She grinned as she pulled something from inside and handed it to Justin.

He blinked down at it as cold aluminum hit his palm. "You bought me an energy drink?" His eyebrow raised, but his heart was pounding in his chest.

Mandy flashed a sheepish smile and looked away. "It's no big deal."

Justin closed the distance between them in one step and put his hand on her chin, leading her gaze back to him. "It's a pretty big deal. This is my brand." He held the can in the air.

Mandy shrugged, but her face was still red. "I saw it in your bag yesterday."

Justin blinked, actually fighting tears. The fact she'd noticed what he liked and took action on it . . . he knew she liked to take care of people, but her taking care of him in such an unexpectedly intimate way warmed his heart in his chest.

Yeah, he was definitely going to fall in love with this woman—and he would fall hard.

If he hadn't already.

CHAPTER SEVENTEEN

Mandy was forever early for everything, so a few minutes after seven on Thursday she was already fully dressed and waiting, a good half hour before her date. She pursed her lips, wondering how she was going to spend the next thirty minutes, then snatched up her phone and shot her mom a text. It had been a few days since their phone call, and her mom hadn't reached out. Which was unusual, despite her recent communication avoidance.

Five minutes later, her mom still hadn't answered, and Mandy was now anxiously tapping her fingers on her table, staring at her phone. She couldn't shake the feeling that something was off, but when a knock sounded at her door, she realized she'd just have to wait until later to find out.

Mandy's eyebrows pinched together as she clicked off the display and glanced toward the door. Would Justin really be this early?

He'd kept his distance Tuesday night, mostly. He had grabbed her hand during the movie and held it for the duration, but despite a soft kiss on the cheek when he left—at a reasonable hour, no less—it seemed he'd been determined not to cross into date territory.

Mandy'd been a little disappointed. She knew he was just being a gentleman—which she loved about him—but she'd pictured him taking her on the coffee table before he'd gotten there, after all . . .

She crossed to the door slowly, shaking her head to clear it. Tonight would be different. At least, she hoped it would.

Mandy gently pressed against the door to look out the peephole.

The hallway was empty.

Mandy frowned then unbolted and opened the door.

At her feet was a dark-yellow envelope. She appraised it for a moment before picking it up and taking it inside, locking the door.

She bit her lip, quickly opening the top and dumping its contents out on her kitchen table next to the three bouquets of flowers she'd gotten once a day since Monday night. Then she grinned.

Scattered across the tiny tabletop were a variety of trinkets with meanings that Mandy could only guess at. A box of matches, an oriental hand fan, a wine cork, a small candle like you'd see on a homemade birthday cake, a fossil with a leaf imprint from eons ago, and a tiny flashlight that fit in the palm of her hand. Mandy laughed aloud and snatched up her phone.

What's all this?

Justin responded immediately. **Clues for tonight's date.**

Mandy scanned the items more intently for a moment before she text back. **As always, I'm confused.**

Justin just sent a winky face.

You coming soon?

You *are* eager, babe. I'll be yours soon enough.

Not soon enough, she shot back, no clue why she felt so emboldened. True, they'd shared an intimate weekend—though not intimate enough for her liking—four months ago, but did she really know him that well? She sighed. Somehow, though her scientific brain couldn't explain it, she'd felt a deep connection to Justin Stanford since May. And she couldn't shake the feeling that they were meant to be together, as terrifying as that was.

She blinked when his text came through. **Start early?**

Mandy bit her lip to keep from smiling. **Absolutely.**

Five minutes?

She stared at her phone. What . . . ? **Are you already here?**

Justin sent a snarky emoji.

Mandy smiled, realizing he already was. **Five minutes. Can't wait.** She followed up with a kissing emoji, again unsure why she was acting so bold but deciding she kind of liked it.

Mandy's grin only widened as she ran to the restroom and checked her appearance one last time. The dark-brown mascara she'd chosen accented her light-brown eyes perfectly, but she wore no other makeup. The man had seen her at her worst, so she knew she could be herself with him.

But that didn't mean she couldn't dress up a little. She hadn't found a necklace that went perfectly with the dress, so she opted to wear just a simple pair of tiny silver studs shaped like the flowers on her dress and a silver bangle bracelet.

She was washing her hands when the knock came. She dried them quickly, hanging the towel on its rack near the sink so it would dry properly, then flew to the door.

Justin was grinning at her when she tore it open, one hand behind his back.

"Hi," she breathed, her chest heaving.

"Hi, beautiful." He pulled his hand out from behind him

and suddenly a massive bouquet of white carnations flooded Mandy's vision.

She reached for them, pulling them to her nose and inhaling their light scent. She stepped back to let Justin in. "Thank you. These are beautiful."

Justin crossed his arms casually as she shut the door. "You know, you're in danger of being easy with those. Carnations are like the cheapest flower out there."

Mandy smelled the bouquet again. "True, but that's why I like them. They remind me to find the beauty in the everyday."

Justin was nodding. "You are definitely a romantic."

MANDY SCRUNCHED her nose at him then headed to her tiny kitchen. She paused for a moment then started rummaging in her cabinets.

Justin stepped into the kitchen, crowding the space. "Don't you have another—" He spotted the other arrangements on the table, all haphazardly standing in water in a mismatched collection of pitchers and large cups. "—a single vase? Aw, Mandy, you don't even have one vase? We'll have to remedy that."

Mandy shrugged, bending over to look around her pots and pans in the lower cabinets. Justin's gaze fell on her backside, and he swallowed hard as he stared, his hand scratching the back of his neck where his collar was suddenly irritating it. Her ass was perfect, just the right size for squeezing.

He was convinced she stayed down there a few seconds longer than she needed to just to turn him on. It worked.

He adjusted himself through his khakis just before she stood, setting a beat-up plastic pitcher in a cerulean blue in the kitchen sink and flipping on the water.

Justin snorted. "Mandy, come on. We have to get you some grown-up stuff. Plates, glasses, silverware—nothing matches. And why don't you have even one vase?"

Mandy's response was quiet. "Never needed one."

Justin was silent for a moment as he processed her meaning. *Oh.* He cleared his throat. "Well, now you will. So we'll have to find you some."

Mandy's eyes lit up. "Ooo! I know just where to go." She flipped off the water, pulling the pitcher to the counter and setting the carnations inside.

Justin chuckled at her enthusiasm. "Get more than you think you need. I plan to keep lavishing you with carnations."

Then his eyes found hers, and he watched Mandy suck in a sharp breath as he took a step closer to her until their chests were nearly touching. Mandy's chest heaved, her incredibly sexy dress brushing against his thin, yellow polo shirt, and Justin thought he would combust if he didn't touch her.

So he reached out a hand, brushing his fingers across her forehead and down her temple to her cheek. He tucked her hair behind her ear, tracing the shape of it before lightly fingering her tiny earrings. "I like these."

Mandy swallowed hard, her eyes widening slightly. "Thank you," she whispered.

He trailed his fingers down her neck and shoulder—though he desperately wanted to trace another route to where the deep vee of her dress was showing off just the right amount of her breasts—then found the skin of her arm with his fingertips. His fingers blazed a trail of fire down her bare skin as he finally reached her hand. He interlaced their fingers and dropped them to his side. "Definitely too damn tempting."

"No, babe, you are." Mandy smirked, echoing his words from before.

Justin flashed the crooked smile he knew made Mandy squirm, and she did exactly that. He chuckled lightly. "Well, this is gonna be a fun night."

He wasn't talking only about what he had planned. The sexual tension building between them since May was growing to dangerous levels, and the time apart had only increased it. If he didn't do something about it soon, they'd both explode into flames.

Though in this moment, looking into Mandy's eyes, that was exactly what he wanted.

But she moved before he could. She leaned in closer to him, her free hand on his chest, until their lips were mere inches apart. "Yes, I believe it will be." Then she pulled away without pressing her lips to his and smirked. "Ready to go?"

Justin whistled, shaking his head. "Damn, babe. You're just way too sexy." He stepped out of the kitchen, dropping her hand. "That dress is . . ."

Mandy grabbed her purse off the counter, slinging it over her shoulder. "Hmm?"

Justin took his time scanning her from head to toe. "Well, let's just say maybe I'll show you how much I'm enjoying it later."

Mandy gasped, putting a hand to her chest. "Justin! I already told you I'm not easy."

But Justin could tell she'd been thinking the exact same thing. "You're not fooling anyone, Mandy. You want me as badly as I want you." His voice was low, and she clenched her legs together in response.

Mandy swallowed hard. "Honesty? You're right. But isn't it too early to, uh . . . do *that* before we've been dating for a while? Isn't there a normal waiting period or something?"

Justin smiled. "We've never been normal, babe. Hell, we slept in the same bed four months ago."

Mandy's cheeks flushed, and Justin's mind was immediately transported to the memory of his hands wrapped around her, her legs wrapped around him . . .

Okay. He had to stop if he was going to get through this night without ripping her damn clothes off her tight little body in public.

Mandy cleared her throat. "Okay. Wouldn't want to ruin what you have planned for tonight anyway." She motioned to the things still spread out on the kitchen table. "Do I need to bring these with me?"

Justin pursed his lips, looking over the items. "Hmm . . . yeah, we'd better bring them. Just in case." With one motion, he swept them all into the nearby envelope and folded it in thirds, stashing it in the pocket of his khaki pants. Then he held out his hand between them, palm up. "Ready?"

Mandy grabbed his hand with a smile. "Ready."

CHAPTER EIGHTEEN

JUSTIN PULLED out of her complex and headed down the road, his windows down. Thanks to a flash storm earlier this afternoon, the air had cooled quite considerably, and the wind tossed Mandy's hair around her face.

Justin reached for her hand, holding it between them on the center console. Mandy loved the feeling of her hand in his. "Looks like we might not need the Chinese fan after all. Or the candles and matches, for that matter. Too windy. And the flashlight was just for you, in case your power goes out again." He grinned over at her.

Her first real clues. Mandy squinted at him, trying to figure him out. He just wiggled his eyebrows.

She punched his arm lightly. Damn—had his arms bulked up over the summer, too? "You're evil, you know that?"

"For you, babe, I'll be as evil as you'd like." He flashed his devilish grin, and Mandy crossed her legs, squeezing them tight.

He chuckled.

"So where are we going?" she asked when he got on the interstate.

"I told you, Mandy—it's a secret."

"How do you know I like secrets?"

Justin shot her a look, his eyes narrowing. "You'll like this one."

Mandy shrugged, staring out the windshield. "We'll see."

Justin laughed aloud.

Several minutes later, Justin found his exit, one of the many that led downtown. Mandy wanted to ask again where they were going, but she knew it wouldn't get her anywhere. She'd just have to wait.

Damn, this man was always making her wait.

He pulled into a parking garage, grabbing a ticket from the unmanned station before driving through the open gate and finding a spot. He put the ticket on the dash then hopped out.

He was at Mandy's door just as her hand reached for the handle. She blinked at him.

"What?" he asked, eyeing her.

Mandy took his offered hand and let him help her out of the vehicle. "No one's ever held a door open for me before. Or bought me flowers. Or picked me up at my door for a date."

Justin pushed the door shut after she'd cleared it, his gaze unfocused. He pressed the lock button on his key fob until the lights flashed then dropped his keys in his pocket. Then he put an arm around her shoulders. "So a night of firsts, then."

Mandy smiled over at him, grateful he didn't bring up what her confession meant about her past. He squeezed her once before letting her go and finding her hand. She was discovering just how much he loved to touch her, and she didn't mind it. Not one bit. "I suppose, yes."

Justin led them out of the garage and onto the street. "I'm

glad you wore flats. This is the closest place I could find to park tonight."

Mandy smiled as they made their way among the sea of skyscrapers just lighting up in the twilight. "I don't mind walking. Feels good to stretch my legs."

"Works up an appetite, too."

"And I'll want food as well."

Justin threw his head back and let out an uninhibited laugh. Mandy smiled, loving the sound. "We've already discussed our mutual *appetite*," Justin commented when he'd quieted down, "but that will just have to be dessert."

Mandy's face heated, but she doubted Justin saw it in the growing darkness.

About five minutes later, Justin slowed as they approached a white-washed, ancient stone building lit impressively with a multitude of floodlights shining up from the lawn in front of it.

Mandy gasped. She knew this building. "We're going to the Orlando Museum of Natural History?"

Justin put his free hand on his chest, his mouth forming an O. He hadn't let go of her hand since the parking garage. "But of course! Where else do two anthropology students go on their first date?"

Mandy grinned widely as they climbed the lighted steps to a bank of glass entrance doors. Justin stopped before opening them.

"Aren't we going in?"

Justin nodded. "In a minute." He pulled out his phone, typed something into it, then shoved it back in his pocket. Then he gazed inside, and Mandy followed suit. What was he waiting for?

Before long, a security guard approached the doors, and

Justin took a step back as the heavyset man unlocked the door and swung it open.

Mandy eyed Justin.

Justin shrugged as they entered. "They're closed on Thursdays."

She gasped. "Then how . . . ?"

Justin extended his hand to the man, who shook it. "Ralph here is a friend, as is the curator. They offered to do me a favor." He smiled at the older man. "Thanks, man."

"No worries, Justin—happy to help." The tanned, balding security guard patted Justin on the shoulder then looked over at Mandy. "This must be a special lady." He winked at her.

Mandy saw Justin's cheeks heat up a little and smiled to herself.

"Ralph, I know we're a little early. How long until we're set up?"

"Give me ten minutes."

Justin nodded and pulled her farther into the museum as the man hurried away as quickly as his considerable girth would allow.

Mandy gasped as they stepped out from behind the partition that blocked their view of the main lobby from the entrance. A full skeleton of a T-rex commanded the space, stretching to the high ceiling made of glass. The lobby was dark, but the moon shone brightly off the white bones and other glass displays surrounding it in an open circle. "Justin . . . this is incredible," she breathed.

She turned to find his gaze and caught him staring at her, smiling.

"What?"

He squeezed her hand. "Nothing. I just like to see you like this." His smile widened.

Mandy blushed.

"So we have ten minutes—where to?"

Mandy gasped. "We can go wherever we'd like?"

Justin chuckled. "Of course! The guys here like me."

Mandy grinned. "Let's go see the Aztec display."

Justin nodded then started off to the left. "That's my favorite, too."

THEY STEPPED into the display room where ceremonial gowns, clay pottery, and precious gemstones filled the glass-covered cases. Justin had been here too many times to count, but he loved it here. Central American culture had always drawn his attention.

Mandy stopped at the first case and peered inside, her eyes wide. The security lights bathed the room in a low glow, but Justin thought it was romantic—he hoped Mandy thought so, too.

She smiled, squeezing Justin's hand and pulling him closer. "Look—have you noticed this before?"

Justin leaned in, his eyes squinting at the artifact she was indicating: a large, gold pitcher with inlaid gemstones. "Hmm?"

She jabbed her finger closer. "Look on the side opposite the handle. You can actually see the marks of the tool that created it."

Justin leaned in closer, then his eyes widened. "Wow." He glanced over at her. "How'd you see that in this light?"

Mandy smiled over at him as they moved to the next case. "I noticed it before."

"How often do you come here?"

Mandy leaned forward to study the intricate designs on an ancient tapestry. "Every other week or so?"

Justin sighed. "So this is a really boring date for you. Sorry." His forehead creased as he frowned.

Mandy turned to him, leaning in closer until their chests were touching and kissed his cheek then smiled again. "This is perfect, Justin. Definitely *not* boring."

He pulled her into a hug and just held her for a few moments. Justin felt the heat from her body warm up every inch of him, and he couldn't help but feel their connection deepening already. This woman was going to consume every part of him, and he was ready to beg for his destruction.

Then he pulled away, kissing her forehead. "Good. Because I still have a surprise for you." He wiggled his eyebrows.

Mandy laughed aloud as they moved further into the room.

CHAPTER NINETEEN

A FEW MINUTES LATER, Mandy saw Justin check his phone. Then he reached for her hand, pulling her toward the lobby and leading her through it to the back of the museum, opposite the entrance. "Time for your surprise."

Mandy followed silently, wondering what could possibly come next on this already incredible night.

Justin led her to the elevator and tapped the button, waiting only a moment before the bell dinged and the door slid open. Mandy followed him on, watching as he pressed the button for the top floor, number four. She raised an eyebrow at him, but he seemed to be ignoring her unasked questions at the moment. As if he hadn't been all evening.

When the elevator let them off in the fourth-floor hallway, Mandy gasped. Across from the elevator was a glass handrail overlooking the massive lobby. Justin just grinned at her but turned to his left and followed the hall until they came to a heavy metal door. He pushed it open, and Mandy spied a utilitarian staircase.

"You okay walking, or should I carry you?" His mischievous grin shot pleasure to her core, and she blushed. She wasn't exactly the working out type, but she did get in some cardio from time to time, enough that climbing a couple of flights of stairs should barely wind her. "I think I'll be fine." She rolled her eyes at him as they started up the steps.

He led her up a few flights, and Mandy was infinitely glad she'd ditched her heels back in May. No tall boyfriend, no need to torture her feet any longer. Besides, Justin was the perfect height in her flats.

She grinned to herself as they turned another corner and headed up yet another flight of stairs. She still couldn't see the top. "We almost there?" She was starting to have trouble catching her breath.

"Almost there, babe," he called over his shoulder. Justin was breathing a little hard, too, which had Mandy gasping for air for an entirely different reason.

She was glad he couldn't read her mind.

They finally reached the top of the stairs and were greeted by another metal door. Justin reached for the handle, pushing it open.

And Mandy gasped yet again.

She stepped through the door, and a gentle breeze tossed her hair around her face. Justin stepped out behind her, leaving what looked like a large dowel in the door so it wouldn't lock behind them.

Mandy surveyed their surroundings, barely noticing the dark shadows of the skyscrapers around them in light of the sight in front of her. She took several slow steps forward, her mouth open as she saw what Justin'd had set up for them.

Several strings of bulb lights blazed brightly over a round table covered in a long white cloth. Two wrought iron chairs sat on either side of the table where two place settings covered with cloches and another bouquet of carnations sat waiting for them.

Mandy put her fingers to her lips, fighting tears. Justin wrapped his arms around her waist from behind then leaned in to her ear. "You like this surprise, baby?"

Mandy sniffed. Yeah, she was definitely crying. "It's beautiful." She turned to look over at him, his face inches away. "Thank you." She pressed her lips to his briefly then pulled back.

But Justin spun her around abruptly, and she fell against him. "Let's try that again," he mumbled, low and seductive. Then he leaned down and claimed her mouth.

She sighed as her entire body fell into the kiss. Being with Justin was exactly that: falling. And burning, scorching. His fire would consume her very being—Justin was fire, and she wanted to get burned.

Justin's lips massaged hers, and soon the kiss deepened. Mandy's lips parted, and Justin's tongue found its way inside her mouth. She matched his fervor, their tongues intertwining, and Mandy struggled to hold herself back from showing him just how much she wanted his body melded with hers. She couldn't get close enough.

So she jumped up, wrapping her legs around his waist and her arms around his neck, never breaking the kiss.

Justin didn't break it, either. He simply wrapped his hands around her thighs, holding her tightly against him as their tongues continued their mutual exploration.

His hands were on her bare skin, scorching her, her dress hiked up from her spontaneous leap. They pulled away for an instant to catch their breath, chests heaving, and Mandy stared deeply into his eyes. They were still out of the circle of light cast by the glowing string lights, so she could barely see them. But she could tell they were sparkling.

Justin's eyes were oceans. She'd sensed it before, but never as much until this moment. She saw the depths of his soul in his eyes, saw his capacity for deep pleasure—and deep pain. And she decided, in that moment, that she would do everything she could to help him avoid the latter.

Justin was still breathing hard, but his voice came out steady. "You ready to eat?"

Mandy bit her lip, and Justin's eyes flicked down to them.

"Okay, another minute." At his verbal concession, he leaned in, his lips connecting with hers in a rush. Mandy squeezed her legs around him, wanting him even closer than he already was. As their lips explored each other once again, their breath intermixing, Justin's hands inched their way up her legs.

Mandy's breath caught as she felt his hands grab her bare ass, and she was glad she'd chosen a thong specifically for tonight. He moaned as he did, and Mandy's core tightened at the sound.

Then Justin suddenly pulled away, his breath coming in short gasps. "Mandy, we . . . we shouldn't do this here. Not yet."

Mandy pouted, and Justin laughed, placing a quick kiss on her lips to erase her frown.

"You know I'm right, baby." He set her down and took a step back. "We should eat now, before the food gets cold. There will be plenty of time for that later."

"You promise?" she asked as she trailed a single finger down his chest.

"Later," Justin responded pointedly, and Mandy silently rejoiced that "later" would be much sooner than she'd thought.

CHAPTER TWENTY

"Can I ask you a question?" Justin asked, eyeing Mandy's beautiful face in the yellow light of the sparkling bulbs above their heads.

She had just finished her salmon cake, garlic mashed potatoes, and Southern-style green beans, so she took a sip of wine before answering. "Sure. Honesty, remember?"

Justin smiled, but it faded quickly. "What made you want to date Dan?"

Mandy took a breath, staring down at her plate. "I don't really remember. We just kinda hit it off in class."

Justin nodded, taking a drink from his wine glass. "Did you know right away?"

"That he was an asshole?" Mandy raised an eyebrow.

Justin snickered. "No. That you wanted to date him."

Mandy cocked her head, eyeing him. "Not right away, but pretty quickly." She took a breath. "Why all the interest in Dan? I haven't thought about him much at all lately."

"Really?"

Mandy nodded, taking another sip from the glass. "Really.

He's my past. I can't change what happened, I can't change that I was ever with him, so I'm choosing to move on."

"To your future?"

Mandy smiled. "Right."

Justin grinned back. "And what does that future look like?"

Mandy stared off into the night sky. "Well, a new apartment for starters. And a master's degree, of course."

Justin chuckled. "What do you want to do after graduation? Are you pursuing your doctorate?"

Mandy waved her hand in front of her, shaking her head. "Oh, no. I'm done with school after this."

"Really?"

Mandy nodded. "Are you not?"

Justin leaned back in his chair, his plate clear, too. "No way. I'm done after this. I'm excited to get into the application part."

"Where do you see yourself doing that?"

Justin pursed his lips. "In the field. Archaeology's my focus."

"Me, too!" She grinned at him.

He grinned back. "So we may just be able to spend some time together on a dig in some faraway land someday, huh?"

Mandy blushed. "I wouldn't mind that at all. I actually don't mind digging in the dirt. I like getting dirty."

"I bet you do."

Mandy snorted. "Always a dirty mind."

"Takes one to know one, babe."

Mandy tilted her head. "I'll concede that." She caught his gaze, and Justin felt it below his waist. He suddenly felt hot despite the cool breeze up here, and he wanted nothing more than to throw everything on the table to the ground and take her right here, right now.

He shook his head, clearing it so he could get up from the table without a rather embarrassing display.

When he'd gotten himself under control, Justin stood and started clearing their table, placing the empty dishes on a covered serving cart nearby. "You ready for dessert?"

Mandy gulped and looked around. "Here?"

Justin laughed loudly. "No, dirty mind, I have actual dessert. Nothing lemon, I promise."

Mandy smiled, then her eyes found the covered dish on the serving cart next to their used plates. "What do we have?"

Justin grabbed the cloth covering the dish and whisked it away dramatically. "Dark chocolate cake with a chocolate ganache."

Mandy clapped in her seat. "Yum."

Justin's shoulders relaxed as he carried the plate over and set it between them. He produced two clean forks from the cart and set them on either side of the dish. "Whew, I'm glad you like chocolate. I figured it would've been on your hate list if you didn't."

Mandy took a bite and groaned, her eyes falling shut. "No, I definitely should add this to my love list."

At the sound of her moan, Justin just stared. *Damn, that was hot as hell.* He felt a fire burn in his eyes as Mandy's opened and found his.

"What?"

"You moan again, and I may not be able to control what happens next."

Mandy's face turned red, but Justin saw a determination flash in her eyes. She had him right where she wanted him—and he was in deep shit.

She took another bite of the cake. "Mmm." She stretched the

word out as she swallowed, closing her eyes again. Then she flashed her gaze to his. "You mean like that?"

Justin growled and flew to his feet as Mandy's fork clinked to the porcelain plate. He grabbed her hand, yanking her from her chair, and pulled her against him. She stumbled into him once again, her hands against his chest.

He reached for her, cupping her jaw and hungrily tugging her mouth to his with a groan.

Their lips met with the force of a hurricane. Mandy gasped against his mouth, stealing his breath. Her mouth was urgent, insistent, and Justin couldn't control himself any longer. He had to have this woman tonight. Soon.

But he was going to wait until it was perfect.

She pulled away slightly to catch her breath. "Justin . . ."

He growled again, his mouth on her neck just below her ear. She tipped her head back as Justin's lips frantically blazed a trail down her collarbone to the center of her chest. He tasted her skin as his tongue trailed down toward the deep vee in her dress.

Then Mandy grabbed the hair at the back of his head and yanked his mouth back up to hers. Their lips met with a simultaneous gasp, and Mandy stumbled, her muscles weakening. Justin smirked against her lips as he realized what his kiss was doing to her—her legs were barely holding her up. He reached for her thighs once again, and she jumped up into his arms like they'd done it a thousand times as he pulled her legs around his waist.

Mandy's core pressed up against his hardness, only her thin panties and his khakis between them, and she gasped. Justin pulled away, just an inch, so they could breathe.

"Mandy, baby . . ."

Her chest was heaving. "Justin," she panted, "take me home."

His eyes found hers immediately, searching them. His own breath was ragged and uneven. "You sure?"

Mandy nodded vigorously. "Oh, yes, definitely." She glanced over at their table. "What do we do about that?"

Justin looked over. "Ralph will take care of it."

"Too bad about the cake."

Justin set her down and strode over to the serving cart. He leaned down, pulling a to-go box from beneath the white cloth covering it. Mandy grinned at him.

"Dessert after dessert." He flashed that wicked grin he knew she loved.

Justin scraped the cake into the box and clasped it shut then reached for Mandy's hand, pulling her toward the exit while handing her the box. She grabbed her purse and dropped the small to-go container inside then trailed him down the steps.

THEY RAN to the car hand in hand, the night air whipping around them and through Mandy's hair. They were back at the Jeep much more quickly than when they'd walked to the museum, but it still wasn't quick enough for Mandy.

When they got to the Jeep, Justin pressed her up against the side of the vehicle in the dark parking garage, their chests heaving from the exertion. His mouth pressed to hers as his hand rested on her thigh, his knee sliding between her legs and coaxing them apart. As his tongue tasted hers, his hand bunched up her dress until he found her bare thigh. He pulled away to kiss her neck.

Mandy moaned as he inched his way up her leg. "Justin, I don't know if I can wait until we get home."

Justin lifted his head to look at her, his hand still on her exposed upper thigh, and growled again. "I want you so badly, Mandy, but I want this to be perfect."

Mandy smiled at him. "It's you—it'll be perfect."

Justin kissed her once. "No, we're doing this right. I want to take my time showing you how much I love this dress."

A thrill ran through Mandy at his words, and she shivered.

Justin ran his free hand along her bare arm. "You cold?"

She shook her head. "Hot, actually. *Really* hot."

Justin grabbed her right hand and pressed it up by her head, against the Jeep window, and let his other hand trace up her leg and around to her backside. Then he grabbed her bare ass and yanked her against him, and she suddenly felt all of him, felt exactly what she did to him. She gasped.

"Babe, you're not the only one who's hot." His lips descended on hers, and he tasted her yet again. Mandy had lost track of how many times their lips had met in the past few hours.

"Hey! Is someone there?"

Justin jumped away from her as Mandy jerked and let out a squeak. She moved to peer around the back edge of the Jeep and saw a flashlight beam headed their way. She giggled.

Justin called out, "Sorry, just trying to find my keys!" He pressed the unlock button, and the car's lights flashed bright in the dark garage, reflecting in the smooth cement floor, thick columns, low ceiling, and a lone car's taillights a few spaces down. Mandy heard the locks click as the doors released.

The man didn't come any closer as Mandy rounded the car to climb in the passenger side. She'd already waved Justin off when he'd tried to come with her to open her door. "Okay, folks. You have a good night."

Mandy waved to him as she climbed inside. Both doors slammed in unison as Justin started the car and backed out of the spot, circling his way to the exit.

Mandy was laughing as they pulled out of the garage. "That was *amazing*."

Justin started laughing, too. "We must have really scared that guy."

Mandy nodded, still giggling.

Justin sped back to Mandy's apartment, pushing his luck with the speed limit. Mandy was a little worried about highway patrol, but she wasn't exactly complaining. Their preview in the parking garage had started something that Justin had to finish, and soon.

CHAPTER TWENTY-ONE

JUSTIN MADE it back to Mandy's house in no time at all, the fact that he hadn't been stopped by the police for speeding well over the limit barely crossing his mind. He quickly popped open his door then sped to her side of the vehicle. He reached inside the car before she could climb out and picked her up, wrapping her legs around him once again. He locked the car with the key fob then carried her toward the building.

Mandy found his gaze as he approached the open stairway. "You sure you want to carry me up all these steps?"

Justin had already started climbing them two at a time. "Yup, babe. This is faster."

Mandy arms tightened around his neck as they made their way to her floor, and Justin couldn't hide his grin. He set her down only long enough for her to find her keys and unlock the door.

Once inside, Justin lifted her again, pressing her against the door to shut it, his mouth closing on hers. But when he clicked the deadbolt shut, he felt her freeze.

He pulled his lips from hers.

"Justin?"

He leaned back only far enough to see her eyes.

"Are you sure about this?"

The question seemed ridiculous in his current state of mind, but he kept that to himself. He bent down and kissed her bare collarbone. "More sure than I've ever been about anything."

Mandy bit her lip, her back against the door and her flowy dress still pooled around her waist like it had been since her legs had wrapped around Justin's torso. "I just want to make sure we're sure."

Justin pulled back and set her down. Her knee-length dress settled around her in a fluttering cascade of cloth. "Where's this coming from, baby?"

"See? That."

"What?"

"'Baby.' That was part of our deal in May. Is it real? Or is this just us reacting to the undeniably seductive lie we told back then?"

Justin kicked off his shoes, leaving them at the door as he took her hand and led her to the futon. He shifted in his seat to face her, her hands in his, his gaze intense. Because he was more serious than he'd ever been. "Mandy, listen to me. This"—he motioned between them—"is absolutely real. We've both felt it. And it's more than just being friends—you know that, too. You are the most amazingly sexy but also the most incredibly fun woman I've ever met. I've loved spending time with you since the moment we met."

"You mean since that night here, in my apartment."

Justin shook his head slowly, his eyes trained on hers. He swallowed hard, bracing himself for her reaction to his next words. He'd promised to be honest, so he would be—even if it scared her away. "No, Mandy. Even before that, when you weren't mine to want. But I did anyway."

Mandy gasped, her eyes widening. "How long?" she whispered.

"Since before Dan."

She just stared.

"I saw you from afar, Mandy, and I've lived for the few conversations we've had over the years about school or our professors or just anything. We had a few classes together, too. You captured my attention even then." He put his hand to her cheek. "I've waited three long years for you to be ready for me. So the question is: Are you?"

Mandy's eyes searched his, as if she was looking for any hint of teasing. She wouldn't find any because it didn't exist in this moment.

She swallowed hard. "I'm ready, baby. I want you."

Justin's face broke into a wide grin. "You don't know how glad I am to hear you say that."

Mandy smirked. "Then why don't you convince me? You promised to show me how much you love this dress, after all."

Justin growled and leaned in for a quick kiss. "I did, didn't I?"

Mandy waved her hands down either side of her body as her voice lowered. "Show me." Her eyes sparkled.

Justin placed his hands gently on her collarbone, lightly caressing the exposed skin there. She shuddered at his touch, and Justin felt himself getting hard again. If just touching her skin like this, fully clothed, was this electric, he couldn't imagine them in bed.

Scratch that—he could. But right now was the seduction.

He trailed his right hand down the center of her chest, slowly, painfully. Just as he reached the peaks beneath her dress, he slowed even further and lightly traced his fingertips over the soft flesh of her breasts peeking out from beneath the low-cut wrap dress, the exposed skin that had been torturing him all night. At the touch, his shoulders relaxed. His hands on her body were a revelation straight from heaven itself.

Justin's hands found her shoulders next. His fingers trailed down her sides, following the seam of the dress, and she lifted her arms above her head to get out of his way. His eyes were focused on her as he discovered exactly how her body reacted to his touch.

His fingers found her thin waist, and his hands followed the belt there to where it was tied off to one side almost of their own accord.

He heard Mandy's breathing speed up as her gaze followed his hands. His breath shook and his hands were trembling as he pulled on the belt, releasing the bow in one motion. He knew what this moment meant for them, and he both wanted it to happen quickly and wanted it to last at the same time.

Suddenly the dress fell open, revealing her matching navy bra and panties and her flat stomach.

Justin sucked in a breath. "Damn, baby. You look positively edible." He lowered to her bare skin, pressing his lips just above her belly button. She shuddered beneath him as his tongue darted out to tease her stomach.

She grabbed the back of his head by his hair as if holding him in place. Justin moaned quietly but deliberately held back. This woman had already captured him, and he was helpless against her, but he would make this the best night of her goddamn life.

Justin raised up a few inches, capturing her gaze over her covered breasts, breasts he'd been waiting over three years to unwrap and devour. He was going to enjoy worshipping them along with the rest of her gorgeous, perfect body.

Justin faced her stomach again, this time blowing lightly on her skin. He teased a trail up her torso until he reached the middle of her bra.

Then he pushed off the couch, holding out his arms to her once he was standing. She furrowed her brow for a moment but extended her hands to him, letting him pull her to her feet. "Why'd you stop?"

"You still have too many clothes on, babe."

Mandy blushed. "Oh." She swallowed hard then looked him right in the eye. "I have a feeling you're about to remedy that."

"Damn right." Justin reached up to where her dress still hung, sliding his hands underneath the fabric and pushing it off her shoulders and to the ground. His eyes scanned her half-naked body as he flashed a devilish grin. "You're incredibly sexy, Mandy."

Mandy took a step back, leaving her shoes in the middle of the dress that was now laying in a pile on the ground. Then she turned around, and Justin sucked in his breath at the sight of her fabulous bare ass.

She smirked at him over her shoulder. "You coming, babe?" She flashed him a grin then sprinted for the bedroom.

CHAPTER TWENTY-TWO

MANDY HADN'T EVEN MADE it to the bed before she felt Justin's arms wrap around her bare waist. She shrieked, laughing as he spun her around.

"You really are going to make me work for it, aren't you?" Justin smirked as he tightened his hold on her, her arms at her sides and body flush up against his.

Mandy nodded, biting her lower lip the way she knew made him hot. He growled then released her slightly so he could lean down and plant a kiss on her lips. She used the opportunity to take a step back after he did, frowning.

"What? What's wrong?" Justin's brow furrowed.

Mandy scanned him head to toe. "You have too many clothes on, babe."

Justin laughed aloud then reached for the collar of his polo, pulling it over his head in one smooth motion.

Mandy moaned when she saw his bare torso, and her hands once again found his skin. "I knew it!" She traced her fingertips across his chest.

Justin's eyes fell closed. "Knew what?"

She waited to answer until his eyes blinked open and he caught her gaze. "You've gotten even hotter."

Justin laughed again, wrapping his arms around her tightly and pulling her into another hug. "Now who's ridiculous?"

Mandy just smirked again as he released her. "What are you gonna do about it?"

Justin's jaw suddenly hardened, his gaze intense and unyielding. Mandy felt a thrill down her spine at the abrupt shift in his mood. "You'll just have to wait and see." He planted a quick kiss on her lips then stepped back. Mandy moved toward him, but he held up his hand. "Nope. My turn."

Mandy shuddered as her core throbbed. "Is that right?"

Justin nodded slowly, his eyes searching her entire body.

Her breath caught, and she found herself issuing a command she'd never dreamed of giving to anyone before. "Tell me what you're going to do."

Justin drew in a breath. "First, I'm going to finish undressing you slowly. Then I'm going to worship that beautiful body until you beg for release."

Yup, she was definitely throbbing.

He took a single step forward. "Then I'll push inside you, baby, and give us both what we've wanted forever."

Mandy just stared, shocked she *wasn't* blushing, but she supposed it was just because he was right—she'd wanted this forever, even before she'd been consciously aware of it.

Justin took the last step to close the distance between them. Then slowly, deliberately, he reached his hands up to the back of her neck. He inched down her spine until he found her bra.

Mandy's breath hitched.

She saw him smirk at the gasp as he unhooked her lacy bra. It held in place for a moment, but Justin slowly, achingly slowly, pulled each strap down her arm one at a time. Then he coaxed it off and dropped it to the ground.

Mandy's skin flushed under his heated gaze, and her heavy breasts ached to be touched. Though it had been way too long before she'd been touched like this at all, she wanted Justin to be the one to help her find her release. She wanted Justin, plain and simple. And the burning desire in his eyes as he stared back at her told her he felt the same way.

Justin's hand found her shoulder again, but this time his fingertips trailed a line directly to her breast. She gasped as his hand closed around it, squeezing gently. Then, with a fire flashing in his eyes, he bent down and took her into his mouth.

She moaned more loudly than she ever had before, but she didn't care. Her neighbors were like eighty and probably didn't have their hearing aids in at this hour anyway.

Not that she cared right now even if they did. Let them listen. She was about to have the best sex of her life, and in this moment, she didn't care who knew it.

Justin moved to her other breast, and she groaned, weaving her fingers in his hair. He pulled away for a second, raising up until they were eye to eye. "You like that?"

Mandy held his gaze and nodded solemnly.

"Good." His mouth returned to her breast while his hand found the other, his fingers teasing the nipple. Mandy couldn't help the moans escaping her, and she wondered how she was still standing.

Then Justin pulled away again. "Next," he stated simply, but his low voice caused ripples of desire to rush across her skin.

"What's next?" She had to ask if only to hear him say it.

He looked down at her thong. "As hot as that is, babe, it has to come off. Now." He growled out the last word, and Mandy felt it travel through her and settle between her legs.

She nodded slowly, her eyes wide. Justin reached for her, placing his hands on her hips, pausing there a moment. His chest was heaving as he pulled at the thin strips of lace holding her panties up. "Damn, girl. You always wear stuff this hot?" He inched the thin, silky fabric down, and Mandy shivered in anticipation.

"Special occasion," she eked out. She tried to shrug, but what Justin was doing made her feel anything but casual. She felt goddamn sexy.

"If you couldn't tell, I approve." Justin's fingers moved back, sliding the thong away from her body and pulling it down her legs. He ended up kneeling on the ground as she stepped out of them.

He gazed up at her, taking in the sight of her naked body. His hand pressed to her stomach for an infinite second, then his breath hitched as he made his way south.

Mandy's eyes fell closed as his fingers found her folds. She gasped as he immediately found her most sensitive part and rubbed against it once, twice, three times . . . she lost count after that.

There was no way she'd stay standing if he kept doing *that*.

Then his fingers stopped, and he glanced up, catching her gaze. He exhaled against her sensitive, swollen middle, and she squirmed. "I want to taste you, Mandy."

She'd never once had a guy want to do that for her, but this was Justin, so she didn't hesitate. "Okay."

But instead of leaning in, he stood to his feet in front of her. He tucked her hair behind her ear, planting a sweet kiss on her lips. "I thought this would be more fun if you weren't the only one without clothes on."

Mandy blushed, nodding. She immediately reached for the top button of his khakis, quickly unbuttoning then unzipping them and pulling them down his legs. Her eyes widened a little at the bulk she spied under his boxer briefs.

Justin chuckled low, the sound reverberating in her being. "See something you like, babe?"

Mandy just kept staring. "Oh, absolutely." She reached for the elastic, sliding his boxers over his considerable length and down to the floor. She gasped—she couldn't help it. He was definitely bigger than anyone else she'd been with.

Justin laughed again, clearly reading her reaction. "Don't worry, babe. I've got you." Then he nodded to the bed. "Lie down."

Mandy obliged, backing up until she found the edge then crawling backward so she didn't have to take her eyes off him. Justin mirrored her motions exactly, climbing over her as she scooted up toward the headboard.

"You're really beautiful, you know that?" he asked as her head found her pillow.

She blushed. "You're not so bad yourself."

"Oh, but I can *be* bad, and that's what counts, babe." His devilish grin was back, and Mandy squirmed at the ache she felt between her legs.

Justin's mouth turned up in the smirk that made Mandy heat up even more. "See, I told you your body gives you away." He backed up then, sliding between her open legs. Mandy let her knees fall toward her plush comforter, and he rested his hands on them as he leaned back on his heels. His eyes stayed trained on hers the entire time, and the intensity in his gaze made something inside Mandy flutter, something she hadn't known existed until this moment. "Let me taste you, baby."

Mandy just nodded.

Justin's gaze shifted to her wet core, and he leaned down until he was just a breath away from her center. Mandy squirmed as the warm air from his delicious mouth brushed her most sensitive spot. Then he glanced up at her, smirking before his tongue connected with her skin.

Mandy moaned, so loudly that she grabbed a pillow and thrust it over her face. She felt Justin smile against her, but his tongue didn't stop tracing circles over her folds. She put the pillow back, swearing to herself that she'd be quieter, and soon she was writhing beneath him.

Justin came up for air a minute later and caught her gaze. He paused, cocking his head as he studied her. "You've never done that before, have you?"

Mandy shook her head. "How do you always know everything about me?"

He flashed his panty-dropping crooked grin. "I know your tells, babe."

She gasped. "I don't have tells!"

Justin's eyebrow shot up. "Wanna bet?"

Mandy bit her lip to hide a smile. She nodded.

Justin lowered down to her center and licked it from bottom to top in one smooth motion. She squirmed, calling out, and Justin chuckled. She could feel his breath against her. "See? I could tell you liked that, for one."

Mandy waved her hand. "That one's easy. Who wouldn't like that?"

Justin nodded. "Okay." He paused for a second then leaned in again, but this time his lips closed over her most sensitive part, and he started sucking. She screamed, but he didn't let up. Instead, she felt his hands press against her inner thighs, spreading them farther apart. He was preparing for something, but she didn't know what. She was focused on not screaming so loudly again.

Then she felt his fingers join his mouth, and she started writhing on the bed. She grasped the sheets in her fists as his fingers played, danced, searched until they found what they were looking for. Then a single finger pushed inside her.

She screamed again.

Justin was smiling against her for a second time—she could tell—but he wouldn't let up. Turned out he did know a thing or two about what she liked, even when she didn't know herself. Damn, that man was good.

Instead of letting her go, he sucked harder, using his tongue to flick and tease her. His finger was joined by another as he thrusted them in and out, his mouth and tongue more frantic on her folds. Then a third finger pushed inside her.

"Justin!!" She screamed so loudly the largely deaf neighbors definitely heard her. But she'd assumed right—she'd never had sex this good, so she was going to enjoy it, dammit.

Mandy could feel her orgasm building as Justin's mouth and fingers worked their indescribable magic. As he thrusted in and out of her in a fury, she felt the fire that was Justin Stanford building inside her. As he sucked and licked and nipped her folds, her back arched and her toes curled. Then she screamed again as her orgasm ripped free, searing through every part of her.

Waves of her own pleasure and Justin's flames cascaded over her as she rode the feeling, her brain exploding and nerve-endings flashing. Then she released and collapsed on the bed.

But Justin still didn't let up. He pulled his fingers out of her, but his mouth was still frantic on her sensitive, swollen folds. As he sucked and nipped at her, she felt a second orgasm, so much stronger than the first, build quickly inside her. Her eyes rolled back in her head as her entire being tensed then released again, another scream tearing from her throat.

Justin finally let go, raising up. He wiped his mouth with the back of his hand. "Damn, girl! I didn't know you were a screamer."

Mandy had collapsed back on the bed, her eyes half open. "I didn't either, actually. Never have been."

Justin smirked. "Good to know."

Mandy waved an arm weakly in his direction. "Don't get cocky."

He wiggled his eyebrows.

Mandy laughed. "Okay, *definitely* get cocky. Right now, please."

Justin moved on top of her, grinning down at her. He took a breast in his mouth in one motion, and she gasped at the suddenness of it.

And soon, she was squirming again. Justin raised up to watch her then leaned in closer, their lips inches apart.

"Kiss me, baby. Taste yourself on me."

Mandy stretched up to urge him closer, and his lips closed on hers. The taste of where his lips and tongue had just been made her core ache in every good way.

Then Justin pulled away for a split second. "You still clean?"

Mandy nodded. "You?"

Justin nodded back. "Birth control?"

"IUD."

"Good. Because I can't wait any longer." Justin guided himself to her opening then pushed inside, thrusting in as deep as he could go.

Mandy moaned, her hips lifting to meet his. Justin inside her was like finally coming home. Justin inside her was passion and safety and fire and wonder and belonging. Justin inside her made everything in the world seem okay, right, good.

Justin inside her was . . . *everything*.

The fire she felt when his skin touched hers was scorching throughout her entire body. Justin was consuming her, just as she knew he would so many months ago.

But she wanted it so badly. Needed it. She needed his fire to burn her from the inside out, scorch her soul and set her body on fire. Because anything less was no longer acceptable. Not when Justin was everything she wanted and needed.

Mandy screamed as he pulled back then thrusted in again. His mouth closed over hers as he found a slow rhythm, his tongue dipping inside her mouth and muting her screams while his steady thrusts worked her into a frenzy.

He shifted above her to hold himself up with one arm while his other hand started at her breast and pressed down her torso to her already swollen middle. She gasped when his fingers found their mark, and he dug in as he thrusted harder, speeding up. His mouth captured her screams as she felt another orgasm building alongside his.

She tightened around him as the flames burned her from the inside out, and Justin tensed then let go just as her toes curled. She gazed up at him as he released inside her, and her stomach clenched at what she saw.

His eyes were squeezed shut, his eyebrows furrowed in indescribable pleasure-pain, and the low groan that emanated from his chest got her wet all over again. He grabbed the pillow beside her and fisted it as he came for her, came inside her.

Mandy felt herself come down from her high just as he relaxed, too, leaning down to steal another kiss. He pulled out of her slowly, almost reverently, then dropped beside her, his chest heaving.

Neither said a word as they worked to catch their breath. Then Mandy broke the silence.

"Holy shit, Justin."

"Language, babe!" He chuckled.

Mandy sighed. "That was . . ."

". . . incredible?"

"Everything."

Justin got quiet for a moment, so Mandy leaned up to look at him, rolling to her side.

"You okay?"

He nodded as he stared at the ceiling, then he looked over at her, catching her gaze. The oceans were back, as vast as the deepest sea. Mandy wanted nothing more than to get lost in them. "I'm more than okay, babe. That *was* everything." He reached up and tucked her hair behind her ear.

Mandy smiled sweetly, letting her eyes fall shut at his touch. His fingers stroked her cheek over and over again, and Mandy thought she could easily fall asleep right here, right now.

Which made her think of the time. She stretched up and looked at the clock on her nightstand. And immediately turned beet red. "It's not even ten o'clock." Mandy leaned back on the bed, throwing her hands over her eyes. "I will never be able to show my face outside again."

Justin snickered from beside her.

"It's not funny! They're gonna kick me out!"

Justin was still chuckling. "Don't worry, babe. You can just move in with me."

Mandy froze. "What?"

Justin leaned up on his side, propping his head up on his hand as he gazed down at her. "I'm gonna start looking for my own place soon. If it gets to be too much here, you can always live with me."

"Justin . . . isn't it too early to be talking like this?"

He shrugged. "Would you want to live with me?"

Mandy's chest tightened. Her head told her this was nuts, but her heart . . . "Of course, I would. I just . . . isn't there an order to these things? An acceptable time period? We barely know each other, Justin."

He sighed. "You say that like it's true."

Mandy shrugged. "Isn't it?"

Justin lifted up to a seated position, his back against the headboard. "Listen to me, Mandy."

She pulled herself up to lean against the headboard beside him, the off-white sheets pooling around her waist.

"I don't care what everyone else thinks or does—I just know that since I've known you, I've wanted you. I waited three long years for you to pick me over Dan, and though it didn't work quite that way, everything happened for a reason. And now we're here, together, and nothing could ever be more right. I've never known anyone like you, Mandy, and I know you feel that way, too."

Mandy swallowed, nodding.

"I don't know where this thing will go, but I do know I want you in my life. For as long as you'll have me."

Mandy's eyes filled with tears. "Justin, I . . ." She searched for the right words then settled on the simple truth. "I *do* feel the same way. I didn't notice you back then, but I'm glad you were there when everything blew up with Dan. I'm glad you had the idea to fake a relationship. And I'm grateful you were willing to hold me until I was done crying and wait for me to get over the breakup."

A tear slid down her cheek, and Justin wiped it away before she could herself.

"You're right—I've never known anyone like you, and after

the past few months, I don't care to keep looking. When I said that was everything, Justin, I didn't just mean the sex. I meant you."

She actually thought she saw his eyes get a little shiny.

"So where do we go from here?" she asked.

Justin smiled, and it was definitely watery. "Wherever we'd like." He reached over, cupping her jaw and leaning in for a kiss. She didn't know if he'd intended it to just be quick and sweet, but as soon as his lips were on hers, she felt that fire again.

Mandy shifted her legs beneath her, raising up to kiss him harder, deeper, locking her arms around his neck and drawing him closer. Then Justin pulled her onto his lap, and she felt him harden beneath her, clearly ready for a second round. He leaned back against the headboard so she straddled him, her tongue slipping inside his mouth.

He moaned in response, and Mandy's core heated up again. His hands stroked her back, traveled down to her backside, cupping the cheeks and giving them a squeeze.

Then he pulled away, and the wicked grin was back. "I wanna try something."

Mandy blinked, her face blank. Where was he going with this? "Okay."

Justin grinned wider then lifted her off his lap, setting her back on the bed on her knees. He climbed off the bed and stood up, circling to the foot of it. "Come here."

She crawled toward him until they were face to face. She pushed up to her knees and kissed him once.

He chuckled. "Turn around."

Mandy blushed, and Justin barked out a laugh.

"Just do it, baby. You trust me, right?"

Mandy nodded, spinning slowly until her back was to him.

Justin grabbed her hips and pulled her toward him until she was at the edge of the bed. Then he pushed against her shoulders.

"Hands and knees, babe."

Mandy gasped, her eyes shooting to his over her left shoulder.

"You haven't had any fun in bed, have you? Good—it's my new mission to make sure you do." He wiggled his eyebrows at her, and she blushed again. "Now hands and knees, baby."

Mandy slowly complied, bending at the waist and placing her hands on the sheets.

"Try leaning further, on your elbows."

She did as he suggested, her ass up in the air in front of him. She still didn't have a clue what he was doing. "This had better be good."

Justin trailed his hand down her back and to her ass, giving it a light smack. Mandy jerked, pleasure shooting to her middle. "You really don't know where this is going?"

Mandy shook her head.

"Good." He yanked her closer to him in one motion, and she gasped when she felt his hard length up against her core. He chuckled under his breath. "Now you see where this is going."

Mandy nodded, swallowing hard.

"You good?"

She nodded again. "Yes. This is actually kinda hot."

"Just kinda?" He shifted his weight so his tip teased her folds, and she started squirming.

"Really . . . hot . . ." She gasped as her body heated up one more time.

Without warning, Justin pushed inside her again. She called

out as they found their rhythm, and Mandy's body felt like it was floating as it undulated as if on the ocean tide.

Justin reached between her legs just as she could sense his orgasm building, and she felt hers crest, too, as he played with her most sensitive part. She managed to be a little quieter this time, but she still cried out when she felt her toes curling and her core clenching around him. Justin came with her again, his fingers digging into her hips.

They crawled up to the pillows and collapsed on the bed yet again. Mandy was certain she was going to be sore tomorrow, but she didn't care. Right now, she was just spent. As Justin pulled her close and held her, just like he'd done four months ago in this very bed, she wondered how she'd gotten so lucky.

As she was falling asleep in his arms, her throat sore and legs wobbly, she realized that Justin's flames had consumed her from the inside out, but his fire had also set her free. And she never wanted that feeling to end.

She just wasn't sure where they'd go from here.

CHAPTER TWENTY-THREE

Mandy woke up early, the sun still hiding below the horizon. She was parched, so she reached for the water bottle she kept by her bed, unscrewing the cap and taking a sip as quietly as she could. She glanced over at Justin, who was lying peacefully on his side, facing her, his eyes closed and breathing even. Mandy smiled. If she was being honest with herself—and ignoring the fear trying to settle deep in her gut—she could admit she'd be fine waking up to this sight every morning.

Then he stirred, probably because she wasn't as quiet as she was trying to be. He moaned as he awoke.

Mandy turned on her side so she was fully facing him as his eyes fluttered open. She'd never noticed how long his blond eyelashes were, how well they framed his bright-blue eyes. Her breath caught.

"Hey, baby," he muttered with a sleepy half smile.

"Hey, babe." She was still smiling.

Justin blinked a few times then opened his eyes wider. "What time is it?"

Mandy rolled over to glance at the clock then turned back to him. "Six-thirty."

He groaned, rolling to his back. "We don't have to get up yet, do we?"

Mandy reached over to run her fingertips across his cheek. "Not if you don't want to."

Justin turned to her, his eyes more clear. "Well, we *did* fall asleep pretty early . . ." He wiggled his eyebrows.

Mandy gasped. "My neighbors don't want to be woken up this early!"

Justin rolled to his side, reaching for her and pulling her closer before repeating her words from months ago. "Then you'll just have to be quiet."

The thought shot pleasure all the way down to her core, and she clenched her legs together to ease it. Justin leaned in and pressed his lips to hers. She moaned contentedly when they connected, as if her entire being had been waiting for this moment. In a way, she supposed it had.

She scooted closer to him as his hand found her hair then traced down the side of her face, his lips massaging hers gently but passionately. She needed to feel his naked body up against hers again.

Which gave her an idea.

Mandy pulled away slightly to catch her breath. Then, just as she had months before, she lifted the covers and swung her leg over him. Justin's eyes flashed as she gazed down at him, her hands finding their way to his bare chest once again.

"Care to try the real thing?"

Justin nodded, his crooked smile making an appearance.

Mandy smirked back then slowly leaned down, bringing her mouth to his chest. Her tongue flicked his nipple, and she immediately felt him tighten beneath her. "Seems like you like that."

Justin's eyes had fallen closed, and he just nodded. "Definitely, babe." His eyes popped open, fire burning in them. "Do it again."

Mandy held his gaze as she flicked her tongue against his hardened nipple, and Justin groaned. At the sound, Mandy closed her mouth around him and started sucking, enjoying the feel of him in her mouth. She bit and teased his nipple, and he moaned beneath her. A smile spread on her face as she switched to the other.

Justin moaned again. "If you're trying to turn me on, you accomplished that a long time ago."

Mandy lifted up slightly to catch his gaze. "Shh. I'm enjoying myself."

Justin raised a hand to his lips, dragging pinched fingers across them like he was zipping them up. His hands slid under the sheets, settling on her bare hips and sending heat to her center.

Mandy chuckled, flicking his nipple once more with her tongue before moving farther down his body.

She kissed her way to his navel then used her tongue to trail a line from his belly button up the middle of his chest. She could feel his body respond beneath her, and a whole new level of passion flared inside her. This was different, but it was still incredible. And somehow even more intense.

Then she had an idea. "Justin?"

His eyes flicked open. "Hmm?"

Mandy blushed at what she was about to suggest. "It's my turn."

Justin blinked. "Your turn for what?"

Mandy scooted further down the bed, positioning her head

just above his cock. She saw his eyes widen, just a little, as understanding flickered across his face. "To taste you."

"You sure, baby?"

Mandy nodded as she leaned down, catching his gaze. "Absolutely. I need to taste you like you tasted me." She reached down and grabbed the base of his length. Justin's eyes slid closed.

She leaned all the way down, taking him into her mouth. She didn't have any experience at this, but once she'd thought about pleasuring him in this way, she couldn't stop thinking about it. She just hoped she was doing it right as she licked up and down, sucking as she went.

Justin groaned, and his hands found the back of her head as she bobbed up and down, speeding up. His fingers intertwined in her hair and she moved even faster, spurred on by Justin's moans.

Then he gently tugged on her hair, pulling her off of him.

Mandy released him with a popping sound. "Something wrong?"

Justin caught her gaze, his heated and full of fire. He shook his head. "On the contrary—you are amazing at that."

Mandy blushed. "Really?"

Justin grinned, nodding. "Absolutely. But I want to let go inside of you."

She moved toward him, stalking her way up his body. "I'm good with that."

He laughed. "Come here, baby." He held out his hands for her, and she collapsed on top of him, her lips finding his.

Mandy squirmed on top of him as he shoved inside her mouth, and she moaned against his lips as her tongue found his. She was throbbing, aching. She needed him inside her—now.

She reached down and grabbed his length, running the tip across her most sensitive part, and tiny sparks shot along her spine. They moaned into each other in unison, and she rubbed him against her folds until she found what she was looking for. Then she rocked back on top of him, taking him in all at once, and she gasped as his length filled her up so completely she wasn't sure where he ended and she began.

She groaned loudly, and her eyes shot open at the sound. Justin chuckled then stretched up to reach her. "Kiss me, baby. Moan into me."

Mandy leaned down, pressing her lips to his. And she did as she was told, moaning longer than she ever had before as they found their rhythm.

Then she pulled back, sitting up with him still inside her, the angle creating a deeper intensity that left her breathless. "I can be quiet. I just need your hands on me, Justin. Please."

He immediately found her breasts and teased both nipples with his fingertips. She clapped her hand over her mouth and let out a muted scream.

Justin's eyes flashed, all heat and sex, and Mandy caught and held his gaze as his fingers explored further, finding their way down to her clit. Her breath caught as their eyes stayed connected, and Mandy felt whatever was between them deepening. She didn't have the need to cry out now—she was too overwhelmed by what she saw in his eyes. As they moved in rhythm, speeding up to their mutual climax, Mandy felt her heart expanding, and she didn't know what to make of it.

She felt her orgasm building just as Justin's was, too, slamming her back into the present moment. Justin thrusted up into her as she clenched around him, and stars sparked behind her eyelids as pleasure ripped through her core. Justin shuddered beneath her, yanking her down to him and smashing his lips to hers as they released together.

They were still panting when Mandy lifted up and laid down beside him. His hand found hers as they lay there, staring at the ceiling.

Suddenly, her thoughts sped up, whipping through her mind in a flurry. She'd never experienced that before, during sex or otherwise: a deep, primal connection to another human being.

No, she couldn't be this connected to him in just a few days. Or a weekend four months ago and a few days. That was just insane.

But as she stared up at the ceiling, the room lightening as the sun rose to another day, she abruptly figured out what was happening.

And it scared the shit out of her.

CHAPTER TWENTY-FOUR

JUSTIN WOKE PEACEFULLY, a slight smile on his face. Their first class was at two fifteen, so he assumed Mandy had shut off her alarm. He appreciated her foresight; after a thoroughly enjoyable yet exhausting night—and morning, as it turned out—they definitely needed their sleep.

He turned to look at Mandy, who was resting on her side of the bed to his left. They'd just naturally chosen sides as if it had already been decided.

Add to that the insane connection he'd felt during sex this morning and his weird, almost premonition-like glimpses into their future, and Justin was convinced more than ever that Mandy was the only woman for him. Forever.

Unable to help himself, he leaned over and lightly kissed her shoulder, waking her. She stretched, a smile spreading across her face, then her eyelids fluttered open.

Her familiar hazel eyes stared back at him, but they were different than last night. Eyes were most definitely the windows to the soul, and Mandy's told him everything he needed to know. Everything that his heart had been telling him all along.

He swallowed, pushing down the revelation. Mandy would need to be the one to voice it first, when she was ready, because he was already certain of how he felt.

Then she leaned in and planted a chaste kiss on his lips. "Good morning."

Justin grinned. "Morning, babe. How'd you sleep?"

Mandy stretched again then rolled over toward Justin, leaning against his chest. He snaked his arm around her naked body and pulled her to him. She sighed. "Perfectly. I could wake up every morning like this."

Justin kissed her hair. "You could, babe. We could start looking for an apartment after class today."

Mandy froze for an instant then quickly thawed, likely so he wouldn't catch it.

But he did, of course. He pulled back, forehead creasing as he searched her eyes. "Everything okay?"

Mandy took a breath. Then she pulled away from him and bit her lower lip, sitting up. The sheets pooled around her waist, exposing her ample bare breasts, and Justin thought she was actually glowing. And *damn*—it was smokin' hot. "Baby, I've loved this. This has been the best night—and morning—of my life." She smirked at him, and he flashed his crooked smile for a few seconds before it faded. He could sense something coming.

"But . . . ?" he asked.

Mandy drew in another slow inhale then released it slowly.

Justin raised to a seated position, leaning against the headboard. "Babe, is everything okay?"

A tear welled in the corner of her eye, and she blinked it away.

"Aw, baby. Please . . . tell me what's wrong." Justin reached up to brush her hair off her cheek.

"Honesty?"

He nodded solemnly.

Mandy paused, drawing in a deep breath. Then she whispered just two words: "I'm scared."

Justin shifted closer, cupping his hand around her cheek. "What are you scared of, Mandy?"

She glanced away, hiding her eyes. Justin steeled himself for what she was about to say, suddenly unsure that Mandy was feeling the same way he was.

Mandy straightened her spine as she turned back to him, her hand waving between them. "This."

Justin dropped his hand to his lap as he froze, a stab of pain shooting through his heart. But then Mandy's face fell, and he felt the tiniest glimmer of hope spark to life. Maybe this relationship *wasn't* crumbling to pieces before it had barely even started.

He blinked. "What do you mean?"

He watched her carefully pull in a breath. "Justin . . . I think . . ." Then she dropped her gaze to her lap, whispering her next words to the quiet bedroom. "I think I'm falling for you."

Justin's entire being relaxed for a split second, then his heart started racing. He knew she'd been scared, but she'd found the courage to tell him the truth yet again. He smiled, and Mandy returned it with her own wide grin. "So you felt it, too."

Mandy gasped. "This morning, yes! But Justin, I . . . it's too soon. I can't be falling for you."

Justin's grin widened, and he reached for her, pulling her into his lap. "Mandy, baby, I've been falling for you since we met."

Mandy blushed as their foreheads connected. "Really?"

Justin nodded against her head. "Absolutely." He leaned in and planted a kiss on her lips then pulled away to catch her gaze. "But why does that scare you?"

Mandy kept her voice low as if it would be less terrifying to speak the words if they were barely audible. "I've never felt this way before. I don't know how to even make sense of what I'm feeling." She took a breath. "And I don't ever want to hurt you."

Justin kissed her again, longer this time. When they parted, he smiled slightly. "Mandy, baby, take all the time you need. Sort it out in your head, do whatever you need to do. I'll be here when you're ready to admit it."

"Admit what?" She pulled back to stare into his eyes.

He smirked, laying everything on the line with one teasing phrase. "That you're in love with me."

Mandy smacked his arm. "You wish."

But Justin could tell by the look in her eyes that she absolutely was.

CHAPTER TWENTY-FIVE

LATER THAT NIGHT, about twenty minutes before Justin was set to arrive to take her out to dinner—and hopefully bring her back here and take *her*—a text finally came in from her mom.

So sorry, sweetie! I got so busy last night then forgot to text this morning and this day's been crazy. I'm good. How are you?

Mandy frowned at the screen. What would her mom be doing to keep herself so busy? **No worries, Mom. You doing okay?**

Her mom's response was quick. **Yeah, honey, just busy with everything.**

"Busy" twice in as many texts. Something was definitely going on. **Mom, are you sure you're okay?**

Amy's response wasn't as quick this time. **I'm okay.**

Oh no. She was definitely *not* okay. **Call you?**

Can't really talk right now, honey, sorry. Going into book club. Talk soon?

Mandy frowned, her stomach clenching as she replied.

Something was definitely going on with Amy Thatcher, no question.

But her mom would say something if she really was in trouble, right?

AFTER A WEEKEND and two days of downright mind-blowing sex—he would have never thought that sex could be this good, but he supposed that was what love did to a guy—Justin found himself considering what the future would look like. He knew he wanted Mandy in it, that was certain, but what did that mean? Wouldn't it just make sense to move in together?

He'd already spent every single night at her apartment—they were basically living together anyway. So why did Mandy still hesitate when he brought up the idea?

Justin glanced over at his phone and picked it up. He still had an hour before his Wednesday afternoon class.

He was currently sprawled out on his bed in David's house. He would be glad to pack up and move out of here at his first opportunity—he and Mandy were going apartment hunting later that week anyway, so hopefully they'd find something perfect.

He shot off a text. **Hey, Mom. Just checking in.**

Her response came only a minute later. **Hey, baby!** She added a smiley face emoji. **How is everything? How is Mandy?**

Justin grinned. **Right to the point, I see.** He added a winky face and sent that text then typed up another one. **She's really good. We're really good.**

How was your date last week? You never gave me any details.

Justin's mind immediately shot to the memory of Mandy screaming at the top of her lungs as she trembled beneath him that first night. He shook his head to clear it. Those were not the details his mom needed. **It was amazing, Mom. She's incredible.**

Justin watched the three dots pop up as his mother typed. **I hope you were safe!**

His mouth fell open as his eyes shot wide. **Mother! I can't believe you just said that!**

His mom just sent the grinning emoji.

Then: **I just want you to be happy, baby. And I know Mandy makes you happy.**

Justin smiled to the empty room. **She does. Very much.** He added a heart emoji.

As soon as the text sent, a video chat request came through. "Mom?"

"Justin Andrew! You didn't tell me you were in love!"

Justin smiled wider—he couldn't help it. "I'm in love."

Jan screamed, bouncing up and down, her bone-straight hair fluttering around her cheeks. Her eyes still looked tired, but her energy levels were obviously up, and Justin's heart warmed at the realization. "Ah! I knew it! Justin, baby, I'm so happy for you two!"

"Well, she hasn't exactly said it yet, so I'm not one-hundred-percent sure she loves me back."

His mother's face turned serious. "Have you told her how you feel?"

Justin shook his head. "Not yet. I don't want to force her to acknowledge it until she's ready. I think she's a little hesitant about committing." Then he paused. "I kinda asked her to move in with me."

Jan's eyes went wide, then she opened her mouth just to close it again.

"What?"

"I just . . . what did she say?"

"That it's probably too soon."

Jan just nodded.

"You think so, too?"

She sighed. "No, honey, I actually don't. *For you.* But for her, she's probably terrified of getting so close to someone again."

"I would never do what Dan did to her, and she knows that."

Jan nodded. "I know, honey, but that fear is probably still there, hiding under the surface." She took a breath. "You need to give her some space."

"I am, Mom. I told her I would."

She nodded again. "Good. She'll come around, baby, and the timing will be perfect."

He smiled at the screen. "I know she will. I've just . . . I've been waiting so long for her, Mom. You know how long I've been waiting."

"Then you can wait a little while longer. It's what she needs, Justin. If you love her, you'll do it for her."

He nodded. "Of course, I will. Because I do, more than anything."

Jan's smile warmed his heart. "I am so glad to hear it, baby." She glanced off to the right, clearly looking for something off-camera—or maybe she was just checking to make sure Roger wasn't in hearing distance. "Now let's talk about your dad's new project. It's ridiculous. He's been in the garage for days and won't show me anything!"

Justin chuckled and listened to his mother's latest "your father is always tinkering in the garage" anecdote. His dad chose to spend his free time—which was substantial, since they were both retired—creating things in their large garage. His mom was forever frustrated that he wouldn't show her his project until it was done because she was relentlessly curious.

Those two were adorable together. Goals.

"OKAY, EVERYONE," Dr. McDreamy—he'd told his students to call him Grady—started as he opened class on Friday. Mandy couldn't focus on the glasses he wore today or the way his dark polo shirt hugged his pecs. She still hadn't connected with her mom to get the full story of what was going on with her since last week—they'd just exchanged a few amiable texts—and Mandy was starting to get really worried. She'd even text Lucy to ask if she thought something was going on, but her sister had been so involved in her classes that she hadn't noticed anything out of the ordinary.

Plus, Mandy still had Justin on the mind . . . and their sexcapade last night. She blushed just thinking about it, the one last night in particular—which involved moves she thought she'd never try with body parts she'd previously considered taboo but were so erotic she had to clench her thighs together even now just thinking about it—plus the several they'd shared over the past week. She felt like she could barely catch her breath, but she didn't mind it one bit.

And he had stayed over every night.

"This semester has a group project," the professor continued. "Each group will compile data from an archaeological project of their choice—from my list, of course—and make a presentation of their research and data at the end of the semester. Your research, methods, analysis, and conclusion will also be submitted as a 5000-word paper. One per group, so I don't go blind reading all of them." He smirked at the class, and Mandy remembered why she'd ogled him all through undergrad. For the right girl, he'd be a dream guy. Turned out, that wasn't her.

She glanced over at Justin and smiled. She was okay with that.

Dr. McGready continued. "The oral presentation will be one-fifth of your grade, and the paper will be another fifth. So choose your partners wisely." He grinned at the class. "Let's take ten minutes and find our groups. Four to five members each."

The classroom erupted in light conversation, and Mandy leaned over to Justin. "Can you please be on my team, Mr. Statistician?"

Justin grinned at her. "Of course. We'll want someone who's good at analysis, someone who loves research—"

"Ooo—that's me!" She cut him off.

Justin chuckled as he continued. ". . . someone who's a good writer, and someone who's good at public speaking." He glanced around the room. "You know this crowd way better than I do. Any ideas?"

Mandy nodded then stood, crossing the room to collect their perfect group members. Five minutes later, all five of them were clustered around Mandy and Justin's table, exchanging pleasantries.

Grady called the class to attention a few minutes later, once all the groups were settled. "Okay, good. Don't forget to exchange contact info before you leave today." He started passing out a single sheet of paper to each group. "I just handed you the list of archaeological projects you can choose from." He glanced down at the copy he'd retained. "What group wants the first one?"

A skinny guy up front raised his hand. "We can take that."

Mandy perused the list over Justin's shoulder. She leaned into his ear, calling to him under her breath. "Justin. Number three."

He nodded so subtly that only she noticed. "I saw that. Perfect."

Justin leaned forward, asking the others for their opinion of the dig in Guatemala. Their group—a dark-skinned girl named Carla who Mandy'd admired in all her major classes for her speaking skills, a middle-aged, mildly attractive man named Doug who was the perfect candidate for analysis since he lived and breathed spreadsheets, and a pretty girl named Tara who could've been Mandy's sister and always got good grades on her papers—all nodded their approval, so Justin spoke up when Grady got to that one.

With their group secured, phone numbers exchanged, and first meeting scheduled, Mandy let out a long exhale as she and Justin packed their things. "Whew. It's gonna be a long semester."

Justin smirked as he shoved his laptop in his backpack and lifted it to his shoulder. "Yes, it will. Why did we do this to ourselves again?"

Mandy grinned as she slung her own bag over her arm. "I don't know—because we love archaeology?"

Justin frowned, shrugging. "I forgot about that."

Mandy laughed as they walked down the tiered platforms toward the front where Dr. McGready was perusing something on his laptop, his bespectacled gaze locked on the screen. He glanced up as he heard them walk by. "Mandy Carlson and Justin Stanford, right?"

They slowed, both turning to face him. Mandy smiled. "Yes. We're excited for this semester. I know Justin is." She smirked and shoved him lightly with her shoulder.

Grady laughed. "And why is that?"

Justin crossed his arms, bumping into Mandy's hip with a grin. "My degree is in statistics. Mandy here thinks I love numbers and data for some reason." He rolled his eyes playfully.

Grady nodded, his eyes crinkling behind his glasses with his smile. "And how long have you two been together?"

Mandy blushed. "Is it that obvious?"

Grady shrugged and crossed his arms over his tight polo shirt. "I am more perceptive than most."

Justin glanced over at Mandy, and her cheeks got even redder. "It's still new," he admitted.

"Ah." Grady reached for his laptop, snapping it closed before sliding it in his shoulder bag. "Well, good luck, you two. I hope it works out." He smiled at them, draping his bag over his shoulder.

Justin smiled at Mandy. "Me, too."

She bit her lip to hide the smile threatening to stretch across her face. "Thank you, Grady."

"You're very welcome. See you both Monday." His things collected, Grady stepped around them and strode toward the exit.

Justin eyed Mandy after their professor left the room. "Still have a crush on Professor McDreamy?"

Mandy blushed again. "I can't believe you'd say that! I've never had a crush on him."

Justin crossed his arms and stared at her. "Riiiiight."

Mandy huffed. "Okay, fine. He's easy on the eyes." She waved her hand in the air to dismiss the notion. "But he's not exactly my type."

Justin pursed his lips. "Considering every guy I've ever seen you with—"

"Literally just you and Dan."

"—I can't say that you have a type."

"Maybe I just finally found my type."

Justin grinned, reaching for her hand and pulling her toward the door. "That makes me the lucky one."

Mandy grinned back, following him out into the hallway.

CHAPTER TWENTY-SIX

JUSTIN HAD another class starting in a few minutes, so Mandy gave him a kiss and decided to wait for him at home. After the short drive to her apartment, she dropped her bag on the floor by her door and kicked off her flats. They'd planned to go apartment hunting when he got out of class, so she had over an hour to kill.

They were looking for an apartment for *him,* and she'd made that abundantly clear. She wasn't ready for that sort of commitment.

She dropped to the futon, frowning as she stared at the wall, lost in thought. But wasn't she ready, really? She'd known Justin since before Dan, and though they'd been acquaintances who'd had a few interesting conversations, looking back, he seemed to spend a lot of time in her circle. Then after Dan had cheated, and Justin'd been there to help pick up the pieces—which was four months ago, by the way—Justin had stolen her breath.

And her heart, too?

No, she couldn't go there. Her heart was still safe in her

chest, not for anyone else to claim. She'd protected it with Dan, mostly, and even with Tom. She didn't let people in, and for good reason. Because they'd leave, just like her dad. Just like Dan.

But Justin's different, her mind answered back. And she wanted to believe it. She *felt* it, for crying out loud, first when they'd had sex last Friday morning, and, truthfully, ever since. She couldn't deny the deep, almost spiritual connection she felt when she looked into his bright-blue eyes. She couldn't deny the connection she'd felt between them even before they'd had sex.

She chewed on her thumbnail. What if this was just hormones, just attraction? Maybe they were just really compatible in bed.

She grinned. That was definitely the case regardless. Every night was a new adventure with him, and she found herself craving him more and more.

Her mind still frustratingly undecided, she pushed to her feet and stalked into the kitchen. Her flowers from earlier in the week were still in their pitchers—he'd kept sending her one a day since early last week. And she'd been so wrapped up in him that she hadn't made time to go get any new ones.

She pulled her phone out of her pocket. She still had just under an hour before Justin would be here to pick her up. She decided to check in with her mom yet again. Maybe she'd finally get some answers.

Hey, Mom, just wanted to see how you were doing.

The answer came a few minutes later. **I'm fine, sweetie. Just busy.**

Mandy frowned at her now-standard answer. **Busy with what? I swear you're busier now with Lucy gone!** She added a smiley face emoji to soften the message.

Her mom answered a minute later. **I'm currently helping with a bake sale at Lucy's old school. The PTA can still use my help, so I said I would for a while.** She added a smiley face emoji, too.

Mandy bit her lip as she contemplated her reply. **Can we talk soon? I feel like we haven't talked in forever.**

It took another minute for her mom to answer. **Sure, sweetie. I'll call when I get a chance.**

Soon, okay?

Okay, baby. Love you.

Love you, Mom.

Mandy frowned again as she set her phone down. She'd just have to wait for answers from her mom. Maybe she was simply reading the situation all wrong—God, she hoped so.

She shrugged to herself. Maybe a little shopping would help clear her head. Sitting here worrying about it for the next forty-five minutes certainly wouldn't.

Mandy grabbed her purse, locked the door behind her, and fought her aversion to driving to head to her favorite part of town once again. She had the errant thought to grab a mocha while she was here as she pulled into the parking lot behind the thrift store.

But as she glanced at her phone on her way toward the front of the store, she realized she probably didn't have enough time. Justin would be out of class in just thirty minutes.

She yanked open one of the pair of glass doors that greeted her at the entrance and took a split second to luxuriate in the plentiful air conditioning before she hurried back to the glass section. This store always had the best selection—it was the largest of its kind in the city, and she saw their clever commercials and eye-catching billboards much more often than the ones from the thrift store chains.

As Mandy perused the rows of glass containers in every shape and size known to man—seriously, there was even one shaped like a hippo—she heard footsteps behind her.

"Mandy! Hi."

She spun at the sound, gripping the one vase she'd already picked out so it wouldn't fall. Her eyes shot wide. "Uh, Logan. Hi."

Logan crossed his tattooed arms over his considerable chest and smiled down at her. She felt an inch tall when she stood next to him, but then again, they hadn't spent much time vertical. He'd been great for one thing: good sex. Though now that she had Justin to compare it to, she was downgrading it to adequate sex. Especially since he'd been kinda, well, *small.*

She smiled back. "How have you been?"

"I've been good. How are you? You didn't respond to my last text . . ."

Uh-oh. She should've known that would bite her in the ass. "Yeah, sorry . . . I just got busy with my work study and stuff, and now the semester's started . . ."

He nodded slowly, but she didn't think he was okay with her lame answer. "It's okay, I get it. Things get busy."

She nodded back, a pleasant smile on her face. She was used to awkward, but good awkward, like with Justin. This was bad awkward, and she couldn't wait to get away.

"Hey, Mandy? I was wondering if you wanted to get dinner sometime."

The response flew out of her. "I'm actually seeing someone now."

Logan raised an eyebrow. "Oh, really? Congratulations."

She smiled sweetly. "Yes. Thanks."

As they wrapped up the pleasantries and Logan waved goodbye on his way to the checkout, Mandy's humiliated heart started sprinting. She'd just admitted to someone that she was in a relationship. She and Justin hadn't even talked about if they were exclusive—she assumed they were, but making assumptions was never a great basis for a relationship—and here she was acting like the ring was already on her finger.

Figuratively, of course.

As she selected five glass vases—that was all she could carry; she'd have to come back later for more if Justin kept this up—and checked out, her mind raced as her thoughts became more frantic. She drove home in a daze.

She'd always believed everything happened for a reason. The fact that she happened to hit up the thrift store on the same day that Logan had done the same thing *plus* her admission that she was in a relationship meant something. She was certain—well, almost certain—that Justin felt the same way. That he wanted to be with her and only her.

He'd told her he'd never slept with more than one woman at a time. He'd told her he'd never cheat.

But then again, Dan had said those things, too.

Stop it, Mandy, she chastised herself. *Justin is not Dan. He's not an asshole. You know that.*

She *did* know that, deep down inside her. Deep down where Justin's soul had invaded. And though it scared her more than anything to be truthful about her feelings, she sensed that she would need to soon.

It was time for "the conversation."

She just hoped she and Justin were on the same page. Otherwise, she may just get scorched after all.

CHAPTER TWENTY-SEVEN

JUSTIN'S late afternoon class on Wednesdays and Fridays was all about the Mayan language. He had Dr. Kayla Harrington for the semester, and she was downright brilliant.

Though he was definitely not looking—he'd been off the market since he'd met Mandy, truthfully—he noticed toward the end of class that she had that classically beautiful vibe going with her deep brown eyes and long, auburn hair. As she started wrapping up her lecture, gesturing excitedly with her left hand to help get her point across, Justin noticed she didn't have a ring on her finger. He wondered how someone like her hadn't found someone yet. She didn't seem like she'd be struggling to find dates.

He shrugged at the thought as another popped into his head. What about Professor McDreamy? They'd be *perfect* for each other. They both were in love with this archaeology stuff—he wondered if they'd ever considered it. They had to know each other pretty well.

He pulled out his phone as the class was wrapping up. **Just had a random thought.**

The text came back a few minutes later. **About what?**

Hypothetical matchmaking.

Mandy sent a laughing emoji. **We've been together a week, and you already want to set someone else up?**

He grinned as he typed his response. **Just hypothetical, babe. But we gotta spread the love.**

You're so ridiculous. He didn't miss that she ignored the "love" comment.

Another text came through fifteen seconds later. **So who are we hypothetically setting up?**

Justin chuckled under his breath as Dr. Harrington released the class. Students sprang to life and started to trickle out of the classroom as he typed back. **Our professors.** He added a smiley face emoji.

Mandy sent him a laughing emoji again. **This should be good. Who?**

Grady and Professor Harrington. Don't you have her this semester, too?

Yeah. Actually . . . The three dots popped up as she typed her next message. **That's actually brilliant, babe. Those two would be perfect together.**

Justin just grinned and packed up his things.

Justin picked Mandy up at her apartment just minutes after their conversation. To save time, she'd come running down the stairs to meet him at his SUV.

When Mandy climbed inside, Justin leaned in and planted a sweet kiss on her lips before sitting back in his seat with a grin. "Where to first?"

Mandy tucked her red-and-white polka dot dress around

her legs, staving off the AC. She already had the apartment hunting app open on her phone, so she started tapping until she found the properties she'd saved. Most of these places didn't require an appointment, so she figured they would hit as many as they could before they all closed for the night.

"Hmm . . ." she mumbled as she swiped through the list. "First stop is north of here. I really liked their layout, and they have two-bedrooms."

Justin winked at her as he pulled out of her complex. "Are we going to be roommates?"

Mandy smacked his arm, trying to ignore the butterflies in her stomach at the thought. She needed to bring up "the talk" soon, probably tonight, and this whole apartment hunt was just conjuring more for her brain to deal with. The fear wasn't going away, it just seemed to lessen in Justin's presence. She took that as a good sign.

She pulled up directions on her phone. "Turn right." Justin nodded, so she continued. "And I told you—this apartment search is for *you*."

Justin reached for her hand and pulled it to his mouth, kissing her fingers. "I heard you, babe, I promise. I just want you to like it, too. I want you to be comfortable there, whether you decide to eventually move in or not."

Mandy bit her lip, nodding as her thoughts drifted. And, of course, Justin noticed.

"What's going on in that beautiful head of yours?"

Mandy gave him the next set of directions, and he made his way to the interstate. Then she sighed. "I ran into someone today."

"Oh, yeah?"

"Yeah." Mandy nodded slowly. "Logan."

Justin's eyebrow shot up. "Really?" Then he smirked. "You going barhopping without me while I'm in class?"

Mandy rolled her eyes, thankful for his penchant for lightening the mood at nearly every occasion. "Of course not. I went to buy vases."

"Oh, good! Because I brought you more flowers in the back." He nodded toward the backseat.

Mandy turned in her seat then gasped. "I clearly did not buy enough."

Justin laughed. "I told you, babe."

"You *warned* me, yes. What—did you buy stock in a flower company?"

Justin laughed again. "No, baby. I just think you deserve it."

"Why?" The question just slipped out. "I mean, you don't have to make up for or prove anything."

Justin narrowed his eyes at her, just a little, but his eyes stayed soft. Then he squeezed her hand. "I know that, Mandy. Can't I just like giving you flowers?"

Mandy blushed. "Of course. But can we keep it to, like, three a week or something?"

Justin's thumb rubbed the back of her hand as he chuckled. "Okay." He raised her hand to his lips once more and kissed her knuckles. "So what happened with Logan?"

His jaw clenched at his question. If she hadn't been staring at his face, she would've missed it. He was actually jealous.

She hid her smile as she answered. "Nothing much, we just caught up. I kinda ghosted him back in June." She threw her free hand over her eyes.

"Damn, girl, that's cold! You ghosted him after *sleeping* with him? Because you *did* sleep with him, right?"

Mandy blushed. "I wouldn't call what we did sleeping, but sure, let's go with that."

Justin snorted. "Now who's ridiculous?" He started laughing loudly, and Mandy couldn't help but join in.

Then they quieted, and the atmosphere in the car shifted. Mandy squirmed in her seat at the uneasiness that skated over her skin, but she couldn't figure out what to say to get rid of it.

Justin broke the silence for her. "You okay?"

"Why would you ask that?" Mandy blinked over at him.

He shrugged. "Seems like something about it freaked you out a little."

"Are you a mind reader or something?"

Justin just grinned back.

She swallowed. "Okay, yeah. It freaked me out a little."

"How so?" Justin pulled into the complex as he asked, making his way to the office. He parked in a "future resident" parking spot hidden from the entrance by a host of leafy trees and bushes and put the car in park. He left the AC on and turned in his seat to face her before she answered.

Mandy took a deep breath. "He kinda asked me out." She muttered, her eyes on Justin's face.

His jaw twitched again. Jealous Justin was actually pretty damn sexy. "What'd you say?"

Did he really not know? "I told him I was seeing someone."

Justin's eyes relaxed only the slightest bit, but Mandy could tell relief was flooding through his system. She loved that she knew him that well. But then he smirked. "Oh, yeah? Who?"

Mandy smacked his arm. "You, you crazy person."

Justin's crooked grin widened.

But then Mandy fell silent, and she could feel the mood change again when Justin—of course—recognized the shift in her.

"Is there more?"

Mandy exhaled. She supposed the time was now. Honesty.

"It just made me think about . . . *us*." She paused before the last word, emphasizing it.

Justin's eyes softened. "What about us?"

He was going to make her ask. "Is there an 'us'? Like, exclusively? We haven't exactly talked about it."

Justin just stared, his gaze penetrating. She shivered. "Would you like there to be?"

"Justin! It's just . . . like I said, it's too soon. We've only been dating a week!"

"Eight days," he whispered, and Mandy could've sworn she heard a hitch in his voice, but his gaze didn't waver. Mandy's chest constricted, and a warmth thrilled through her as she saw the depth and the truth of his feelings in his ocean-blue eyes.

She knew his every unasked question, and he knew her every unvoiced confession. She didn't know how she knew; she just did. The tension between them sparked, filling up the vehicle, as Mandy tried to find the courage to tell him the truth. Because she knew her excuses about time were absolutely inane—she didn't need to wait any longer to realize what she truly felt for him.

She drew in a deep breath. "Justin . . ." She hesitated, searching for the right words.

"Mandy, if you're not ready for us to be an 'us,' that's okay."

"Justin, no, I—"

"Just be honest with me. You promised to always be honest."

She'd never seen this side of him, the one that told her his heart was in her hands.

And suddenly, looking at Justin's pain, she wasn't scared anymore. Relieving his pain was more important than holding on to her fear.

She pulled her hand from his so she could reach over and

cup his face. "Justin, baby . . ."

He caught her gaze, and Mandy saw his eyes getting shiny.

"Justin, listen to me."

He nodded once, and she dropped her hands, but her eyes held him in place.

"Honesty?" She took a deep breath. "I want there to be an 'us.' You're it for me."

At once, Justin cupped his hands around her jaw and pulled her to him. Their lips met with a spark, fire burning Mandy's tongue as Justin's slipped inside. She loved how sweet he tasted.

A minute later, he pulled away. "Mandy, I've wanted nothing more than for there to be an 'us' from day one. I know it's really soon, and I know it seems like we haven't known each other that long, but that doesn't feel true to me. We've been drawn to each other from the beginning—I know you feel that. It defies logic, but it's undeniable. It's why we spent that amazing weekend together then picked up right where we left off when we saw each other again, four months later."

Mandy nodded, tears filling her eyes and clouding her vision. She laughed as Justin swiped one from her cheek, and she grabbed a few tissues from the glove compartment to wipe her eyes.

Justin stared through the windshield. Mandy followed his gaze, noticing how secluded they were back here, blocked from the view of the office by some bushes on one side and a forest of palm trees on the other.

When his eyes flew to hers, she knew they'd had the same thought.

Justin wiggled his eyebrows at her. "Care to try something fun?"

Mandy bit her lip, nodding. She glanced at the backseat. "Is there enough room for us back there?"

Justin reached for his car door and exited the Jeep only to open the back door and climb in, yanking it shut behind him. He gingerly laid the flowers on the floor mat behind his seat as Mandy scooted in on the opposite side, her insides threatening to crawl out of her skin. Butterflies were swarming in her stomach at the mere thought of Justin taking her right here in this parking lot.

He grabbed her hips, sliding her across the seat to him until she was seated in the middle of the backseat. "We'll make room." He shifted to lean over her, pressing her back gently until she was lying across the seat. He settled between her legs, her dress bunching around her waist. His hand found her thigh as if it were a magnet, and he slowly dragged his palm up to her panty line.

Mandy's eyes fell closed as his finger slid her panties to the side then slipped inside her. She moaned quietly.

"Babe, as hot as it is when you scream for me, you're gonna have to be quiet."

She opened her eyes wide and found his, nodding at him. She stared as he unzipped his pants, sliding his already hard cock out of his boxer briefs, and she felt the butterflies take flight inside her chest.

"You ready for me, baby?"

Mandy nodded vigorously. "Yes, Justin, please. Fuck me."

Justin's eyes flashed, and he leaned in to kiss her, his mouth hard and hungry on hers. Then he pulled away for just a second. "Damn, babe, it's hot when you cuss."

She caught his gaze again, feeling the heat between them intensify, then mouthed the words again, slowly this time, emphasizing every syllable. "Fuck. Me."

Justin growled, guiding himself inside her as he connected

with her lips, then he groaned. Mandy moaned into him as he slid in slowly at first, but his movements soon became hard and fast, desperate. His hand slipped below her neckline and under her bra to fondle her breast as he thrusted harder, pushed deeper. She gasped against his mouth. Her hands snaked beneath his shirt to caress his back then slid around to the front to feel his chest.

As Mandy felt herself nearing her release, she pulled away for a second, searching out Justin's eyes as they moved together. When she found them, she held them. "Justin, baby, look at me while I come for you."

Justin nodded then thrusted twice more, and his body tensed as he found his release. His eyes never left hers, and that was all it took for Mandy to clench around him, her own orgasm cresting. She wanted to cry out, wanted to close her eyes, but she held his gaze tightly. She had to see all of him.

Then she released, her back arching when he thrust into her one last time, and sparks ignited throughout her body, exploding into every cell. The intensity of her orgasm stole her breath as the love in Justin's eyes stole her heart and everything else.

Mandy stilled as Justin held himself up above her, still inside her. Their chests heaved in unison yet their gazes never wavered, and the weight of the moment enveloped Mandy's entire being like a warm blanket on a cool night.

"Justin . . ."

"Yeah, baby?"

She took a deep breath. "I think I'm in love with you."

Justin's eyes softened, and the corners of his mouth turned up. "I'm in love with you, too, Mandy. I have been since that morning in your apartment. I just didn't want to tell you until you were ready to say it back."

She nodded slowly. With his eyes trained on Mandy's face, Justin pulled out of her, reaching for the tissues she'd set on the console between the front seats. Mandy's eyes welled as Justin cleaned her off and gently moved her panties back into place. No one had ever taken care of her like this, and she felt like her heart might explode in her chest.

He cleaned himself up and discarded the tissues on the floor then pulled Mandy's dress down over her so she wasn't exposed. Well, her body wasn't. Her heart was open and vulnerable, but she realized, in that moment, she was more than okay with that.

"You ready, babe?"

Mandy nodded, wiping away the tears. "Yes. Let's go find our apartment."

Justin froze on his way out the door then turned back to her. "Did you just say . . . ?"

Mandy pushed up to a seated position and grinned. "Yup. Let's move in together."

He abandoned the door handle and reached for her suddenly, pulling her toward him for a hard kiss. Mandy was laughing as he pulled away.

"I love you, babe, more than you know."

She grinned wider. "I love you, too, baby." She kissed him once then moved to climb out of the backseat. Once she'd crossed around the front of the vehicle and he'd secured her hand, she smiled again, nearly skipping to the entrance. "Well, we've already christened this place. Maybe that's a good sign."

Justin wiggled his eyebrows at her. "Maybe we'll just have to christen them all, increase our chances." He reached down and smacked her ass. Mandy yelped but leaned into him, her hands grabbing his muscular bicep as they crossed the parking lot to the office.

CHAPTER TWENTY-EIGHT

MANDY VENTURED into the office first, but Justin was close behind. He grabbed her hand as they walked in, a little bell on the door dinging.

A middle-aged woman stepped out of the office to their left. "Good afternoon! How are you both today?"

Justin smiled at her. "We're here to look at an apartment."

The woman's kind eyes lit up. "Of course! I'm Natasha." She extended her hand.

"Justin." He took her offered hand with a wide grin.

"Mandy."

Natasha nodded at them, shaking Mandy's hand. "Nice to meet you both. Would you like to see what we have available?"

Mandy was already nodding at Justin's left. "Yes. I liked the two-bedrooms I saw online. Do you have any of those you could show us?"

The woman nodded, heading into her office and motioning for Mandy and Justin to take the seats by the door in the tiny space. She circled her desk and sat down in the rolling chair as Justin dropped to the chair nearest the exit. "Yes, I believe so.

Let me check." She pulled a thick, three-ring binder from a desk drawer and perused it.

Out of his peripheral vision, Justin saw Mandy cross her legs then start bouncing her top foot up and down. Justin reached over and put his hand on her knee. She eyed him and mouthed "sorry" with a smile, but he just grinned back. He left his hand there, rubbing ever so slightly, enjoying the feel of her soft, smooth skin.

Mandy's cheeks reddened, and his smile widened. She had to know what he was thinking, had to know how she made him feel with just one look, one touch. Not that he was hiding it very well.

The suited woman looked up. "Oh! I have the perfect one to show you. It's actually available right now, too. How soon were you two looking to move?"

Mandy caught Justin's gaze, and he sensed he would need to take the lead here. "I can move as soon as possible. Mandy . . ." He realized they probably should've talked about this before they came in.

She took it in stride. "My lease is month-to-month, so I can move in by the end of September." She glanced over at Justin. "It's not like I have that much stuff to move anyway."

Justin chuckled then turned back to Natasha. "We'd love to see that unit."

After making a copy of their driver's licenses, Natasha grabbed a set of keys from a lock box across the room then headed to the front door. "Just follow me. I'm in the Acura."

Justin nodded as they walked to the car, waiting until Natasha had shut her car door before speaking. "Mandy, I'm sorry about that. I realize now we should've discussed it before we came looking."

She waved him off as they climbed in the car and Justin

pulled out of the spot to follow Natasha to the unit. "Not your fault! I only decided to move in with you what—like ten minutes ago?"

Justin laughed and reached for her hand. "After some pretty incredible sex, I might add."

Mandy bit her lip, and Justin felt his cock twitch. "Damn right. Care to reprise tonight?"

Justin grinned as he pulled into a parking spot next to Natasha's. "Oh, definitely. Though I think you're out of food at your house. We'll have to grab dinner on the way home." He liked the thought of home where Mandy was concerned. It just felt right.

Mandy smiled over at him as they hopped out and met in front of the Jeep. Justin grabbed her hand and let Natasha lead them up the open stairs.

The apartment was on the second floor, but Justin didn't mind that. As long as it was quiet and smoke-free, the second floor would provide an added level of security. Not that they'd need it here—this looked like a decent neighborhood—but they couldn't be too safe, especially if Mandy would be here alone at night.

He'd try to keep that to a minimum, of course. He was anticipating several nights of copious amounts of sex—and mornings, too. He adjusted himself as they stepped into the apartment. He really needed to get those thoughts under control.

MANDY GASPED as she entered the apartment behind Justin and Natasha. The front door opened into a large room that boasted a coat closet off to the right. A tiled floor delineated a small entryway which opened into a rather large living room, much larger than Mandy would have expected. She spied two tall windows on either side of the far wall that she knew would fit her TV perfectly. Wait—did Justin have a TV, too? So many unanswered questions . . .

She turned to her left. The breakfast nook—it had a breakfast nook!—was immediately to their left, with the kitchen further down. Not quite an open concept, but the two large entrances to the space came pretty close for an older-style building. Mandy supposed the bedrooms were off the hallway to the right.

The leasing agent smiled at her exuberant exhalation. "This one does show well. It's actually an end unit, which means windows on three sides and a little extra square footage, plus this building only has two stories, so you won't have any neighbors above you."

They stepped into the living room, and Mandy noticed a glass door off to the right, close to the windows on the far wall. Her eyes shot wide.

Natasha smiled again at her unasked question. "Yes, there is also a porch. With an outside storage unit as well." The friendly woman pushed open the door so Mandy and Justin could step outside. They barely fit on the porch side by side, but Mandy didn't think they'd spend a ton of time out here given the near-constant heat anyway. She took a peek into the storage unit, which seemed pretty big, but it wasn't like they had a ton of stuff. *Something to grow into,* she supposed then smiled to herself at the thought.

Justin kissed her lips lightly before they stepped back inside.

Natasha led them into the kitchen next, and Mandy's mouth dropped open at the sight. The kitchen had so much more square footage than her own, though that wasn't exactly hard to achieve.

Extending perpendicular with the entrance was a full wall of cabinets and countertop that held the sink, stove, dishwasher, and fridge and ended at a cute, decent-sized window that matched the one above the sink.

Justin came up behind her and snaked his arms around her waist as she took in the connected breakfast nook—and a third window—that had an entrance near the front door. The windows in the kitchen brought in a ton of natural light that lit the space beautifully.

Mandy turned to Natasha. "This is beautiful, thank you. Can we see the bedrooms?"

The woman smiled. "Yes, of course! Right this way." She motioned for them to head out of the kitchen first.

As they followed Natasha through the living room, Justin reached for Mandy's hand. She squeezed it as they entered the hallway and held on tight.

"This is the second bedroom, technically the smaller of the two." Mandy stepped through a doorway to their left into a bedroom she thought was a decent size for an apartment. The room had two windows and a full closet, too, which would be good for storage. That was the only nice thing about her apartment—the walk-in closet was nearly as big as her kitchen. Clothes were the one thing she probably bought too much of—okay, one of two things if you counted her candles. And vases now, apparently.

Natasha led them back into the hallway and pulled open a set of accordion doors, presenting a full-sized washer and dryer. Mandy's eyes widened, and Justin squeezed her hand. She smiled over at him. "No more laundromats?"

Justin pulled her into him, planting a kiss on her forehead. "No more laundromats."

Mandy grinned back at him as Natasha headed toward the end of the hall to what could only be the master suite.

As soon as she stepped through the doorway, Mandy's heart nearly stopped. The ceiling was vaulted and boasted a recessed, surprisingly modern ceiling fan. Off to the right was first a door to the bathroom—she'd check that in a minute—and beyond that was another door. She hurried over to it.

Mandy gasped when she flipped on the light in the closet. This space was three times the size of hers at home.

Justin chuckled behind her. "Enough room for my designer shoe collection, babe?"

Mandy laughed and smacked him lightly in the chest. Natasha's eyebrows pinched together as she looked down at Justin's off-brand cloth boat shoes. Mandy chuckled again, catching the other woman's gaze with a sheepish grin. "Inside joke."

Natasha's face smoothed as she smiled. Mandy went back to checking out the rest of the room.

Two windows brought in bright sunlight on the wall opposite the closet and bathroom, and that seemed to be it, except . . . Mandy spied a set of accordion doors lining the wall next to the door. Her eyes flew to Natasha's.

The middle-aged woman chuckled. "Yes, there are two closets in here. We actually added that as a selling point a few years back when we did renovations to update our units. But as you can see, we didn't lose much in square footage."

Justin crossed the room, opened and closed the closet doors, then spun on his heel to catch Mandy's gaze. "Babe, we should check out the bathroom."

She nodded at him and met him at the ensuite door. Mandy

stepped into the bathroom first, and yet another gasp escaped her lips. She just seemed to keep doing that here.

Though this was the only room in the house without a window, Mandy found she didn't care. A long, granite-topped vanity held double sinks and so many drawers that Mandy figured they'd never be able to fill them. Beyond the toilet—which was hidden by a half wall on the far side—was an actual jetted tub. Her eyes shot wide as she hurried over to it.

Justin chuckled behind her again.

Mandy turned to flash him a wide grin, noticing then a large walk-in shower, a small linen closet, and another door on the wall opposite the sinks and the long mirror. She turned the handle to open it and found herself back in the hallway. "Oh, that's convenient for guests," she muttered, but it was quiet enough in here she was sure both Justin and Natasha heard her.

They followed her out of the bathroom, and the trio was soon back at the front door. "Well, what did you both think?" Natasha asked politely.

Justin snickered. "You probably don't need to guess what Mandy was thinking." He grinned over at her, so she smacked his arm.

"This place is really nice." Mandy smiled sweetly at the leasing agent as she tucked her arm around Justin's waist.

Natasha turned to Justin. "What did you think?"

Justin surveyed the space one last time. "I like the vibe here."

Mandy nodded beside him. That summed it up pretty well.

She let her eyes wander as Justin asked about the price and fee structure. From what she heard, the price was reasonable. She'd only kept a small apartment because she didn't need the room and liked the proximity to the university, not because she couldn't afford it. Plus, with two of them paying for the place, it probably wouldn't even be a stretch.

"Thank you, Natasha," Justin was saying as he outstretched his hand. The leasing agent shook it. "We'd like to look things over at home and make a decision after we sleep on it. Are you all here tomorrow?"

She nodded. "Ten to six."

"Perfect." Justin smiled at her then looked over at Mandy. "You ready, babe?"

Mandy glanced around one last time then nodded. "Ready, babe."

Natasha handed them a packet with all the information they'd need then followed them out to lock up.

CHAPTER TWENTY-NINE

Justin couldn't stop smiling. Watching Mandy check out that apartment was adorable. The way her eyes lit up as she saw each room made his heart expand in his chest. He desperately wanted to give this place to her, desperately wanted them to move there together and make it their own, make it their home. He was ready for that—he'd been ready for a long time now.

Mandy grabbed his hand once they got on the interstate. "I really like that place, Justin."

He chuckled. "I could tell. I'd hate to have you at a negotiation."

She smacked his arm. "Oh, stop, you know the price is the price. Besides, I could see us making a home there." She glanced over at him.

"Me, too, baby. I could definitely see us there." Justin kissed her hand. "But are you sure you don't want to check out a few others to compare?"

Mandy frowned, cocking her head before she shook it. "Nope."

Justin laughed.

Mandy nodded. "So it's decided. We'll take it."

Justin took a breath. "Uh, Mandy?"

"Hmm?"

Justin smiled. "Hate to be the practical one here, but we probably have a few things to discuss first."

Mandy's head bobbed up and down. "Like if you have a TV."

Justin barked out a laugh. "Well, sure, okay. But I was thinking more about finances."

Mandy sobered quickly. "Oh."

He kissed her hand again. "Look, we can go into as much or as little detail as you'd like. We really just need to decide who covers what bill."

Mandy nodded, taking a deep breath. "I'm actually okay with showing you everything if you want to see it. Like I said, you're it for me. No sense keeping secrets between us."

Justin grinned widely. "I was kinda hoping you'd say that."

He pulled into her apartment complex a few minutes later, and they climbed the stairs in silence. Once inside, Mandy went to the kitchen to grab her pad of paper and a pen. Justin noticed she'd spread the flowers around her apartment—one was on the kitchen table, one was on the coffee table, and he thought he spied a couple in the bedroom—and they all had proper vases. Mismatched, but he was beginning to sense that was her style.

"I like the vases."

Mandy grinned at him as they crossed to the futon. He sat down beside her.

"So seems like we have a lot to discuss. You'll stay the night." She grinned at him as she repeated her comment of four months ago. At this point, he was basically living in this shoebox with her anyway. A shoebox that felt even smaller now that they'd seen their new place. At least, he hoped it would be.

Justin grinned back, loving that she remembered so much about their early relationship. Made him think that she'd been as into him as he'd been into her. "Okay, I suppose I can handle *one night* with you."

Mandy smacked his arm. "Time to get serious." She pursed her lips at him and squinted her eyes.

Justin laughed out loud. "You are just as ridiculous as I am." Then his laughter died down. "To answer your question from before, I don't have a TV."

Mandy blinked. "Really? I thought every guy had to have a TV. You know, for sports and stuff."

He shrugged. "I don't really follow many sports teams. I'll watch BMX once in a while, but only if it's on."

Mandy sighed dramatically, pressing her hand to her chest. "You're my dream guy."

Justin chuckled again, reaching to tuck her hair behind her ear. "I love you, you know."

"I love you more, baby." Mandy smiled at him, and Justin smiled back, loving the words on her lips. She turned her head to kiss his palm then turned back to him. "So I get a stipend from my mom and Bill every month. They've told me how much they'd cover, which is way more than this place costs. I just didn't feel right taking a bunch of money I didn't need." She shrugged. "I shouldn't have any trouble covering half the rent and utilities—and I could probably cover more if needed."

Justin waved her away. "My parents have money set aside for my education plus room and board. My mom will be ecstatic that we're moving in together anyway, so she won't mind helping out at all."

"Really? You told your mom about me?" Mandy blinked over at him.

Justin nodded, offering her a sweet smile. "Of course. I talk to my mom about everything."

Mandy blushed. "Everything?"

He laughed aloud. "Well, our sex life is off-limits, but almost everything else."

"When?"

"When what?"

"When did you tell her about me?"

Justin paused, wondering if this would be the thing that finally freaked her out and sent her running. "Well, when she was in the hospital this summer . . ."

Mandy nodded slowly. "And?"

She didn't miss a thing. "And . . . before that."

She cocked her head. "How much before?"

Justin looked away then whispered his confession. "She's known about you from the beginning."

"Three years ago?"

"Three and a half, actually."

Mandy's mouth fell open slightly. "Before Dan?"

He nodded. "Yeah. You first caught my eye in calculus, freshman year."

Mandy gasped. "I didn't know you were in that class! I'm so sorry I didn't notice you back then."

Justin smiled. "No worries, baby. We're together now, and that's what matters." He leaned in to steal a quick kiss. "So are we done with this list yet? Since you didn't write anything down anyway?"

Mandy tossed the pad and paper on the coffee table then turned back to him, a mischievous grin on her face, her eyebrows raised. "Why? What did you have in mind?"

Before Justin could respond, Mandy's phone rang. Her phone was usually silenced, so she must've turned it on because she was expecting a call, but from whom, he didn't know.

She leaned over to where it was sitting on the coffee table and checked the caller. Then she snatched her phone up and stood. "Sorry, babe, I gotta take this. It's my mom."

He laid his hand on her hip and gazed up at her, his brow furrowing. "Everything okay?"

She frowned down at him. "I'm not sure. Something's been weird with her lately. Guess I'm about to find out." She turned and stepped into the bedroom, shutting the door behind her.

CHAPTER THIRTY

JUSTIN JUST STARED as Mandy walked away. What had happened? She hadn't mentioned anything going on with her mom until just now, but it had clearly been concerning her for a while. Did Mandy not trust him enough to tell him that she felt something was wrong?

The lines on Justin's forehead deepened. And why did she feel the need to leave the room to have a potentially difficult conversation? He wanted to be there for her—hold her hand, maybe, or pull her into a hug like he'd done when Dan had all but destroyed her this past spring—but she seemed determined to keep him at arm's length. A couple shared their feelings, their concerns, not just their bed, after all.

Or maybe he was reading way too much into it. Maybe it was nothing.

He leaned back on the futon and sighed into the still room, Mandy's voice quiet and muffled through the closed door. Regardless of her motivations, he just wished she would've shared this with him, let him help carry the burden. But maybe she wasn't ready.

Maybe she wasn't ready for any of it.

A wave of nausea crashed over him as his stomach lurched at the thought. Maybe his insistence on moving in together so soon had pushed her away. Maybe he'd been forcing this relationship to be what he'd been imagining for the past three and a half years instead of letting it develop naturally. Maybe Mandy needed more time. Maybe she was terrified.

Her hesitance would be understandable after Dan. She said she'd healed, and he had no reason to think otherwise, but being cheated on by someone who she thought was going to propose had to bring about a plethora of trust issues.

Justin sighed again, stretching his arms out on the back of the futon and leaning his head on it, closing his eyes. Maybe it *was* too soon to move in together. Any logical person would've agreed. But he knew how he felt—and how she felt, too. But still . . . how could he know for sure what the right thing was?

She loved him—she'd admitted as much, and he'd seen it in her eyes—but as the phone conversation lengthened and Justin watched the minutes tick by, he started to wonder if that was enough.

"Mom?"

"Hello, Amanda."

Uh-oh. Her mother *never* used her full name. Growing up, she'd almost been convinced the name on her birth certificate was "Mandy." "Mom, what's wrong?"

Her mother sighed, and Mandy sensed she wasn't going to like the next words out of her mother's mouth. She crossed to the bed and sunk to the edge of the mattress. "Honey, Bill and I . . . well, we're having some problems."

Mandy gasped, her stomach knotting. "Oh no, Mom! Are you okay?"

Amy sighed again. "Not really, baby. He . . . well, he doesn't seem to want to be in this marriage any more. And neither do I."

Mandy felt tears threatening. "I don't understand, Mom—you were so in love. You both seemed fine in May!"

Amy paused before answering. "Honey, sometimes things go south. Looking back, we were having problems even then."

She had to ask. "Did he cheat on you?"

"Oh, no, honey, nothing like that. He's a good man. It's just . . . he's been working so much, we barely spend any time together. I guess you could say we drifted apart."

Mandy wasn't understanding. "What are you saying—that your love just . . . died?"

Her mother's voice cracked. "I'm sorry, honey, but yes, I suppose. In a way. Unless something changes drastically, we're both feeling like it's time to move on."

"But . . . I . . . uh, I'm . . . Have y'all been fighting or something?" Mandy's Southern accent showed up when she was under stress. "I just don't understand. You're just going to throw away five years of your lives together?"

Amy sighed. "It's been over for a while, honey. I just didn't know how to tell you."

"But . . . you can't work it out?"

"We just don't want to anymore, baby. I'm really very sorry."

Mandy stared at the wall, unseeing. She didn't have a clue what to make of any of this. Even after her mom had said goodbye and hung up, Mandy just dropped the phone in her lap and kept staring.

Nothing made sense anymore. Her mom and Bill had been

so in love—he'd said she was what he'd been waiting for after his wife died. They'd been happy together. They'd loved each other. Where did it all go wrong?

Mandy didn't know how many minutes had passed when she heard a soft knock at the door. Dammit—she'd forgotten Justin was still here. She supposed she owed him an explanation, at the very least. She'd kinda disappeared.

Mandy rose from the bed and dragged her feet the two steps it took to cross the room and opened the door. Justin's eyes were wide as he took in her countenance, and, of course, he read what she was feeling. She didn't know how he did it—he just did.

He extended his arms. "You look like you need a hug."

Mandy nodded, slowly at first, then sped up as tears started to fall. Mandy crashed into his chest and started crying, sobs wracking her body.

A few minutes later, since her tears weren't stopping, Justin led her over to the bed so they could sit down, and he pulled her onto his lap so he could hold her. And as if they'd been transported back in time to last May, Mandy just held onto him and wept.

JUSTIN HAD no clue what was going on, but in this moment, it didn't matter. Whatever her mom had told her had rocked her to her core. Was Bill okay? Lucy? Or was that someone calling about her mom?

Questions cluttered his brain as he held her against his chest, smoothing her hair with his hand. He kissed the top of her head at periodic intervals, his attempt to show her he was there. That no matter what had happened, they would deal with it together.

When Mandy's tears finally subsided, he set her on the bed and reached for the tissues on her nightstand, handing her the box.

She smiled slightly, sniffling. "Thanks."

Justin smiled back, tucking her hair behind her ear to get it out of her eyes. "You okay, baby?"

Mandy shrugged, coughing a little as she wiped her eyes. "I'm not sure. Mom . . ." She drifted off, and Justin had to ask.

"Is she okay?"

Mandy shook her head. "Not really. She and Bill are over."

Justin felt a sharp stab in his chest. "Are you sure?"

Mandy nodded, her lip quivering. "Sounds like it. She said they just don't love each other anymore." She turned watery eyes to him. "How can two people who love each other just fall out of love like that? How is that even possible?"

Justin reached for her hand and squeezed it. "I don't understand it either, baby. But I'm so sorry."

"It's just . . . they were so in love! I don't understand. How can they just give that up?" Her eyes were filling again, and she sniffed as if to keep the tears at bay.

Justin put his arm around her and pulled her to his side, repeating his last words. "I'm so sorry, baby." He didn't have a clue what else to say.

MANDY SENT Justin home shortly after that. She needed to be alone to process this. She realized he'd spent every single night here since they'd gotten together, so she almost felt like she was kicking him out of his own house, but he understood.

At least, she hoped he did. Because she didn't.

Why was she pushing away the man she loved? She knew she could lean on him, trust him through the hard stuff—he'd proven that in May, even before they were together for real—so why did she send him home?

As she settled into her position against the headboard, staring at the wall, everything fell into place.

When you loved someone, they left. That was how the world worked. She'd been too young to even remember her dad, but her mom had to love him at some point to marry him, right? She'd never been given any indication that she'd been born out of anything but love.

Then, after so many years of being alone, she'd found Bill. He'd taken care of her, loved her—hell, she even moved across the country to be with him! And now they just "decided" they didn't want to be married anymore? How was that fair to her, to Lucy, to their family, to themselves?!

When people committed to each other, that was supposed to be it. Nothing short of death should make them leave each other. "'Til death do us part," right?

Her stomach clenched. That was how she felt about Justin. Though it had only been a little over a week, she'd been following her instinct, the one that told her he was the only one for her. She'd dated the wrong guy—a few of them—but now she was ready to commit.

Or she had been, a few hours ago. Now, she wasn't so sure. And she hated it.

At some point, probably out of mental exhaustion more than anything else, Mandy laid out on her fluffy comforter and cried herself to sleep.

Her bed had never felt so empty.

CHAPTER THIRTY-ONE

IT WASN'T fair to Justin to leave him hanging—she knew that—but Mandy just couldn't deal with anything at the moment, so she waited to talk to him until his text came through the next morning.

Hey, Mandy. Just checking to make sure you're okay.

Mandy smiled in spite of herself. That man really did love her. And, despite her misgivings in light of everything she'd learned last night, she loved him back, with her whole heart.

But how could she commit to him now, when she'd just learned the hard way that love wasn't enough?

I'm okay. Sorry about last night.

Justin's response was quick. **You know you never have to apologize for what you feel. I'll always be here for you to cry on if you need it.**

She wanted to believe him, but how could he know he'd always be there for her? How could he promise that he'd never leave?

He couldn't.

I know, Justin, thank you.

He took a minute to reply. **Do you want me to stay away today?**

Mandy could feel her heart break at his question. She knew how much she meant to him, and she couldn't keep pushing him away. It wasn't his fault her mom and stepdad were breaking up.

So she sent one word. **No.**

I'll be there in ten, babe.

Mandy nodded to the empty room then went back to bed.

JUSTIN WAS at Mandy's apartment in ten minutes as promised, and he tapped repeatedly on her door when he got there, chest heaving from his sprint up the stairs and the stress of the situation. Mandy hadn't had a spare key to give him, and Justin had to shake off the idea that she definitely wouldn't give him one now, not after this.

She didn't answer right away, and Justin's stomach tightened. He knocked again, more insistent this time. Maybe she'd fallen back to sleep?

She answered the door several seconds later, swinging it wide with the speed of a snail.

His heart broke when he saw her. Her eyes were red and swollen, the dress she'd worn last night was still on her body and terribly wrinkled, and her face was sunken and drooping.

He stepped inside slowly, carefully. He wasn't sure he should touch her, wasn't sure how she'd react. And he hated it.

Mandy closed the door behind him almost robotically. The gnawing in Justin's stomach increased.

"Would you like something to drink?" Mandy stumbled in

the morning light streaming through her single living room window, wiping her face as she sunk to the couch in a daze.

Justin hesitated a moment then sat down beside her, ignoring her question. "Baby, please talk to me. You look like you had a rough night."

Mandy nodded but wouldn't make eye contact. His gut clenched—that wasn't good. "I'm okay."

He leaned down until his gaze caught hers. "You're not. You know I know you better than that."

Mandy blinked at him then resumed staring at the single shelf for books she had up on the wall between the front door and her tiny coat closet.

He waited a minute before trying again. "Mandy?"

She drew in a breath. "Justin, I can't move in with you."

Justin's heart broke again, but only partly for himself. His heart was breaking for Mandy—she'd been so shaken by this that she couldn't take the next step in their relationship. She'd been so sure last night, but now everything in her world had been turned upside down.

He swallowed hard, shoving down the feelings that told him her rejection of moving in with him was her rejection of *him,* that it meant she didn't want to be with him anymore. "That's okay, Mandy. I think I'll take it, though."

She nodded, still avoiding eye contact. That killed Justin more than her decision not to move in with him. He was at a loss. How could he help her if she refused to let him in?

Justin took a breath. "What can I do?"

Mandy wiped her nose, glancing his way. For one brief moment, he caught her hazel eyes, and that moment was all it took to see the depth of her pain. For her mother, for her family . . . but he saw another pain, a deeper pain, in her gaze. This was personal loss, and Justin sensed it had less to do with her mother losing Bill and everything to do with Mandy pulling away from him.

He couldn't breathe. He loved this woman with everything he had, and she was it for him. He'd thought she'd felt the same way, and maybe she did. But what about now? What could he do to help her see that they could get through this together if only she'd let him help?

Where did they go from here?

MANDY SLEEPWALKED through the weekend and her next few days of classes. She didn't know what she wanted out of life, and indecision haunted her every waking moment. It was exhausting.

She'd been so sure that she was meant to be with Justin on Friday. She'd been ready to move in with him, share her life with him, become a committed couple in nearly every sense of the word. But now . . .

How could her mom do this? How could Bill? How could they do this to *each other*? How could they just give up?

As she sat in Dr. Harrington's class Tuesday morning, no closer to any kind of resolution, she saw her phone light up in her lap. Her eyes flicked down to check it out of habit—she knew who it would be without even looking. He was the only one that texted her anymore since her conversation with her mom.

Hi, babe. Whatcha doin?

Mandy wanted to roll her eyes, but this class was on the small side, and she was near the front. She typed her reply under the table and hit send. **In class. Talk in 15?** She turned her attention to Dr. Harrington's lecture until her phone lit up again.

She glanced down. **Sure, babe. I'll hold you to it.**

Mandy sighed, flipping her phone over so it wouldn't distract her anymore. She needed to pay attention to this lecture—this was going to be her life's work, after all, if she could ever pass this admittedly difficult class—but her mind once again returned to her unrelenting dilemma. She just needed to make a decision already.

The problem was that neither option was acceptable. If she broke up with Justin, she'd miss out on the indescribable connection they had and, quite possibly, give up the love of her life. But on the other hand, staying with him meant giving him her heart completely, and, given everything that was happening with her mom, that option felt utterly impossible and downright terrifying.

So fifteen minutes later, as she threw her backpack over her shoulder before stepping into the bright, sunlit hallway, her mind was still as confused as ever. She smiled at a fellow grad student she recognized as Dr. Harrington's TA—Jackie, she thought—when Justin's next text came in.

It's been 15 minutes, babe. I've missed you.

Despite the fact that her brain was begging her to push him away, Mandy's heart warmed at his text, and she felt a smile pull at her lips though it never actually sprang to life. She quickly tapped her lock code into her phone, pulling up her messages to type out her reply as she hurried toward the front doors.

But she couldn't think of what to say, and her thumbs hovered over the keyboard. This had been happening frequently. Her heart told her to flirt with him, continue their teasing banter until he had her panting and begging him to take her to bed. Her brain told her to snap at him, push him away until he couldn't stand the sight of her anymore.

So since neither option was good, she'd settled for cool indifference most of the time. She was a coward. **Sorry. What's up?**

Can I take you out tonight? A boring dinner date at Palermo's?

Mandy almost smiled again. She really wanted to let herself be happy, but her heart/brain war had stolen most of her joy these days. **Sure.** She sent that text then scolded herself. Palermo's was the nicest, most expensive restaurant in town. Justin wasn't holding back.

So she sent a follow-up text. **Sounds nice.** She even added a smiley face.

Great! Pick you up at 7?

Mandy just sent a thumbs-up emoji. God. He probably thought he was talking to a dude or something for all the lack of emotion in her noncommittal texts. He really deserved better than this. He deserved someone who would love and commit to him without hesitation. He deserved the world.

Mandy sighed as she slipped her phone in her pocket and headed to her car. As she climbed inside and turned the key in the ignition, she decided that tonight would be the true test. Tonight, she would keep her eyes open for clues. Maybe she'd spot an older couple who seemed to be in love for decades, or perhaps she'd see a breakup go down before her very eyes. Either way, she'd make a decision tonight. And then she'd learn to live with it.

She nodded to herself as she pulled onto her street. Yes. That made sense. Since she couldn't figure things out for herself, she'd let someone else decide. That was always a good choice, right? Let someone else make the decision for her?

She frowned as she climbed the stairs to her apartment. *Dammit, Mandy.* You *are the only one that can make this decision, and you know it. Anything less wouldn't be fair to Justin.*

Yes, well, sometimes life isn't fair, she argued back. She knew that better than anyone.

CHAPTER THIRTY-TWO

MANDY HAD BEEN PULLING AWAY from him since Friday; Justin could tell. And it broke his heart. So tonight, he planned to woo the shit out of her and win her back.

First step: carnations. Of course. That girl deserved endless flowers, but since that wasn't physically possible, he'd settle for bestowing them upon her at every opportunity. And a date presented the perfect one.

So at precisely six thirty, Justin was headed out of Dave's apartment and to the flower shop he probably single-handedly kept in business. He'd donned the suit he'd worn at graduation in May and had paired it with a black shirt and accessories. He might not have the designer shoe collection Mandy had teased him about, but he *did* know how to dress to put his body on full display.

The body he knew Mandy loved, even if she had been keeping her distance lately. He hadn't slept over since Friday, and Justin missed how they'd been together—missed *her*—like crazy. He hadn't been lying about that.

When Mandy answered her door, Justin's breath flew right

out of his chest, and he could've sworn his heart stopped. Mandy had donned the perfect little black dress—the skirt flared out and reminded him of the dress she'd worn to their first date, made him remember how the skirt had pooled around her waist . . .

She had even painted on some matte red lipstick to match the dark-crimson heels that kickstarted Justin's heart and got it racing.

Maybe he had a chance tonight, after all.

Mandy was staring, and he realized he should've said something already. "Uh . . ." He cleared his throat. "Mandy, that . . . you are absolutely breathtaking."

Her cheeks blushed in that adorable way he loved, and he reached up to brush his fingertips across one without thinking. She didn't flinch away, but she didn't lean into his touch, either.

Okay, so maybe tonight wouldn't be as easy as he'd thought.

JUSTIN WAS DEFINITELY PULLING out all the stops.

Mandy'd left the two dozen white carnations he'd brought her in water before she led the way to his Jeep. He'd accompanied her to the passenger side and opened the door for her, even offering her his hand to help her in. Then he'd flashed that damn panty-dropping crooked smile before hurrying to his side of the car and pulling out of her complex and into traffic.

Mandy had to clench her thighs together at the sight—she couldn't help it. Despite everything, Justin still held the keys to her heart. And other things, apparently.

Focus, Mandy. Look for signs.

She knew it was stupid, but she was convinced that she'd see something that would help her make up her mind tonight.

Dinner was spectacular, and Mandy actually enjoyed herself. Justin kept their conversation light, and Mandy was grateful he wasn't pushing her to make a decision. She'd never dealt well with people telling her what to do.

Or maybe he needed to—maybe *Justin* should be making this decision. But she knew what he'd choose, and her brain was fighting that option fiercely.

"So what would you like to do next?" Justin asked as the server walked away with his credit card and the bill.

Mandy bit her lip. What *did* she want? The question felt more loaded than Justin probably intended, but she answered honestly anyway. "I'm not sure."

Justin just nodded as their server came back. He signed the receipt, then he led Mandy with a hand to the small of her back out of the restaurant and back to his Jeep.

When they were both settled inside, Justin pushed the key in the ignition but didn't turn it. Instead, he let the rest of his keys dangle as his hands dropped to his lap. Then he let out a loud sigh.

Mandy's eyes flashed to his. What was going on?

"Um, Mandy?" He glanced over and caught her gaze.

"Hmm?"

She watched him draw in a deep breath as if he was nervous. Perhaps he would be deciding for her, after all. Why didn't that make her feel any better?

"Can we talk?"

Mandy nodded slowly though she didn't want to. In the last five seconds, she'd decided her plan to make a decision tonight was ill-conceived, and she'd postpone. "What about?"

"Us."

Oh. "Um, okay?" She phrased it like a question, though she wasn't sure why. It came out sounding a little more sarcastic than she'd intended it to.

"See, that."

"What?"

"You know what." Justin's eyes narrowed at her.

Mandy turned and glared through the windshield. She *did* know. She just wasn't admitting that she was a goddamn coward out loud.

"Mandy, talk to me! Just a few days ago, we were ready to move in together, and now I barely feel like I know you at all."

Mandy's chest heaved. If this was her sign, tonight would not end well. "That's not fair! You know I'm dealing with stuff!" She raised her voice—she couldn't help it. And she hated it.

"I know that, baby, but when you're in a relationship with someone, you let them in. You let them help." His voice was gentle, but Mandy could feel the tension crackling in the car, and she just lost it.

"Maybe I don't need your help! Did you think of that? Maybe I'm good with handling this on my own!" As soon as the words were out of her mouth, she wanted to take them back. She wanted to stop this night from turning out to be the disaster it already was.

Justin was staring out the windshield now, and his jaw was clenched so tightly Mandy was worried he'd chip a tooth. The car was silent for a few moments, then Justin gritted out a response. "If that's what you want."

Of course, that's not what she wanted. But she couldn't tell him that right now. She was too busy being angry at him, at her mother, at Bill, at the situation, at everything and everyone. At . . . herself. "Justin . . ." she scratched out, her voice rasping,

"I . . . I just . . ." Her eyes searched the SUV's tan ceiling for the right words. "Justin, I don't know what to do. If we stay together, you could leave. If we break up . . ." She couldn't finish the thought.

Justin's words were soft. "Do you want to break up?"

No. No. *No.* "I don't know."

Justin ground his teeth—Mandy could see the motion through his chiseled cheek. The cheek she desperately wanted to hold while she told him she loved him and would be with him forever. But that couldn't possibly be true. Because no one could promise forever, could they?

"Mandy, I need to say something to you."

His eyes blinked over to her before he continued, so she nodded once.

"I get that you're scared; I really do. I can't guarantee that we will be together forever. But I do know that you're it for me. If you don't want to choose us, it will kill me, but I'll respect your decision. Just please . . . *please* don't keep stringing me along. If you won't let me in . . ." He took a deep breath. "Then let me go."

Mandy's anger flared again, and words flew out of her mouth before she could stop them. "Are you seriously playing the martyr right now?"

Justin's eyes shot wide. "Of course not!"

Mandy scoffed. "Yes, you are! You're acting like you're the perfect one, like you'll take the bullet and be all noble about it."

"Mandy, I . . ."

She waved a hand between them, cutting him off. "No, Justin. You don't get to do that. You don't get to make me fall in love with you then act like you'll let me go if that's what I need. You don't get to play the perfect boyfriend while I'm the asshole who lets you go."

"Now who's not playing fair?"

Mandy growled. She actually growled. "Justin—seriously? You insisted on us so strongly that I couldn't resist you. You wanted this so badly that you made up all that stuff in May to get me to fall in love with you."

Justin smacked the steering wheel. "Dammit, Mandy! If you weren't so fucking terrified of letting yourself love me, we wouldn't even be having this conversation! We wouldn't have hardly spoken in days, and we wouldn't have barely even touched each other in all that time. We wouldn't be acting like we can live without each other!"

Mandy wanted this all to go away, reverse, somehow become the exact opposite of what was her world imploding. But she just kept burying herself alive. "You made me love you, and now you're guilting me into staying with you!"

"No!" Justin shouted. "You don't get to do that. I have *never once* forced you to do anything. You're too damn stubborn for that!"

Mandy shook her head vehemently. "You're wrong. You took advantage of my situation with Dan! You jumped at the chance to act on the unrequited crush you had on me when I was vulnerable."

Justin actually gasped. "I would never do that to you, Mandy! I can't believe you would say that!"

Mandy ground her teeth together and stared out the windshield. "Justin, you need to take me home."

"So you're just not gonna talk to me now?"

"I think I've already said enough."

And just like that, everything she hadn't meant to say was out, and she couldn't take any of it back. In that instant, Mandy felt all the air rush out of the car along with what was left of her heart.

Justin turned the key in the ignition and headed back to her apartment without another word.

The rest of the ride was silent, but as they pulled up to her apartment, Justin spoke to the airless car. "If you need anything, Mandy, I'm still here."

Mandy's heart was breaking, and she'd been fighting back tears the entire ride home. If he'd said that twenty minutes ago, she'd have bit his head off. But now . . . all she could give him was a nod as she met his gaze.

But though it was only for a second, the pain she saw in his eyes stole her breath, and she flew out of the vehicle and up her stairs before she could break down completely.

CHAPTER THIRTY-THREE

JUSTIN SMACKED his palms against the steering wheel again, harder than before. That damn woman! How dare she say those things? How could she believe he'd forced her into anything? His head felt like it might explode—he'd never been so angry in his life.

There was no way he was going to bed any time soon, so he found himself driving to a bar his frat brothers had frequented a semester or two ago but now usually avoided. He could've gone somewhere else, but he had just started driving, and that was where he'd ended up.

He shuffled in silently, his head hanging, and took a seat on the closest barstool. The bartender was a cute brunette who Justin thought he'd seen before, perhaps even ogled before, but he was in no mood to flirt. He just barked out his order, and she backed away slightly with a curt nod, clearly getting the hint. Bartenders were always good at reading people, and Justin's demeanor was obviously telling everyone to fuck off.

He was on his second refill when he felt someone drop to the stool beside him. At first, he wanted to yell at the guy to pick a different seat. But then he got a good look at his new neighbor.

"Grady?"

His professor motioned to the bartender, who poured him a glass of the whiskey Justin was having and set it down in front of him. "Justin, hi."

Justin was not feeling particularly social, but perhaps talking about something other than Mandy would help get him out of this shitty mood. "How are you?"

Grady took a sip from his drink. "Drinking on a Tuesday. Can't be that good, right?"

Justin sniffed a laugh.

"How's Mandy?"

"I'm drinking on a Tuesday, too, remember." He hadn't meant to be so snippy, but he couldn't help it.

Grady put his hand up in the air between them. "Ah. Say no more."

Justin actually smiled as he took a sip of the amber liquid that he could finally feel mellowing him out, just a little. "So what brings you to this fine establishment on this eventful Tuesday evening?"

Grady chuckled. "Same as you."

Justin blinked. "Woman problems?"

The other man raised his glass. "You could say that."

"What happened?" Justin wasn't sure how chummy his professor would want to get with one of his students, but perhaps they were both here for a reason. Maybe they both needed someone to talk to.

Grady shrugged as he took another sip. "Another less-than-stellar date, unfortunately. Not that I thought she would be 'the One' or anything, but not ending the evening in her bed and instead ending the evening in a bar alone—excepting your lovely company, of course—is honestly depressing."

Justin shook his head. "I feel ya, man."

"What happened with you?"

Justin sighed. "Mandy and I just had a huge fight."

"What about?" Grady appeared to actually be interested, so, with the encouragement of the alcohol, Justin decided to open up.

"Her mom is getting a divorce."

"Ah."

Justin's eyes shot to his. "Do you understand everything?"

Grady laughed. "Not nearly as much as I should. But I get it. She's scared to commit."

"Yup." Justin raised his glass then put it to his lips, finishing it off before motioning to the bartender for another refill. She eyed him but poured another glass.

"And you told her that?"

"Yup," Justin repeated, laughing loudly.

Grady chuckled as he shook his head. "Not too smart, man."

Justin snorted. "I know that now."

"What'd she say?"

"That I forced her into a relationship with me."

"Did you?"

Justin's eyes shot to Grady's mid-sip. "What—are you a professor of psychology or something?"

Grady smiled. "Just observant, like I said."

Justin nodded, swallowing his sip then setting the half-empty glass down on the wet napkin. He took a breath before answering. "I'm not sure."

His professor nodded knowingly. "Sounds like you should figure that out."

Justin just nodded back, staring at the rows of liquor bottles across the bar from them.

They drank in silence for a few minutes before Justin spoke up. "Uh, Grady?"

"Yeah?"

"Can I ask you a personal question?"

"Seems only fair at this point."

Justin chuckled. "Have you ever dated Dr. Harrington?"

He swore Grady's jaw tensed at the name. "No."

"Never?"

Grady met his gaze. "Nope."

"Have you thought about it?"

Maybe it was the alcohol spurring on his honesty. "Just about every damn day."

Justin's eyes widened, just a little. "Really?"

Grady nodded. "She's way out of my league."

Justin shook his head. "I don't think that's true. I don't know her much—other than the fact that she's brilliant and beautiful—but you are both clearly on the same intellectual level. You work together, for heaven's sake."

"Precisely the problem."

"Why? Does the school have a thing about you dating colleagues?"

Grady shook his head. "No. But it would make things . . . complicated."

Justin nodded. He completely understood—if he and Mandy didn't survive this fight, they'd still have to see each other three days a week. In Grady's class, no less. "Some things are worth the complication."

"Is Mandy?" Grady shot back.

Justin was starting to really like this guy. He grinned. "Abso-fucking-lutely."

Grady smiled back. "Then it's your job to figure out if you need to do anything to fix it. Maybe she just needs to sort things out for herself." He took a sip. "Does she love you?"

Justin nodded. "I know she does."

"Then give her time."

"That's what my mom tells me."

Grady raised his glass. "Wise woman."

Justin chuckled. "Any reason to think Dr. Harrington would be worth the complication?"

Grady smirked, his lips hiding behind the rim of his glass. "Maybe someday."

As he paid his bill and called a cab, Justin replayed the conversations of the evening over and over in his head. He was actually really grateful he'd run into Grady—the man seemed to be more insightful than just about anyone else he'd ever met.

Because he was right—Mandy needed time. She needed space. And because he loved her, he'd give it to her.

CHAPTER THIRTY-FOUR

THOUGH IT WAS BARELY past nine, Mandy was ready to call it a night. She didn't feel like crying, and since she'd spent the last few days alternating between punching her pillow so many times she'd lost count and bingeing her favorite show while consuming so much wine her headache had been near-constant for the past two days, she felt too spent to do much of anything else.

She was about to head to the bathroom to brush her teeth for bed when an alert for a video chat sounded on her phone.

Mandy sniffed, fighting back tears that hadn't shown up as of yet, and climbed up on her bed, sitting cross-legged atop the comforter as she grabbed her phone off the nightstand. When she saw the name on the display, she tapped to answer it, holding the phone up at eye level.

"Mandy? Are you okay?"

Mandy gave her sister a sad smile and sniffed again. "I'm fine, Lucy. Why do you ask? Are you okay?"

Lucy offered a smile, her straight, black hair falling around her shoulders and onto her red-and-black flannel shirt. When did she start wearing flannel? "I'm good. I just . . . I was just wondering what was going on with you, so I thought I'd call, see if you wanted to talk."

Mandy's chuckle was watery, and she suspected the tears weren't too far away now. "Fortuitous timing, Lucy."

Her sister grinned. "Maybe I'm telepathic."

Mandy nodded, chuckling again even as her eyes started filling up. "Maybe you are."

Lucy swiveled in what had to be her desk chair. "Do you want to talk about it?"

Mandy took a breath, willing back the tears. She'd never been close to Lucy—they'd never even lived under the same roof—but the timing of her call was a little too coincidental to ignore.

"If it helps, I can tell you my guy woes before you fill me in on yours."

Mandy's mouth fell open. "How do you know I have guy woes?"

Lucy smirked. "Just a hunch. I saw you and Justin together in May, you know."

Mandy nodded. She tried to smile, but Lucy's words were hitting a little too close to home. And she realized she wasn't quite ready to share. "Why don't you tell me your story first."

Lucy shifted in her seat again. "So I met this guy, Rafael, like the first week of school. He's kinda scrawny, but he's tall and he's got tattoos and piercings everywhere—like, *everywhere*—so he's totally my type. We hooked up for a few weeks, then he just ghosted me like two days ago. I haven't seen him anywhere, haven't heard from him, nothing."

Mandy gasped with what energy she had left. "Did you ask any of his friends what happened?"

She thought her sister might actually have blushed.

"Well . . ." Lucy's voice drifted off as she glanced off-camera for a split second then turned back to the phone. "We didn't really do much together outside the bedroom. I didn't even know his last name."

"Lucy!"

"I know! I know!" Lucy's face was definitely red, and she covered her cheeks with her hands. "But he was just so talented with his tongue that it didn't matter."

Now Mandy was blushing. "Oh my God, girl! What has college done to you?"

Lucy's grin was shameless. "Made me a sex-positive woman who knows what she likes. I mean"—she leaned closer to the camera to stage-whisper her next words—"*he had a tongue piercing*."

A laugh burst out of Mandy. Like, an actual laugh. "Good for you." Then she sobered. "But I'm sorry he ghosted you."

Lucy shrugged, but Mandy could tell she was anything but okay. "I'll get over it." She sat up straighter. "But now it's your turn."

Mandy stiffened, knowing she was right but hating that it was time to share all the sordid details of her relationship with Justin and its probable dissolution. She drew in a deep breath and started at the beginning.

By the time Mandy got to the events of Tuesday night, hot tears had finally broken through and were flowing freely. "So I told him he forced me into dating him, into loving him. I told him he was guilting me into staying with him, that he took advantage of me when I was vulnerable."

Lucy gasped, which had been her sole response throughout Mandy's story. Mandy had even shared the truth about her fake relationship with Justin back in May, but Lucy had just kept listening with wide eyes. Mandy wasn't sure why she hadn't confided in her stepsister sooner.

The air between them fell silent for a moment as Mandy let Lucy process everything. Then Lucy spoke up. "Was all that stuff you said to him true?"

Mandy shook her head, a fresh wave of tears rushing out of her. Seemed once they started, they wouldn't stop. "Not at all. He never forced me into anything. I was grateful when he stepped up to help me in May, and I wanted him then, just like I do now. It's just . . . everything with Mom and your dad has me all messed up." She'd confirmed her sister had heard about the divorce before she'd shared the details in her own story. "I just don't know how I can commit to being with Justin knowing he could one day leave me, hurt me."

Lucy was quiet for a moment, gazing past her phone at something Mandy couldn't see. Then she stared back into the camera. "Look, Mandy, I'm not going to pretend to be some wise woman who has the best advice for you. But I do know this—we can't make decisions based on fear." She took a breath. "I was terrified to leave home, move away for school. Did you know that?"

Mandy shook her head.

Lucy nodded. "I was. Since my mom died, I never wanted to leave that house. I mean, I did for school and my job, but I spent as much time as I could there. Even when your mom moved in, I stayed. Because that's where my mother was for me. That was where I could still feel her, remember her."

Now Mandy was crying for another reason. "What made you finally decide to leave?"

Mandy spied a tear on Lucy's cheek. "I realized my mom would never want me to stop living my life to feel close to her. I had so many good years with her, so many good memories, and I knew that she was with me wherever I went."

Mandy didn't respond for a moment. When she did, her voice was soft, tentative. "Was it hard for you when my mom moved in?"

Lucy hesitated for a moment before nodding. "A little. It took me a while to get used to the idea, but that was another reason I found the strength to move out. My dad had found a way to get on with his life, so I figured I should, too."

Mandy just nodded, not sure what to say.

"I realized that it's healthy to move on. We can't stay stuck —without moving forward, we're just existing. My mom wouldn't have wanted that for me or my dad. And Mandy, as your sister and brand-new confidante, I don't want that for you."

Mandy wiped at her eyes. "That's sweet."

Lucy smiled. "That's what I'm here for." She took a breath. "But seriously, Mandy . . . it sounds like you and Justin have something incredible. Something once-in-a-lifetime, maybe. I would hate to see you give that up because our parents can't figure out how to make their relationship work."

Mandy nodded, sniffling. "Thanks, Lucy. I'm really glad you called."

Lucy smiled sweetly. "I am, too. We should definitely do this more often."

Mandy chuckled through her tears. "Definitely. Though maybe with less crying next time."

Lucy laughed. "Sounds good to me." Then her laughter died off. "So what are you gonna do about Justin?"

Mandy bit her lip. "I'm not sure, but I'll keep you posted."

Lucy nodded once. "And I'll keep you posted about Rafael with no last name."

Mandy chuckled. "Seriously, Lucy, thanks. For everything. And I hope everything with Rafael works out."

Lucy pressed her palms together and bowed slightly.

Mandy was still laughing after they signed off.

CHAPTER THIRTY-FIVE

THE NEXT DAY, Justin got to Grady's class just as it was starting. Despite his decision to give Mandy the space she needed—part of why he'd made a point to not come to class early over the past three days so he wouldn't be tempted to talk to her—he missed her. He hadn't seen her outside of class since their blow up, and it was killing him.

He was still upset over the things she'd said to him, the things she'd believed about his motivations, but he understood. Mandy had the softest, sweetest heart, but her past had shown her that not everyone could be trusted with it. And her mom's shaky relationship, in her mind, just reinforced that fact.

But though he knew she needed space to sort all this out, Justin couldn't wait any longer to fix this. He needed Mandy like he needed air to breathe. He'd resolved to give her time, but he was done waiting. He'd waited over three years for her—he couldn't wait any longer.

And it seemed fate was on his side. Though he had a class right after this one with Dr. Harrington, Grady had let the class go early, and Justin had a good fifteen minutes before he needed to head out.

He crossed the room to where Mandy was packing her things, and she turned toward him when he placed a gentle hand on her forearm. "Justin?" She abandoned her half-packed bag on the table and tucked her hair behind her ear.

When she averted her gaze, Justin's heart involuntarily squeezed. "Can we talk?"

Mandy didn't answer. Instead, her bottom lip trembled, and she bit her lip as if trying to stop it.

Justin's heart broke all over again. "Look, Mandy. Tuesday night was . . . well, it was a shitty night. We both probably said things we didn't mean—I know I did. But I . . ." What words wouldn't push her away further? "I miss you."

Mandy's lip trembled again, and he desperately wanted to rewind time to last week, back before he'd ever had to see Mandy fighting so hard to maintain control past the hurt he'd, in some ways, caused. It was time for him to own up to that.

"Mandy, I am really sorry. Those things I said . . ." He took a breath. "You didn't deserve any of that. But I meant what I said before you got out of the car: I'm still in this. If that's what you still want, I'm here." The words—and the possibility that he *wasn't* what she still wanted—stole his breath. His chest constricted, strangling him.

"Justin." His name was quiet on her lips, yet it echoed in the now-empty room, surprising him with its conviction. "You promised you'd never lie to me. Honesty, remember?"

Justin felt gutted, but he nodded.

"Then tell me honestly, please. I just need to know. Do you still love me?"

Justin didn't hesitate. "Of course, I do, Mandy." Of course, he loved her. If nothing else in the world ever made sense to him again, he'd still know that.

"Then why . . ." Her voice trailed off, and Justin's head cocked to one side, his brow furrowing.

"Why what?" He wasn't sure he wanted to know, but he had to ask.

Mandy sighed, her shoulders collapsing. "Why is this so hard?"

Justin's face crumpled, and he reached out to place a hand on her shoulder. She didn't flinch away from him, so he took that as a good sign. "Mandy, you know I'll always be honest with you. And honestly? Relationships are hard. We fit together, but it will take work. I believe we're worth it. I know *you're* worth it. You know how I know?"

Mandy shook her head, urging him on.

"Because I love you with every single part of me. I always have, and I always will. You are beautiful and captivating and sweet and powerful and strong and caring and you love so fiercely. From the moment I met you, the moment I laid eyes on you, I couldn't escape you. Though I tried to move on, I never could. Because I knew you were it for me. Only you. Honestly, it's always been you."

Mandy's eyes welled, and tears started streaming down her cheeks. "I love you, too, Justin. I didn't mean those words I said. You didn't force me into anything." Mandy raised her hands to wipe at her cheeks.

He took a shaky breath, stepping closer to cup her face in his hands. "Please, Mandy, please come back to me. I'm begging you. This has been the most miserable week of my life because you haven't been in it."

Mandy sniffled. "I know, Justin, and I'm so sorry. But I . . ."

She glanced away as her voice trailed off, and Justin's heart leapt into his throat.

"What, baby?"

Mandy blinked away her remaining tears and met his gaze. "I'm so scared. I don't know how to do this, be your girlfriend, when we could one day break each other's hearts. It feels like too much."

Justin's heart broke at her confession, and he dropped his hands. "Love is scary sometimes, Mandy. It's a risk. But that's what makes it worth it."

Mandy just stared at him, her light-brown eyes searing into his, searching his soul. And as the moment lengthened, Justin saw the truth in her eyes, and he finally understood. He'd been forcing this from the beginning. He'd been pushing her too hard. She had wanted to make him happy, had wanted this to work, so she'd set aside her own needs to take care of his. Like she always did.

He knew what she needed now. She needed to take things slow. He didn't like it, but this wasn't about him. It never really was. This was about putting her needs first.

This was about being the man she needed him to be.

Justin stepped back. He drew in a deep breath, and, for once in his life, he wasn't going to come back with a witty retort or deflect what he was truly feeling—he was going to finally acknowledge the truth that he hadn't been willing to admit, the one that forced him to look deep inside and be brutally honest with himself: He'd been trying to control their relationship, and he had to stop.

He couldn't force the outcome he wanted, couldn't guard his heart by holding Mandy too close. If they were going to do this, for real, they both had to be in this with wide open eyes and wide open hearts.

So he was going to actually give her the space she needed, whatever that looked like. And it was fucking terrifying, because it meant she might decide she didn't want this. She might decide she didn't want him.

But maybe that's what love really was.

He took another breath, steeling himself, then spoke from the heart. "Mandy, I get it. I understand now. You need to take this slow. You were telling me that all along, but I wasn't listening. I was pushing you, and I'm sorry. You were right."

Mandy teared up again, and her shoulders relaxed then hunched over as she started sobbing right there in the middle of their classroom. Deep, gut-wrenching sobs shook her entire body, and Justin couldn't take it anymore. He wrapped his arms around her, dropping to a chair before pulling her into his lap, and just held her while she cried.

When they had just five minutes before his next class started, Mandy's sobs quieted, and she turned her red, bloodshot eyes to his. "Thank you, Justin. I'm so sorry for everything I said and for not being there for you this past week."

"Baby, it's fine, really. You never owe me anything." Justin smoothed her hair then moved his hand down to cup her cheek. "I'm so sorry I pushed you. It won't happen again."

Mandy shook her head. "I think I needed to be pushed a little." She smirked through her tears.

Justin chuckled lightly. "Maybe our fight was what forced us to finally be truly honest with each other—and ourselves."

Mandy sniffed. "Probably." Then she glanced at the clock on the wall, and her eyes shot wide as she leapt off his lap. "Justin, you have class!"

He stood up next to her, but he shrugged. "I have like three minutes to get down the hall."

But Mandy picked up his backpack and shoved it into his arms anyway. "You need to go!"

Justin slid the strap of his backpack over his shoulder casually, but instead of leaving, he caught her gaze, placing his hand on her cheek once again. "In a minute. First, I need to kiss my girlfriend. That is, if she still wants me." Justin had never felt that empty feeling in his stomach as strongly as he did right now, the one that told him this woman held his heart completely in her hands. Talk about terrifying.

Mandy's eyes held his as she nodded. "I do, Justin. I love you so much, and I want to be with you. We just might need to take things at my pace, slow things down a little. Is that okay?"

Justin smiled, the first real smile he'd felt in what seemed like forever, and leaned in close. "Of course, baby. Whatever you need." He pressed his lips to hers, wishing they had the time to make up properly, then pulled away a few moments later, much too soon.

Mandy's cheeks were red when he opened his eyes, and his smile was back, just like that.

"Okay, I really do have to get to class. But Mandy?"

She blinked out of her stupor. He grinned—he loved knowing he still had that effect on her. "Hmm?"

"Would you wanna have dinner with me tonight?"

Mandy just stared for a brief moment, then she nodded, and Justin's heart warmed.

"Awesome." He grinned, but then he remembered a key detail and his face fell. "Uh . . . so I guess I need to tell you something." He reached up to scratch the back of his neck and glanced away. "So since the apartment was open, I kind of moved in on Wednesday."

Mandy gasped. "That was fast!"

Justin caught her gaze. "Yeah, they were motivated, I paid cash, and I didn't really have much to move." He shrugged.

"Do you have any furniture yet?"

One corner of Justin's mouth turned up as he ticked off items on his fingers. "Just a couch, a kitchen table with two chairs, a bed, and a nightstand. Oh—and I have a coffee table in the back of my SUV to unload."

Mandy's mouth was still open. "So you've been busy."

Justin nodded as he shoved his hands in his pockets.

"I'd like to see what you've done with the place." Mandy's shy grin warmed Justin in places he hadn't felt her touch in much too long.

"I'd like to show it to you. Chinese takeout?"

A wide smile spread over Mandy's face. "I'd like that."

"Good." Justin leaned in to peck her on the lips then strolled toward the door feeling a thousand pounds lighter. "See you at seven?"

Mandy nodded and was still waving at him as he stepped through the door and out into the hall.

CHAPTER THIRTY-SIX

MANDY KNOCKED on Justin's door—the door to the apartment that should've been *theirs*—right at seven. Her stomach had been doing somersaults all day, and she'd spent the afternoon thinking about this past week, wondering what it all meant. Wondering what she truly wanted.

She was still freaked out over her mom and Bill's impending divorce. She was still worried that Justin might one day leave, or that she might hurt him. But Justin was right—love could be scary sometimes.

So she was nervous about tonight, sure, but she was also excited. She really loved this man, and he deserved all of her. He deserved someone who would commit to him completely, love him with their whole heart. And she wanted so badly for that to be her.

Justin answered the door with a bouquet of what had to be two dozen red carnations. Mandy leaned in to smell them before she even crossed the threshold, letting her eyes fall closed and pulling in a big whiff. Justin was watching her with a curious expression when her eyes fluttered open, but he quickly stepped back so she could enter before she had time to ask what he was thinking.

"These are beautiful, Justin; thank you." Mandy smiled at him over the lightly fragrant bouquet as she took it from him. She knew instinctively he'd chosen red on purpose. Red for passion, fire, heat—all the things she felt when she was alone with him. All the things that had been missing between them for a week. All the things she desperately wanted back.

And she realized as he led her into the living room and showed her around the sparsely furnished apartment she loved even more now that his things were in it, that she could have it all. She could feel that passion again. She could give in to it fully. She could have every part of Justin. As long as she gave him every part of her.

But how exactly could she do that?

The doorbell rang just as Mandy had taken a seat on the perfectly worn brown leather couch Justin said he'd found on a resale listing site for UCF students. It was the exact couch Mandy would have chosen for the place, and she wondered if Justin somehow knew that as he answered the door.

Justin came back with an armload of white paper containers, and Mandy popped up to help him, laughing. "How much did you order?"

Justin grinned as they laid the spread out on the large, glass-topped coffee table. "Enough for an army, apparently. Or at least a lot of leftovers."

Mandy nodded as she finished opening the last container. Beef lo mein, her favorite. "Smells amazing."

She settled back into the comfy couch with a smile on her face, and Justin dropped down beside her, offering her a set of disposable wooden chopsticks. "Ladies first."

Mandy caught the sparkle in his eye as she grabbed the

chopsticks, ripped the package open, and snapped the sticks in two. Then she snatched up the lo mein without hesitation and dug in.

Justin laughed as he reached for the Kung Pao Chicken. "A woman who knows what she likes. Gotta say, Mandy, that's pretty hot."

Mandy felt blood rush to her cheeks as she chewed on the tasty beef and noodle dish. That was so "Justin" of him to say.

They engaged in light conversation as they ate, Justin keeping her laughing most of the meal, and Mandy realized just how much she'd missed this. How much she'd missed him. How easy it was to be around him. How safe he made her feel. How loved.

As she finished her meal—only stopping when she felt her stomach couldn't hold another bite—she finally figured out what she wanted. She wanted this, him, all of it. She didn't want to give in to the fear any longer.

She'd mourned, she'd been sad, and now it was time to move on—to the man she loved more than anything in the world. She was still terrified that something could happen to tear them apart, and she knew they would move as slowly as she was comfortable with, but she was going to try to take Lucy's advice and stop simply existing. She was going to try to move forward, live her life, and choose to be happy.

Joy was a choice.

"Wanna watch a movie?"

Mandy eyed the empty wall between the two windows that showed the darkening sky beyond them then raised an eyebrow at him.

Justin grinned, shrugging. "We can watch on my laptop."

Mandy pursed her lips for a moment then realized that sounded like the perfect thing. "I would love that."

Justin stood and started collecting the leftover containers of food. "I'll clean this up; you pick the movie. Hang on." He disappeared into the kitchen with the containers and came back with a laptop. He dropped to the couch, opened it up, signed in, then handed it to Mandy with the browser open to their favorite streaming service.

Mandy stared after him as he took another load of food to the kitchen. She wasn't sure why, but this felt like a whole new level of trust. Not that Justin didn't trust her before, but you had to really trust someone to just hand them your laptop, right?

She picked out a romantic thriller and started it, pausing it at the beginning as Justin came back into the room.

He dropped to the couch beside her, keeping a little distance between them, but only a little. Mandy thought it was probably an intentional move. He seemed to be giving her the space to call the shots, and she was grateful.

"Ready?"

Mandy smiled, nodding as she clicked play. "Ready."

Justin grinned back. "What'd you pick?"

Mandy smirked. "You'll just have to see."

Justin took a sip of the drink he still had left over from dinner—an energy drink, predictably, though Mandy couldn't figure out how he'd sleep tonight—then situated himself on the couch. He put his feet up on the coffee table and pulled the laptop off Mandy's lap, setting it on his outstretched legs.

Mandy took her cues from him and stretched her feet out beside his, settling closer to him until their bodies were touching. She needed to feel him close to her.

Sometime during the movie, while the characters were both discovering that the other was secretly a spy, Justin got up for a refill and flicked out the lights on his way back. Mandy's skin prickled at the thought of being alone with Justin in the dark. Everything that man did set her heart racing and her core tightening. It had been way too long since she'd felt him inside her.

So when the movie ended, Mandy turned to him, reaching her hand out and laying it gently on his chest. She felt him tense beside her, and instantly she heated up. "Justin," she breathed into his ear, her fingers trailing across his hard chest the way she knew turned him on, and she saw his eyes fall shut at her touch.

She grinned, flicking her tongue out to tease his earlobe. His moan was nearly silent, but she heard it.

"What are you doing to me, Mandy?" Justin whispered, his hands gripping his legs, almost as if he was waiting for express permission.

She was ready to give it. "Seducing you, of course." She trailed her lips down his neck and across his collarbone, exhaling slightly to tickle his skin. Then she breathed him in, and his scent filled her entire being. She moaned as she kissed her way up his jaw.

"Are you sure?" Justin asked, but Mandy could tell his resolve was waning.

She nodded against his cheek. "Yes, Justin, take me to bed."

That was all he apparently needed to hear. In one move, Mandy was laid out on the couch, and Justin's body covered her completely as his lips found hers.

This kiss was better than she'd ever had in the past. More. This time, their love was deeper, stronger than before. Because they'd been through something hard, something real, and they'd come out on the other side. This kiss meant that they'd committed to each other even when it wasn't easy.

And Mandy couldn't lie to herself any longer.

She wanted Justin, all of him. She wanted to give every part of her to him, too. She didn't want to give in to the fear anymore. She wanted to fully live, fully love, by his side. She just had to figure out how.

Then Justin pulled away. "Let's get out of here."

Mandy blinked up at him, his hardness pressing right into where she wanted him, just ideally without any clothing between them. "What—now?"

Justin shook his head. "No. Right now, I'm going to fuck your brains out." Mandy felt the fire behind his words between her legs, and she squirmed beneath him. "This weekend, tomorrow. Let's get away together."

Mandy nodded. "Okay. Where?"

"What about a quick trip to the coast? My favorite surfing's in Cocoa Beach, and it's only an hour away."

Mandy just nodded again.

"It's decided then: hot sex on the beach."

Mandy laughed. "Whatever you say, babe. As long as we have some hot sex right now."

A wicked grin spread across Justin's face, and the fire flaring in his eyes set her core tightening and stole her breath. "I know you asked me to take you to bed, but do you wanna christen the tub?"

CHAPTER THIRTY-SEVEN

"YOU GONNA TRY SURFING, BABE?" Justin grinned at Mandy as they pulled into their hotel parking lot the next morning. She was adorable in her oversized sun hat and bikini covered only by the shortest pair of jean shorts he'd ever seen. He silently thanked whomever had invented those as he shifted the car into park.

Mandy gasped as she hopped down out of his Jeep. "No way. You've seen me cooking—coordination is not one of my talents."

Justin laughed as he hoisted their luggage out of the back of the Jeep then slammed the tailgate closed. "Okay. You can just ogle me all day."

Mandy nodded vigorously. "You know it." She grinned widely.

Justin laughed again, rolling their bags toward the entrance.

They got their keys—thank God for early check-in—and were in their room ten minutes later. Mandy must have loved that it had a balcony overlooking the beach—that was her first stop.

Justin joined her, snaking his arm around her waist as he pulled her close to his side. Mandy smiled over at him. "Do you usually stay here when you come?"

Justin shook his head, looking out over the gray-blue water. He could hear the waves crashing from here. "No. There's a small motel a little further up the coast, and I usually stay there for cheap." He kissed the top of her head. "I wanted something a little nicer for our first trip together."

Mandy wrapped her arm around him and leaned her head on his chest. "I love this, baby. The ocean is so calming. Like your eyes."

Justin chuckled. "What?"

She glanced up at him, shrugging. "I always thought your eyes were like the deepest oceans. I can see all your emotion, all your depth in them. I can see your soul."

Justin blinked down at her. Shit, was he tearing up? "Damn, girl. You know how to hit a guy in all the feels."

Mandy pushed away from him and shoved his arm. "Then let's go to the beach. I can't wait to see you in your thong."

Justin snorted as they went inside. "You wish."

Mandy smacked his ass as she crossed the room to her suitcase and pulled out her cover-up and flip-flops. "No, you're right. You can't show off the goods to everyone on the beach. That wouldn't be fair."

Justin threw his head back and laughed loudly. He stepped over to her and pulled her close. "I love you, you know that?"

Mandy nodded, looking up at him, her hands on his chest. "I do, actually. And I love you, more than I ever thought possible."

Justin shrugged. "Well, I am awesome."

Mandy tapped his chest. "I'll be the judge of that, babe. Let's see you surf first."

Two hours later, Mandy was lying comfortably on a bright-blue lounge chair shaded by an umbrella, compliments of the hotel. Her skin was so fair that she had to be careful in the sun.

She set down the steamy romance novel she'd been reading and lifted up to look for Justin out on the waves. Though she knew absolutely nothing about surfing, he'd claimed the waves were "gnarly" today, whatever that meant. All she knew was that he was having the time of his life, and he'd even found a few other "bros" to surf with.

She scanned the waves for his bright-blue wetsuit—the wetsuit he'd rented from the hotel that matched her chair, incidentally—but she didn't see him right away. Her heart started racing as she spotted his friends a little ways down in their black suits, but she didn't see him . . .

Oh, there. Mandy's chest released, and she exhaled. His head popped up above the surface as he paddled on his stomach to his next wave.

But she was starting to feel jittery. She'd watched one too many wipeouts, both from him and his friends. She knew he loved this—and had been surfing pretty much his entire life so he knew what he was doing—but the thought of Justin out on the waves still caused her stomach to dip. He could really get hurt if things went sideways.

She pulled up the word "gnarly" on her phone, surprised she hadn't thought to do it earlier. She had a bad feeling she knew what it meant, but she hadn't been concerned until now.

Her heart stopped when she saw the word "dangerous." She jolted up in her seat, scanning the horizon for him again.

That was when she heard the shouting.

She bolted to her feet and sprinted to the water as fast as her short legs would carry her. Justin's surfing friends were running out of the water, and Mandy noticed the last two were dragging a body between them.

The body had on a bright-blue wetsuit. And it wasn't moving.

"JUSTIN!" She screamed at the top of her lungs and flew to his side. His friends let him go before they made it to dry ground, and Mandy dropped to her knees beside him, splashing in the thin layer of water covering the wet sand.

She searched Justin's face for any sign of life, but his eyes were closed. Since she didn't think it was right to shake him, her hands caressed his face, brushing his hair out of his still-closed eyes as she silently pleaded with him to wake up.

How could he look so damn peaceful when he wasn't waking up?

Mandy's gaze shot to the crowd surrounding them. "What happened?!" She was screaming, but no one said anything. No one would tell her anything. Why the hell weren't they saying anything?!

A lifeguard came sprinting up the beach then and dropped down beside him. He pressed two fingertips to the side of Justin's throat, likely testing for a pulse, then he leaned down until his ear was an inch from Justin's lips.

Mandy couldn't breathe. He had to be alive. She couldn't survive it if he wasn't. *Please be alive, baby. You can't leave me now, not when I just got you back. Justin, baby, stay with me. Please. I can't live without you.*

"He's breathing," the lifeguard spit out, and Mandy's breath whooshed out of her. He glanced in her direction. "You with him?"

She nodded, tears stinging her eyes.

An obnoxiously yellow four-wheel drive SUV pulled up

beside them. Two women in matching yellow swimsuits jumped from the truck and pulled out a stretcher from the back.

The male lifeguard turned to her. "We're taking him to the hospital."

"Why?"

"Standard procedure, ma'am. He hit his head."

Mandy gasped as she noticed the gash on the top of his head for the first time. The saltwater must've washed away any blood that had soaked his hair . . .

She leaned over him to get a better look. There was a pool of blood swirling in the thin layer of water atop the sand. "Please . . ." she eked out, her voice strangled. "Please save him. He's my whole world." The threatening tears finally spilled over, and she started sobbing as they hoisted Justin on the stretcher and carried him to the SUV.

The lifeguard gave her the name of the hospital then ran off, and Mandy sat back in the waves and cried.

CHAPTER THIRTY-EIGHT

MANDY WAS at the hospital ten minutes later. Justin was in the ER, but no one would tell her anything. They'd just given her forms to fill out.

Name: Justin Stanford. That one was easy, though she'd have to ask his middle name.

DOB: No clue. She didn't even know his birthday?

Next of kin: Um, his mom? Jan Stanford, she assumed . . . She wrote it down.

Address: Whew. One she knew. Or, at least, she knew where to find it. She pulled it up on her phone where she'd saved it until she could memorize it.

Phone number: Yup, she had that one, too.

Emergency contact: Was it too soon to say her?

Insurance: Damn. She barely knew this guy.

That wasn't true. She just only knew the important stuff. That he loved her, that they were meant to be together, that she'd felt a deep connection to him from the night he'd comforted her after Dan had cheated on her.

She wiped her eyes, setting the clipboard on the seat next

to her.

Then she realized his wallet was in his Jeep. She ran out to retrieve it and was back seconds later.

Middle Name: Andrew. She liked that—it suited him. And his driver's license pic was adorable.

His date of birth was next, so she wrote that down. He was just a few months older than her.

She found an insurance card, too.

She'd grabbed his phone as well—also in the glove compartment of the SUV—and he actually didn't have a code set up to lock it. She found Jan's number and wrote it down.

His mom needed to know what was happening. But before Mandy could call her, *she* needed to know what was happening.

She carried the clipboard to the front desk, still fighting tears. She handed it across the chest-level counter. "I . . . I don't know his medical history, but this is everything I could find."

The nurse across the desk nodded her thanks but didn't say anything.

"Is he okay?"

The nurse looked her over, surveying her disheveled hair and undoubtedly tear-stained cheeks, and seemed to take pity on her. "I'll go find his doctor, sweetie. Just have a seat."

"Thank you," Mandy whispered then returned to her corner of the waiting room. This plastic chair was surprisingly comfortable, but she couldn't relax until she knew what was going on. Until she knew that he was okay. She crossed her legs, the top one bouncing erratically as she waited.

The nurse was back a few minutes later but without the doctor. Mandy lurched to her feet when she saw the woman heading her way. "What'd the doctor say?"

The nurse's face fell, and Mandy's gut twisted. "It seems

they're still treating him. She will be out when they're finished."

"But is he okay?"

"I really don't know, dear. I'm sorry."

Mandy just nodded as she walked away then sunk into her seat. Then she pulled out her phone.

She hadn't talked to her mom since that night. She'd been too angry.

But it was time for them to get past this. Time for *her* to get past this. And besides, right now, she really just needed to hear her mom's voice.

"Mandy, sweetie? Is that you?" Her mother's voice was soft, gentle. Kind.

Sobs tore at her throat at the sound. "Mom."

"Mandy, honey? Are you alright?" Mandy could hear the strain abruptly injected into her voice like a switch had flipped.

"No, Mom . . . it's Justin."

Amy gasped. "Baby, what happened?"

Mandy was full-on crying now, and she couldn't stop. The story started tumbling out through her sobs. "Justin was in a surfing accident. He was unconscious, and he wouldn't wake up, and now he's in the ER, and I'm here, too, but no one will tell me anything, and I'm so sorry I didn't call sooner, and I'm sorry I—"

Her mother cut her off. "Mandy, calm down, sweetie. What's wrong with Justin?"

Mandy sniffed. "He hit his head. There was blood . . ." Her voice cracked.

"Oh, honey, I'm so sorry. Is he okay?"

"I don't know—I think so?" Mandy choked back tears. "They said they're still working on him and will let me know when they're done. That's gotta be a good sign, right?"

"Of course, sweetie," her mom soothed. "I'm sure he'll be just fine. Is there something we can do?"

Even in the madness, Mandy caught it. "We?"

Her mother's next words were delivered with a smile—she could hear it. "Bill and I."

Mandy gasped. "You're back together?"

"We're working on it. You made me realize that I shouldn't give up so easily. Turns out both of us wanted to try again, we just thought the other didn't want to. Communication is so important in a relationship, baby. You have to be honest and speak your truth."

Mandy felt her mother's words like a punch to her gut. "Speaking of being honest . . ."

"Yes, baby?"

Mandy took a deep breath. Now was as good a time as any. "Justin and I haven't been dating since May like you thought."

"What?"

Mandy launched into the whole story, glad for the distraction.

"Amanda Lenae, I cannot believe you lied to me! To all of us!"

"I'm so sorry, Mom. Really. I just . . . Dan had *just* cheated on me, and Justin was willing to step in and cover for me so I could sort things out in my head that weekend. He was there for me, Mom, when I needed a friend more than ever."

"And now?"

"Oh, he's definitely more than a friend. We've been dating for a few weeks now. And, Mom . . ."

"Yes, honey?"

Mandy's next words were whispered. "I love him."

Her mother squealed, just like Mandy did when she got really excited. "Oh, baby. I'm so happy for you! I could tell you both had something special, even back then." Then her voice abruptly mellowed. "But listen, honey, because I don't know why, but I feel like you need to hear this." She took a breath. "Don't let your fear of getting hurt hold you back from loving him, from committing to him. Even if Bill and I don't work this out, it was worth it to love him. I wouldn't trade my time with him for the world."

Mandy was crying again, and she sniffed. "Thanks, Mom." She took a breath, her next words quiet, somber. A confession she never wanted to admit aloud. "I almost let him go."

Amy gasped. "Oh, honey, I'm so sorry."

Silence stretched between them as Mandy considered everything her mom had said. And she realized her mom was right. Her fear was stopping her from committing to Justin with everything she had, from going all in. If Justin didn't make it, she would regret never embracing their life together fully, never moving in with him, never accepting that she couldn't really predict how things would eventually turn out.

She could only decide what she would do next.

Trying to move forward wasn't the same as actually doing it. Saying she was committing to Justin while still "moving slow"—because if she was being completely honest, keeping her apartment was just giving herself an out—wasn't commitment at all. And suddenly she knew that while jumping in with both feet and no safety net was terrifying, it was the only way to truly experience the fullness of what life could be. Life with Justin.

She needed him in her life. She wanted him there. In every single part, one-hundred-percent, no equivocations.

She wasn't going to allow her fear to call the shots any longer.

Just then, a doctor walked in, searching the waiting room.

Mandy watched the nurse grab the doctor and point at her. "Mom, I have to go. I think Justin's doctor is here."

"Keep us posted, baby. Hope he feels better soon. Love you."

"Thanks, Mom. Love you. Hope everything works out with Bill."

"Me, too, honey."

The nurse approached, doctor in tow.

"Hello, dear. This is Justin's doctor."

The doctor extended her hand. "Hello. I'm Dr. Rawat. And you are?"

Mandy shook her offered hand. "Mandy. Is he okay?"

She eyed her. "And your relationship to Mr. Stanford?"

Mandy blinked. "I'm his girlfriend." Under any other circumstances, that confession would've warmed her heart. But the fact that the first time she'd had the opportunity to admit it aloud was in a hospital where he could be just beyond those huge double doors fighting for his life made her blood run cold.

The doctor nodded. "I can't give you specifics, Mandy, but he's stable."

Mandy exhaled in a rush, the relief overwhelming. "Can I see him?"

The doctor nodded. "Yes. I'll take you to him." She turned, and Mandy followed her back through the wide double doors that read "ER Staff Admittance Only."

Mandy entered the room behind the doctor and gasped, her heart squeezing so tightly in her chest she thought she might faint.

Justin's head was wrapped in a large, white bandage that covered about half of his blond hair. His eyes were closed, but the heart monitor beeping at steady intervals released Mandy's chest, just a little bit. He was okay. He was gonna be okay.

His eyes blinked open, sweeping the room. The ocean-blue irises softened as soon as he saw her, and he lifted his hand weakly. Mandy walked over and took it.

"Babe, you scared the shit out of me."

Justin smiled, chuckling slightly. Then he winced, and Mandy felt his pain echo deep inside her. She reached for him, brushing a stray hair from his forehead. "I'm okay, baby. Right, Doc?"

The woman came over to the bed, smiling. She nodded. "Yes."

"What happened?" Mandy asked her.

She looked to Justin, who nodded.

"He has a rather large laceration on the top of his head, but we were able to close it with stitches. He also has a mild concussion, but that's to be expected. We'll monitor him for a bit, but he should be able to travel by tomorrow. He shouldn't drive, though." She scanned his chart. "You aren't local, are you?"

Mandy shook her head, wiping her nose as she sniffled. "No, we live in Orlando."

The doctor nodded. "That should be fine as long as you can drive him home. We'll give him a treatment plan to help keep the wound clean and manage pain." She turned to Justin, patting his leg through the blanket. "You should be just fine. Just skip surfing for a bit, okay?"

Justin smiled, nodding. "Sure, Doc. Whatever you say."

She rolled her eyes at him with a smile then looked over at Mandy. "You have your hands full with this one, I see."

Mandy offered a watery chuckle. "Yeah."

The doctor slid the clipboard in her hand into a compartment on the wall then opened the door next to it. "Someone will be in shortly to go over next steps. Take care, Justin, and feel better."

He nodded slowly at Dr. Rawat as she left, but Mandy's eyes were on him, so she saw the swirling behind his eyes, the pain causing them to squint ever so slightly.

"How do you feel?" Mandy hadn't let go of his hand since she'd entered the room.

He leaned his head back, closing his eyes. "Nauseous, and I have a killer headache. Doc said that was normal."

Mandy nodded, not that she knew if that was normal or not. "What happened, babe?"

Justin sighed, his eyes blinking open. "Everything was going really well until it wasn't. A wave caught me in just the wrong way, and I wiped out. Must've hit my head on a rock or something."

Mandy was tearing up again. "I never want to see you hurt. It killed me. And they wouldn't tell me anything—I didn't even know if you were alive!"

Justin frowned. "I'm so sorry, baby. I hate that you had to go through that."

Mandy straightened, squeezing his hand. "But you're okay, and that's what matters. I don't know what I'd do if I lost you."

JUSTIN CAUGHT Mandy's gaze and captured those beautiful hazel eyes with his. Though she didn't know it yet, she'd been his anchor through all this—his only thought during the whole ordeal, at least when he'd been conscious, was that he couldn't leave her. Turned out, she'd been thinking the same thing.

The connection they shared was more than special—it was downright supernatural.

"Mandy, baby, I am so sorry. I shouldn't have been out in those waves."

Mandy shook her head, tears dripping down her cheeks. "No, babe—we can't avoid living just because it might be scary." She smiled. "But you have to be more careful."

He nodded slowly, his head swimming with the motion. His eyes slid shut.

"Babe, I can let you get your rest."

His eyes shot open. At least, he tried to make them open quickly. He sensed it was much slower than he'd intended—the pain meds they had him on must have been kicking in. "No, baby. Stay with me." He glanced at the plastic chair behind her.

She snatched it up and pulled it over, dropping into it when it was in place, close to the bed. "Okay. Not gonna argue with that."

He smiled.

"Uh, Justin?" she asked.

"Yeah, baby?"

"So your birthday's in April, huh?"

Justin chuckled, but it made his head throb, so he stopped quickly. "Yeah, the fifth." He smiled. "When's yours?"

"August fifth."

"Crazy."

Mandy smiled through her tears. "Yeah." Then she cocked her head. "Um . . . should we call your parents? I put your mom as your next of kin, which made me think of it. But I didn't want to call to worry them until I knew what was going on."

He squeezed his eyes shut. "Yeah, we should." Then he opened them to gaze at the woman he loved more than anything in the world. "You wanna talk to them?"

Mandy's eyes widened. "You mean like meet them? Over the phone?"

Justin smiled. "Yeah, silly. My mom would be thrilled to get to know you. Since you're the most important person in her son's life and all."

Mandy wiped her tears from her face and nodded. "Okay. Let's do this." Then she froze. "Uh, before we do that, you don't have any weird diseases or anything, right?"

Justin laughed, but the throbbing in his head was less noticeable than last time. The meds were definitely working. "Why do you say that, ridiculous girl?"

Mandy smiled at him. "Just realized I didn't know your medical history. They gave me all these forms to fill out, and I didn't know a lot of the answers."

Justin tightened his grip on her hand. "Babe, we have our whole lives for that. You know the important things about me. The other stuff will come with time."

Mandy nodded. "I know. I just wanted to make sure you weren't dying or anything." She smirked.

He grinned back. "Not that I'm aware of."

The room fell silent for a second. Then: "Hey, baby?"

"Hmm?"

Mandy shifted her weight. "I was thinking . . . I'm sure you'll need some care when we get home. Maybe I should just move in, you know, to take care of you." She shrugged but kept her pointed gaze on him.

His eyes shot wide. "You want to move in with me?"

Mandy nodded. "I don't want to move slow anymore. I want to go fast. You're my future, Justin Stanford, and I'm ready to run into it, no reservations. Because if I'm being completely honest, I can't live another minute without you."

Justin smirked. "And you'll stay even after I'm better?

Because I'm going to get too used to you being around all the time."

Mandy chuckled. "Of course, babe. Like I said before, you're it for me. I just let my fear make me forget that."

The widest smile Justin had ever felt stretched across his face. It hurt, but he didn't care.

"I love you, my beautiful."

"Honesty? I love you more, babe."

He laughed. "Not possible." He wanted to kiss her, but he couldn't reach. So he just squeezed her hand. "Now let's call my parents before these pain meds make me too loopy."

Mandy chuckled, pulling his phone from her purse. "Let's do this."

Justin's grin widened. He really loved this woman.

And when she introduced herself to his mother as "Mandy Carlson, the woman in love with your son," he realized that no matter what happened in their life, no matter what they faced, if they faced it together, it would all be okay.

EPILOGUE

Three Years Later

"MANDY! PHONE!"

Mandy looked up from the suitcase she was packing and made a face. She flicked her strawberry blonde hair—which had grown out over the past three years—away from her neck. Though she loved Justin more than anything, she knew he knew it, too; that was the problem. Lately, he'd been taking her for granted—and she hated the aggravating way this sometimes made him act. *I'm not an animal,* she thought. *You could've asked nicely. Or, heaven forbid, actually bring me the phone.*

She sighed. He didn't actually take her for granted. He actually showed her that he loved her every day, even keeping up the regular carnation bouquets—he'd just mellowed to twice a week. She was just frustrated that he hadn't offered to help her pack.

She found her boyfriend in the living room, holding the cell phone she'd left on the coffee table. His eyes never moved from the wall-mounted TV as she snatched the phone away from him over the back of the couch. She glared at him on her way to the kitchen, though he was too enthralled by the TV to notice.

"Yes? This is Mandy Carlson."

"Ms. Carlson, this is Dean Stewart." The caller wasn't really a surprise. Her "teacher's pet" reputation at school had begun to include the deans as well.

"Hello, how are you?" She kept it formal. The man was kind and gracious, but Mandy still found him a little intimidating, even over the phone.

"Fine, fine. I have a request, if you don't mind."

"Sure, what is it?"

He hesitated almost imperceptibly, but she caught it. "Do you know Drs. Harrington and McGready?"

Her heart jumped a little. A knee-jerk reaction—a subconscious habit she couldn't suppress whenever she heard his name. "I was in one of Dr. McGready's classes last semester. Is he okay?"

Another moment of silence, this time glaringly obvious. When the dean didn't respond, Mandy asked another question. "What happened?"

She heard him sigh. "Ms. Carlson, Dr. Harrington and Dr. McGready are missing. They were at the Lamanai dig, working, and they seem to have found something. But as they were heading to the airport in Belize City this morning, they were . . ." He paused then tried again. "Well, by all accounts, it looks like they were *ambushed*."

Mandy's next word came out a whisper. "What?"

Dean Stewart cleared his throat. "I'm sorry to drop this on you so suddenly, but I knew you were headed to Lamanai tomorrow anyway, so I wanted to ask if you would head up the search party."

Mandy smirked at the kitchen cabinets. Finally, her years of making nice with the teachers were paying off. And if she were the one to find them . . . "I would be happy to." Since she'd fallen in love with Justin, her crush on Professor McDreamy was a distant memory that she'd matured and grown out of, but she was still concerned with his well-being—probably a little more than she should be.

Maybe she hadn't grown out of it as much as she'd like to think.

The dean sighed again. "Please find them. Our school can't afford to lose such great archaeologists—or such great people."

Mandy smiled. She knew Dean Stewart well enough to know he really did care about his people. "Justin and I were just packing for our flight in the morning. Should we leave sooner?"

"No, the morning's flight is the first one headed that way. Please let me know what you find out. We're all concerned for them; any news would be greatly appreciated."

Mandy smiled, her dimples making an appearance in the empty room. "Will do."

He hung up without another word.

Mandy's smile faded as she let the situation sink in. She always looked forward to Grady's classes—what was wrong with a little ogling? The man could fill out a shirt—and had had a class with him nearly every semester in grad school. She vaguely remembered Professor Harrington—she'd had a few classes with her after the initial one in her first year, and she'd tried more than once to figure out if she'd been interested in Grady, though the woman didn't seem approachable enough to ask—but Mandy couldn't quite recall what she looked like. It had been a few years, and Mandy was always more attentive when it came to the opposite sex.

"Justin!" she yelled too loudly, smirking as she returned his earlier favor. *See how you like it.*

Unfortunately, as she had come to expect, he didn't notice her subtle rebuke. He simply loped into the room, energy drink in hand. "What's up? What'd the dean want?"

She rolled her eyes at her less-than-attentive boyfriend. A byproduct of whatever he'd been watching so intently, she was sure. "Something happened at the dig. Grady McGready and Professor Harrington were attacked on the way to Belize City. No one can find them, so they want us to head up the search."

Justin grinned. Mandy knew without asking that he would be overly excited about such an adventure—and though she would never admit it, it was one of the reasons she put up with him. Okay, one of the many reasons. "Cool!" He took a large final swig from his drink then chucked it into the recycling bin with a large, dopey grin. "Let's go pack."

He sprinted ahead of her into their bedroom. She followed with the intention of finishing up her own packing, but when she got into the bedroom, Justin was near the door. He growled, reaching for her tiny waist to pull her to him. He leaned in, flipping her hair out of the way as he pressed his lips to her right shoulder. "Have I told you how much I love your dresses?"

"Justin, what are you doing? We need to pack." She bit back, her eyes flashing. "Besides, I'm worried about Grady and Professor Harrington."

At her words, Justin pulled back and caught her gaze, his hands gripping her upper arms lightly. His ocean eyes had gone from seductive to solemn in two seconds flat. "I'm sorry, baby. Of course—I'm worried about them, too." He took a deep breath. "Did the dean say anything else?"

Mandy sighed, leaning back against the wall near the door. Justin's arms moved to cage her in, the man she loved invading her space. "Not much. Just that they found something at the dig, and now they're missing."

He just nodded, inching closer.

"What are we getting ourselves into?" She couldn't stop her voice from shaking.

Justin smiled sweetly, lifting one hand from the wall to cup her cheek. "This is what we wanted, baby. Adventure in a faraway land together, remember?"

A smile tugged at Mandy's lips—she couldn't help it. "Okay, fine. But we still need to pack."

A wicked grin flashed across his face before he leaned in, his lips finding the bare skin of her neck as his hand slipped under the collar of her dress and traced a meandering path south. "We can later. Right now, I want to show you how much I love this dress. You wore it when we first came to tour this apartment, remember? You don't wear it much anymore."

Mandy nodded slowly, and the fire she always felt when Justin touched her flared across her skin. Even after three years, he knew how to turn her on, and though she tried to hide it sometimes, just to get under his skin, she absolutely loved it.

But she loved him more.

So she moaned lightly. "You may have mentioned it." Then her eyes flashed to his, and a familiar ache settled between her legs. "Maybe you should show me."

MANDY BIT HER LIP, and Justin grabbed the back of her head and pulled her lips to his in a rush, kissing that devilishly sexy expression off her lips. Their kisses were urgent, and he wanted to take her right here.

But as he backed her to the bed, their lips still attached and tongues searching, he had a better idea—something he'd been wanting to try for a while. He pushed her gently onto the bed then pulled away for a second to stand over her. "You really want me to show you, baby?"

Mandy's teeth found her lip again, and she nodded slowly with her eyes wide as she stared up at him. Justin wanted to tear her clothes off and rip away the innocence she was faking —well, he might add.

"Okay, babe. Hands up."

She blinked at him, lying back on the bed and lifting her arms above her head. He guided her to the cushioned headboard and pressed her hands against it. She gripped the edge of the taut fabric. "You good, babe?"

Mandy nodded, eyes still wide.

Justin sat on the bed beside her and ran his fingertips lightly from her wrists down the inside of her arms. When he reached the flowy cap sleeves, he trailed down over the dress, his hands brushing her nipples lightly. She moaned at the featherlight touch.

Justin smirked then reached for a pillow. "Okay, lift up."

Mandy pulled her knees toward her, planting her bare feet on the mattress and lifting her hips. Her dress pooled around her waist. Justin slid the pillow beneath her, propping her hips up.

Justin caught her gaze, saw her passion for him sparking in her hazel irises. Sometimes he hated taking things slow, but he knew from experience that the wait was always worth it. He just had to keep reminding himself of that.

He reached down, thankful for the stretchy fabric of this particular dress. He pulled the neckline down until it cupped her covered breasts. Mandy gasped.

Justin flashed the crooked grin he knew she liked. "Oh, we're just getting started, babe."

Mandy nodded, eyes wide. "Just hurry, baby, before I burst into flames."

Justin nodded then reached for her silky black bra. He pulled the cups down, exposing her naked breasts to the air. Her nipples instantly hardened, and Justin felt himself do the same as he leaned in to worship them, sucking, nipping, and biting a little harder than he ever had before. She'd asked to be shown how much she turned him on, and by the breathy moaning emanating from her, she liked it.

Mandy was a dream in the sack—Dan hadn't had a clue. She just kept getting better and better.

His left hand found its way to her bare thigh and trailed up her skin, his mouth still focused on her left breast. When his fingers found her panty line, Mandy drew in a sharp breath. She was ready for him.

He lifted his head. "You want it, baby? You want me inside you?"

"Yes, Justin, please . . ." she begged.

In one smooth motion, he pushed aside her panties and shoved two fingers inside her. She called out.

"Tell me what you need, Mandy." Justin's fingers thrusted into her hard, rough, and his teeth found her nipple again as she moaned.

"I . . . I . . . I need . . ." Her words disintegrated into the air as Justin picked up the pace. Before long, he felt her whole body tensing, and he knew she was close.

As she liked to do, Mandy warned him before she exploded. "Justin, baby, don't stop. I . . . I'm gonna come for you."

Justin grinned, moving his thumb to her clit, knowing it

would push her over the edge. "You'd better, baby. Come hard for me."

Mandy nodded, then Justin felt her clench around his fingers just before she let go.

She moaned loudly as she did, though she'd quieted down some since that first night. Her pleasure was still intoxicating, arousing. And Justin would chase it for the rest of his life if she'd let him.

Justin yanked his fingers out of her then got up and quickly undressed. Mandy started to reach for him, but he scolded her as he dropped his pants and boxer briefs in one motion. "Nope, hands up."

Mandy's face flushed, and the fire was back in her eyes as she did what she was told. She liked being ordered around in bed—that was new—and his entire body throbbed with sheer need at the thought.

Justin pulled her wet panties off quickly then spread her legs wide, his eyes on hers the whole time. Mandy was breathing heavily, her bare chest rising and falling in a picture of pure seduction. He kneeled on the bed between her legs, her hips right at the perfect height for him to drive into her hard and fuck her brains out.

"You ready for me, baby? You gonna come again for me? Because if not, I may have to punish you until you do."

Mandy's eyes flashed again, brighter and hotter this time, and Justin couldn't stand it any longer. He pushed into her with a groan, and he could feel himself expand into every inch of her. They exhaled together in a rush as if they were finally home. Because they were. *Finally.*

Justin thrusted into Mandy quickly, desperately, as she slid up and down on the bed. Her breasts bounced with the motion, and Justin's lips and hands soon found them again. He caressed, squeezed, nipped, bit, and sucked until Mandy was ready to release for him all over again.

She tightened around his cock as she called out, and Justin could've sworn he'd never felt anything better in his life. As she released with him inside her, and he joined her seconds later, he was convinced that no matter where they were headed tomorrow or what they'd find in the jungles of Belize, he'd finally found the woman of his dreams.

Honestly.

Want to find out what happens to Mandy and Justin in Belize?

Start The Codex Series today with *The Secret of the Codex*!

For the latest news on upcoming releases, writing advice, and random life updates, follow me on Instagram at @melissafreyauthor or sign up at melissafrey.com/sign-up to stay up-to-date!

#honestlyalwaysyou
#codexseries

Loved the book? Leave a review!

Independent authors like me rely on online reviews from our readers to help others find our books. Please take a few moments to visit Amazon or Goodreads and leave a review of *Honestly Always You*. I would really appreciate it!

www.melissafrey.com

ACKNOWLEDGMENTS

My first thanks always goes to my husband and true partner, Andrew Frey. Your continual love and encouragement are integral to my success in business and in life. Thanks for believing in me when I have a hard time believing in myself and for supporting me even when what I dream up doesn't always make sense. You're forever my real-life Grady, and I love you!

To my sister, Amanda, the inspiration behind the character of Mandy Carlson. You gave me an incredible jumping-off point for Mandy, and I'm grateful just for you being you. (And also for the advice on what class Mandy would hate in college.)

To my alpha reader, Eve, my author friend and constant encouragement. You gave me the courage to write the romance novel I wanted to write as well as amazing advice that made this book so much better than it started out. Thank you for all you do (and for keeping me sane through the process)!

To my critique partner, Meghan. Your notes are ALWAYS invaluable, and you helped make this book the best it could be. Thank you for always fangirling over my manuscript when I'm not sure it's even worth publishing. You're amazing!

To my beta reader, Lilian. Your comments on the story came at just the right time, and you gave me the encouragement I needed to finish my edits (the value of which cannot be understated)! You helped me iron out some things that needed correcting, and I cannot be more grateful.

To my interior formatter and author friend, Melanie. Thank you for creating such a beautiful book and for your kind words about my writing that mean more than you know!

To my cover designer and long-time author friend, Taylor. Thank you for this gorgeous book cover and for your friendship over the past few years!

To the Badass Author Babes. Though we don't talk as much lately, I still think about and appreciate all of you. Some of you are now my closest friends, and I am so grateful I met all of you! And a huge thanks for the random conversations that birthed the idea for this book in me.

To the Instagram author and book community. I will forever be grateful to all of you for your support, encouragement, and the positive environment you foster in a space that is often negative! I am so grateful for the friends I've met there, fellow authors and book lovers that help me believe my dream of becoming the author I want to be is possible.

To my readers. I cannot possibly express how grateful I am for each and every one of you. The fact that you picked up my book out of millions and spent time with my characters means so much. THANK YOU, from the bottom of my heart.

To the aspiring writers, the frustrated writers, the unsure writers, the discouraged writers, the hopeful writers, the new writers, the imperfect writers. KEEP WRITING. Someone out there needs to read the words you were given to write. Even if that someone is you.

To everyone. Keep doing brave things. Life is much too short to stay small.

ALSO BY MELISSA FREY

The Codex Series

The Secret of the Codex

The Prophecy of the Codex

Non-Fiction

How to Work from Home (with Andrew Frey)

ABOUT THE AUTHOR

Melissa Frey is the author of the supernatural action-adventure Codex series, the Codex companion romance, *Honestly Always You,* and the non-fiction book *How to Work from Home*. When she's not writing, her passion is helping fellow indie authors with writing, editing, and publishing their books at indieauthorlearning.com and teaching them all about Show vs. Tell. You can find her online at melissafrey.com, connecting with readers and other authors on Instagram, and editing books and anything else she can get her hands on. She's a new transplant to the Pacific Northwest and loves yoga, the mountains, super-dark chocolate, and her husband, Andrew.

www.ingramcontent.com/pod-product-compliance
Lightning Source LLC
LaVergne TN
LVHW091107080826
845145LV00008B/1841
* 9 7 8 1 7 3 2 4 3 3 5 6 4 *